Hayner Public Library District-Alton

0 00 30 0398747 0

RECEIVED
MAY 1 1 2006
By _____

D1114957

HAYNER PUBLIC LIBRARY DISTRICT
ALTON, ILLINOIS

OVERDUES .10 PER DAY MAXIMUM FINE
COST OF BOOKS. LOST OR DAMAGED
BOOKS ADDITIONAL $5.00 SERVICE CHARGE.   BRANCH

the boyfriend from
hell

Also by Avery Corman

A Perfect Divorce
Kramer vs. Kramer
The Old Neighborhood
50
Prized Possessions
The Big Hype
Oh, God!

the boyfriend from hell

avery corman

St. Martin's Press 📚 New York

HAYNER PUBLIC LIBRARY DISTRICT
ALTON, ILLINOIS

THE BOYFRIEND FROM HELL. Copyright © 2006 by Avery Corman, Inc. All rights reserved. Printed in the United States of America. No part of this book may be used or reproduced in any manner whatsoever without written permission except in the case of brief quotations embodied in critical articles or reviews. For information, address St. Martin's Press, 175 Fifth Avenue, New York, N.Y. 10010.

www.stmartins.com

Design by Sarah Maya Gubkin

Library of Congress Cataloging-in-Publication Data

Corman, Avery.
    The boyfriend from hell / Avery Corman.—1st ed.
      p. cm.
    ISBN-10 0-312-34979-3
    ISBN-13 978-0-312-34979-0
      1. Women authors—New York (state)—New York—Fiction. 2. Satanism—New York (state)—New York—Fiction. 3. Man-woman relationships—Fiction. 4. Psychological fiction. I. Title.

PS3553.O649B69 2006
813'.54—dc22

2005044805

First Edition: May 2006

10 9 8 7 6 5 4 3 2 1

F
COR

b17198926

the boyfriend from
hell

1

This was the forum. The date. The "who-are-you, what-are-your-interests" venue. He reminded her of one of those preening males on the reality television shows where the women compete for attention, desperate to get to the next staged round. His blond hair was treated with something—she wasn't sure which particular hair product guys used to make their hair sit perfectly—gel, something. The hair was great, out of F. Scott Fitzgerald, and he was wearing an elegant pinstriped double-breasted suit she figured cost more than half her wardrobe; light brown eyes, narrow face; a former squash player for Williams College, which he wedged into the conversation, now a squash champion on the squash circuit. And a mergers-and-acquisitions champion, unusual for only twenty-nine, he told her. He needed to tell. He had a big day at the office and she happened to be his Monday night blind date. So he spun tales of himself, business warrior tales, converting the bar at the restaurant into his campfire, glowing with himself, a blondish, gel-ish glow.

He knew she had gone to Brown, so he seemed to place her some-where within his social class and assumed she cared one whit about cor-porate life, or *his* corporate life. He rolled on, Lou Dobbs on *Money Watch*. With his credentials on the table he finally focused on her, obliged, according to the rituals, to show interest. She imagined him at this point with a Rockette, asking, "And how, exactly, did you learn to kick so high?"

He asked his questions and she answered. She was finishing an arti-cle for *Vanity Fair* about the new generation of young theater actresses. And how did she first get into writing? In high school. And where was that? Bronx Science. He nodded, saying nothing, and she surmised he had never heard of the place, or never met anyone in his life who went anywhere with a Bronx in it. He told her he once thought about writ-ing for his high school paper—at Exeter. *Exeter. Squash.* They didn't play squash in her old neighborhood.

He was actually not completely terrible, this Sean. He went several minutes asking about her and seemed to be listening. She had sat for drinks with worse. What wasn't good was the smugness, the self-importance. He knew he looked terrific, he was doing well in the lists, making sure that she knew and, lucky girl, on a blind date she drew him. Did she have any idea what the odds were in this city to draw *him*? He never let on that he might have been lucky to draw *her*.

She was twenty-four, five feet four with a slender frame, small shoulders and a slim waist, modest breasts, ample enough as they were developing in her teenage years to save her from being taunted as flat-chested by the sidewalk savants in the neighborhood who were appren-ticing to become jerks. She lacked the gym-sculpted upper body and neck muscles she recognized in some of the young actresses she had in-terviewed, and that was fine with her. She disliked the look and was bored in gyms. She ran around the Central Park reservoir a couple of times every few mornings, listening on a Walkman to National Public Radio. She knew it was elitist on her part, but she sized up her lover-aspirant as someone who never listened to National Public Radio, ex-cept for possibly *Car Talk* on a Saturday morning while driving through the Hamptons in his BMW.

"Do you own a car?" she said abruptly.

"Why?"

"Just curious."

"I do."

"What kind?"

"A BMW."

"What color?"

"Blue."

"Nice."

"Did you want me to drive you someplace?" he said, suspicious of her line of questioning. "Help you *move* something?"

"No, I was just asking. General background."

"And what does that tell you about me—as general background? You have me as one of those BMW guys?"

"But you are."

"But that's only part of me."

"Who said it was more?"

Her dark, nearly indigo hair was cut short with loose bangs, a contrast with her fair skin and pale green eyes, and she had a small pug nose. "My little colleen," the next-door neighbor, Mr. Flaherty, called her during her childhood years. The BMW owner was appraising her looks, calculating whether to go for another drink at the bar or offer dinner, applying his spreadsheet sensibility to whether or not he could get her into bed in the near enough future for it to be economically viable.

Smart enough to realize she had him down as a type on the car, defensively he went to his strength, his business wonderfulness. Claiming to value her opinion, he described a new company that he was helping to capitalize, movies on demand by computer. A long day spent transcribing interviews and now this champion—everything was apparently on a loop, right back to where he started, only with different corporate names, and she wanted to be in bed, alone. Not a terrible guy, just, well, who cared.

"I'm wasted. Maybe we could try this again another time."

"You don't really mean that."

"I do. The maybe part."

"Fascinating."

"What is?"

"I know it didn't work out and I know you're just saying maybe when you mean no way."

"I mean maybe."

"I haven't struck out like this since I was about fourteen."

"Then you're doing great. You've got nothing to worry about."

"You could've had a wonderful life with me."

"That's terrific. That's *humorous*." She took his shoulders as if she were a coach at a football game and shook him. "You could use more of that."

They parted outside the restaurant and she thought he showed a little flash there at the end, but she could see the signs. This guy needed a woman directly from his social background, someone who would be thrilled to listen to his CNN business riffs, or a B-school graduate working on her own riffs, not Veronica Ronnie Delaney from the Bronx.

Nine weeks since the end of the relationship and someone as good-looking as the squash champion didn't have a chance when she compared him to her portly, defiantly unathletic ex-boyfriend. She had met Michael Ruppert at a restaurant opening, an invitation that came through her roommate. Michael, thirty-one, was the chef, round-faced, cherubic, with an endearing smile, five feet eleven and clearly on the wrong side of appropriate weight charts. He chatted with her until he was pulled away by the restaurant owner, not before Michael asked for her phone number. He called and offered to cook dinner for her at his place on his night off and she wondered why he would want to cook when he wasn't working and he said, "Because you're beautiful and I'm nothing to look at and cooking is what I do best in the world, so it'll make me look good."

Michael lived in a SoHo loft with spare furnishings, but for the professional island kitchen. He made a salad with fresh ingredients from the

Union Square Greenmarket, and spaghetti Bolognese from scratch, not a fancy meal at all, which she found spectacular. His hands were lightning fast as he chopped ingredients, talking her through the preparation, savoring every element, and she identified a quality in short supply in the New York dating scene, a passion for something, as opposed to a passion for one's self. He was also of the world, political, on the left side of the spectrum, a young chef who read *The Nation* magazine. "I know it reads quirky at times, but who else is saying this stuff?" When she went home that night she imagined being able to write a piece on "How I Fell in Love on the First Date with an Overweight Chef."

Ronnie and Michael began seeing each other immediately and exclusively. Michael was discovered while working as a caterer at a dinner party attended by a restaurant entrepreneur. He opened Stars and Stripes in SoHo, engaging Michael, who created a variation on a comfort food/road food menu that was an immediate success with critics and the public. After a year and a half Ronnie and Michael were both coincidentally in the same issue of *New York* magazine. He was in a group shot and included in a cover story on hot new chefs. She was in on a more mundane level with a piece she wrote about a zoning dispute on the Upper East Side.

The hours in dating and sometimes living with a chef were maddening to her. She was not a nocturnal person and liked to start the day early, the jogging and the National Public Radio. When she slept at his apartment she routinely set her clothes out in the living room the night before in order to make her early departures. He usually wandered in around 2:00 A.M., later if he went for a chef's night out with his colleagues. They made love as often when she was roused from sleep by the night owl as they did starting out together, as it were.

She couldn't equate how a *Nation* subscriber could be so aggressive professionally, so capitalistic. He was publicity-driven, no interview too small: cable television, radio, magazines, newspapers, conferences in other cities. Sometimes he invited her to travel with him, sometimes he said that she would only be bored.

"*The Nation* runs these cruises and they go to places like Alaska," he told her when they were at Pastis Restaurant on a Saturday, his breakfast, her lunch, "and they have lectures. And the thing is, the people who go, a lot of them are rich lefties. There's no contradiction between liberal politics and money. And I want to be successful."

"You already are."

"Not Emeril-successful. You get about two minutes at this."

"Andy Warhol said fifteen."

"Whatever. This is my moment. You have to know when your moment is."

Ronnie felt a specific bond existed with Michael. Both their parents were gone. Michael's mother died of leukemia five years earlier. He hadn't seen his father in twenty years; he didn't even know if the man was still alive. Ronnie's father, who worked as a botanist for the Bronx Botanical Gardens, died of a heart attack three years earlier. Her mother died when she was eleven. Ronnie's only living relative was an irascible uncle in Saratoga, New York, a retired horse trainer, whom she never saw. She called him each year at Christmastime and on his birthday and sent him gifts on both occasions. He did not reciprocate.

She lived with a roommate, Nancy Briggs, also twenty-four, a sturdy blonde of five feet four, a former lacrosse player at Brown, with wide bright blue eyes and freckles, so sunny and all-American-looking she could have been a poster model for women's sports. Nancy worked as an assistant to a literary agent. Ronnie and Nancy's apartment was in an old building on West End Avenue and 111th Street, a two-bedroom rent-stabilized place, courtesy of Nancy's boss, Jenna Hawkins, whose son owned the building; New York insider stuff. They both fashioned home/office setups in the bedrooms, decorated from the Workbench. The living room and small dining room featured hand-me-downs and flea market items.

Nancy's boyfriend was Bob Fox, a lawyer who lived a few blocks away, and Nancy slept at his house frequently, so on nights when Ronnie was not with Michael the apartment was essentially hers. As Chef Michael rolled along on his careerist track he and Ronnie were together about twice a week, usually sleeping at his place. They introduced each other as boyfriend and girlfriend. Then, with disastrous consequences for the relationship, he made room on his plate for another girlfriend.

He was working on developing a *Cooking with Michael* show for the new Dining-In Network on cable. Ronnie was enthusiastic; what could be more accessible for the general public than Michael's variations on basic home cooking? She was convinced he would be a great success with it. But he was unavailable to her for three weeks as the show went from production meetings to taping.

Nancy called Ronnie from work. She needed to go right out and get a copy of the current *Time Out* magazine. She did so and found a photograph captioned, "Rosetta Dupree, the cabaret singer, and ace chef, Michael Ruppert, at her opening." They posed cheek-to-cheek for the camera.

Furious, she made several calls and couldn't reach Michael; she left messages. She considered going to the restaurant and confronting him and decided against it for her personal dignity. She was going to give him the following day to call back, and *then* she would walk in on him at the restaurant.

He called the following morning at ten thirty.

"Hey, you were trying to reach me."

"Hey, I saw *Time Out,* Michael."

"The paparazzi. They escalate things."

"No, they take pictures."

"Main thing is, they gave me a green light on the show."

"Congratulations. And how long have you known this? Have you already celebrated with Rosetta what's-her-name?"

"Ronnie, I've been under a lot of pressure."

"Yes?"

"At odds and ends."

"And is this Rosetta an odd or an end? Are you sleeping with her, Michael?"

"That's not the issue."

"How can that not be the issue?"

"The issue is I need to be open to new things these days."

"New things?"

"Like the show. And new people. And new business opportunities. And I care for you too much to just string you along while I go through all this."

"You mean your moment?"

"For however long it lasts. I think an exclusive relationship feels a little too exclusive right now."

"So what are you saying, you want to sleep with me *and* sleep with her, or just sleep with her? And how exclusive can it be if we haven't been together in weeks?"

"Ronnie, this is hard to say. I think it would be better all around if we were just friends."

"You don't end a relationship, eighteen months, Michael, with a phone call. There are things to talk about, feelings to be honored. I'm coming over."

"No."

"Is she *there*?" He didn't respond. "She is, isn't she? And she's using soap *I* bought."

"That's not so funny."

"I mean it not so funny. A cabaret singer. I get it now. You keep the same hours."

"You're a tremendous person, Ronnie."

"I thought you were, too, but you just got less tremendous. All the best with the restaurant and the new show and the new girlfriend, or girlfriends, and the new business opportunities. Did I leave anything out?"

"Ronnie, this isn't going the way I wanted it to."

"It could get worse. I could take out one of those personals in *The Nation* and tell all your fellow readers that you and your cuisine only *seem* proletarian. Good-bye, Michael."

———

He sent flowers and called, not looking to get together again with her, rather to offer a rewrite on the break-up, which he felt he handled badly. He even clumsily offered for her to eat in his restaurant anytime, to bring a guest if she wanted.

"I think he may have blundered into giving me a lifetime comp," she said to Nancy over breakfast on the run.

"You should do it. Just keep showing up."

"The hell with him. It's a weird culture, to parlay meat loaf into celebrity."

Ronnie and Nancy discussed online dating as a means of meeting someone new and she went so far as making an exploratory move, registering with a Web site. It seemed daunting to her, going through the e-mail gamesmanship, marketing herself electronically. The clincher was an article in *The New York Times Magazine,* which suggested relationships that came by way of the Internet often had a way of rapidly ending, as if someone hit a delete button. She experienced the departure of Michael as akin to a "delete text." She wasn't eager to repeat the experience. Nancy offered the squash champion via her boyfriend as a way of Ronnie getting past Michael. Ronnie was untroubled that it didn't work out with the guy. She found work was turning out to be the best antidote. She worked hard on the article for *Vanity Fair,* it was accepted and scheduled for the March 2005 issue.

Ronnie Delaney was virtually the writer equivalent of the new generation of young actresses she interviewed for the *Vanity Fair* piece. In college she wrote for *The Brown Daily Herald,* largely features about campus life. She intended, upon graduation, to get a job with a newspaper, and then circumstances fortunate and unfortunate conspired to direct her toward becoming a freelancer in New York.

In her senior year she queried *The New York Times Magazine* about doing a piece on political correctness within the Ivy League and was given the assignment. Researching and writing carried her through the time of her graduation into the summer and she stayed in her apartment near school.

The writing style she developed was breezy, colloquial, and, with guidance from a good writing course in college, grounded in research. Her editor at *The Times Magazine* suggested that none of the major metropolitan newspapers in America would be likely to hire her as a feature writer, a level at which she was already functioning. She had gone past conventional entry-level jobs. *The Times Magazine* was publishing her piece and they wanted to use her again. She never even got her résumés into the mail. The piece ran and she was given another assignment. Then her father died. He suffered a heart attack while walking through the sylvan grounds of the Bronx Botanical Gardens. That he died there, in a place of calm, on a mild summer day, doing nothing more than strolling, she considered a statement by her father, as if he had willed himself to die. With the small inheritance from her father's insurance policy she could help support herself and try to make a go of it as a freelance writer, the level to which she had already evolved, rather than step back into an apprentice job.

She moved in with Nancy, a literature major who had come to New York from Wilton, Connecticut. Ronnie worked on a variety of pieces, dated around, usually men introduced by friends of friends from school, or people she met at parties. She had zero tolerance for bars and clubs and wrote a piece for *The Village Voice* on "The Latest Terrible Opening Lines at Bars and Clubs." She and Nancy bought shares in a group house in Fire Island, which resulted in Nancy meeting her boyfriend and Ronnie meeting no one. She followed this with a piece in *The Village Voice* on "The Latest Terrible Opening Lines at the Beach." Over the next two years she wrote articles for various publications and attracted attention among editors as a lively new writer.

While researching the *Vanity Fair* piece she asked each of the actresses to tell her, if they cared to, about "the wiggiest guy they ever dated." One of the actresses described a weekend relationship with an otherwise "semi-ordinary guy," a musician who revealed "an unbelievably strange side."

He turned out to be a member of a satanic cult which held Black Masses on 129th Street.

Ronnie looked into the cult, the Dark Angel Church, unashamedly featured on the Internet and highlighting its leader, Randall Cummings, at Darkangelchurch.org. She called her editor at *New York* magazine and pitched an article on the basis that the city was amazingly fragmented with special interest and demographic groups, but this was *beyond* beyond.

She was assigned the article and placed a call to Randall Cummings. He was smooth spoken and articulate, invited her to a mass, and was perfectly willing to be interviewed. He loved the idea of an article in *New York* magazine, as befitted the head of a satanic cult so modern that it had its own Web site.

The Dark Angel Church was located in Harlem in a narrow one-story brick building on 129th Street near the overhang of the West Side Highway, the exterior painted black with a small black plaque near the front door identifying the church. Harlem was known for its many churches, so it made sense to her that an anti-church group would not draw heavily from the minorities who lived in the area. Of the sixty or so people who entered the building while Ronnie observed, most were Caucasian. The worshippers wore unfashionable clothing, several men in work shoes, giving her the impression of a predominantly working-class crowd.

She waited for the stragglers to enter and approached the door. She was confronted by a bone-thin man of five feet six in a black suit, black tie, black shirt, and black shoes. The blackness of his appearance was broken by the man's complexion, nearly ghostly white. Ronnie detected makeup.

"What do you want?"

"I'm Veronica Delaney. I'm here at the invitation of Mr. Cummings."

"Last row. No tape recording. No pictures."

"I'm going to take notes. That's what I'm here for."

"Do it quietly." And he stepped aside allowing her to pass.

The interior of the church was painted black, the space illuminated by candelabras with glowing black candles mounted along the side walls. The worshippers were sitting in pews. Randall Cummings, their leader, stepped to an altar, an imposing six feet two, wearing a hooded black robe, and she amused herself by wondering if he might be wearing black underwear with little Calvin Klein logos. He peered at the congregants before speaking. His face was elegant from what she could see of it, with a long, thin nose. The voice, as on the phone, was soft, resonant, Middle Atlantic announcer style. No, better than that, she decided, good enough for a voice-over on a PBS nature special on seabirds. She was having difficulty taking this seriously, it was so Halloween to her.

"My fellow worshippers, it was a good week for the forces of evil. But then it always is. And yet, does that translate into your everyday lives? In hard cash? In business opportunities? In a level playing field for people such as yourselves who are not the entitled heads of corporations, the CEOs who get rich on the backs of those who do the work, the Wall Street boys in their private jets and their weekend houses and their fancy boats and their fancy cars, and their lawyers in *their* weekend houses and fancy cars with their mistresses and lovers, in a system where the rich get richer and the hardworking work harder?"

In college she had taken a course on modern political movements and as she listened she thought it could have been an updated Socialist Party speech by Eugene V. Debs from 1920.

"But it doesn't have to be thus," as he began to depart from Debs. "You can channel a force greater than all the forces on earth—and do unto others before they do unto you. You can level that playing field. You can be allied with the power of darkness, which exists, as you know. As you all know."

The ghostly doorman wheeled out a cart with a television set attached to a DVD player, flipping it on with a remote. A fast-cutting series of images flashed on the screen, brutal images: war scenes, concentration camp scenes, American GIs dead in the streets of Iraq, dead or malnourished African children, crime scenes, an unremitting montage of civilization's inhumanities, the worst of Mankind, torture scenes, lynchings, floggings; and on the bottom of the screen, flashing repetitively, a crude attempt at subliminal messaging, the words: "Satan lives . . . Satan lives . . . Satan lives." She made a note for herself on the use of the footage for proselytizing—"unconscionable."

"Is there any question in your minds," Cummings said, as the five-minute film came to an end, "that evil—pure, constant evil—exists on this earth? It didn't just get here. It didn't just show up one night. It is the handiwork of the Prince of Darkness, whose power we are here to harness. And you will."

Cummings then encouraged participation, for people to stand and bear witness to the injustices done to them that week, a litany of slights at checkout counters, work settings, parking spaces, doctors' offices. The injustices, she noted, could easily have been from a Larry David routine on *Curb Your Enthusiasm*. But these people were in earnest. In each case Cummings offered words of encouragement of a perverse nature, that the aggrieved parties should lie, cheat, steal—summon the powers of evil to even the scores against them—and then he added that they should be sexually adventurous, too, illicit, if need be, to get their due in the world. Ronnie thought that was a tidy bonus, an invitation to sex folded into a satanic message.

She sensed that he walked an interesting legal tightrope, never overtly encouraging violence, keeping the fires banked on his particular modified view of evil, perhaps with an eye toward avoiding jail if any of his people were arrested for their actions.

Most of the testimonies from cult members were trivial, although some people expressed genuine pain over the illnesses and the deaths of loved ones. For these he offered a consistent form of guidance—take action. One congregant lost her husband in a farm accident in upstate New York.

"Your husband, what was his name?"

"Tom."

"Your Tom's unnecessary death proves the very existence of Satan. This week do something evil. Steal something. Take something that does not belong to you or something you have not paid for. There is nothing you can do about your husband's death. What you can do is learn from it and empower yourself—through Satan. Be powerful through evil. Channel the evil that took him. What will you channel?"

"Evil."

"And whose power is with you?"

"Satan."

"Amen," he said. "Whose power is with her?" he asked the congregation.

"Satan," was the answer in unison.

"Who?"

"Satan," they said, louder.

"Who will you win with?"

"Satan."

"Win with Satan."

He shook his head in the affirmative and she had an image of them pouring out of the church as if they had all been in a football locker room and were collectively going to rob a liquor store.

At the conclusion of the dozen testimonials, which lasted an hour, Cummings brought the service to an end by instructing them to join hands as he led them in chanting, "Satan is power, Satan is power, Satan is power."

She left the building quickly to get ahead of the cult members leaving. Her intention was to stand outside the doorway and pick up any random conversation. Everyone departing was concerned with a scene unfolding across the street. A police barricade was set up with a squad car parked nearby and two police officers on duty. Behind the barricade three men and two women were shouting, "Go to hell, go to hell!" They looked more rabid and unstable in their anger than the people leaving the satanic mass. A van bearing a NEW YORK NEWS logo was parked curbside, a camera crew shooting the proceedings.

Cummings came up alongside her outside the building.

"Are you Ms. Delaney?"

"Yes."

"A little commotion for your article."

"Apparently."

Across the street several cult members shouted back at the demon-strators. The two sides yelled at each other for a couple of minutes. Under pressure from the police, the cult members dispersed and the protesters, without a target, shouted a few epithets, random barks wind-ing down, and trailed away themselves.

The camera crew turned their attention to Cummings and walked toward him as he stood near the doorway, in his robe, hood up, prepos-terous in most settings; comfortable, though, in his own skin, under his hood, against the backdrop of his church. The crew consisted of a cameraman, a sound man, and a woman reporter in her twenties, a perky brunette. Here was a street demonstration protesting a satanic cult, which she was dealing with as if covering the Thanksgiving Day Parade.

"Mr. Cummings?" the reporter said, beaming. "I'm Sonya Brill."

"Randall Cummings."

"A pleasure."

Ronnie leaned back against the church wall, observing.

"Could you tell us, what are your goals with your organization?"

"We worship Satan, darling. We respect Satan. We make a study of Satan's work and we extract life's lessons."

"Which are?"

He launched into his speech with the do-unto-others portion, em-powerment through evil acts.

"How long have you been in existence?"

"Two years."

"And how did you come to this?"

"It came by way of a gradual awareness. When I realized that evil is endemic to our society. So we worship its dark creator to channel evil, to combat evil with evil, to level the playing field for our members."

"I see. Well, those people across the street, they didn't approve of you worshipping Satan."

"They have every right to protest against us and we have every right to congregate." And then in an apparent bid to use the television coverage to snare some new members he added, "We will win with Satan. We're here every week at our church and every minute on the Internet at Darkangelchurch.org."

"We have been talking to Randall Cummings on 129th Street, where protesters objected tonight to a satanic cult within their midst. Live for *New York News,* this is Sonya Brill."

She shook hands with Cummings and was off with her crew.

Ronnie turned to Cummings.

"You don't mind if I add to that, do you?"

"Ah yes, print versus TV. I'm sure you have a few other questions."

He led her along the outside of the building to a rear entrance, opened the door, and showed her to his office. The room contained a sleek black desk, a built-in television screen above an elaborate stereo system, gray walls, black Venetian blinds; the room was illuminated by an aluminum ceiling fixture and a stainless steel desk lamp for Cummings's work area, which included a computer and printer.

"It's a modern Satan we're dealing with, I see," she said, positioning a mini tape recorder on his desk.

"No, a timeless Satan. But to reach people today, you do need to be up to date."

"And how many cult members do you have, Mr. Cummings? It is *Mr.* Cummings, isn't it? There's no formal title?"

"A little sarcasm there, Ms. Delaney? That would be beneath you."

"Yes, a little, nonetheless—"

"It is Mr. You-can-have-fun-with-us. Shooting fish in a barrel. So easy to belittle the simpletons with their Satan worship, their *cult.* A sophisticated New York girl like yourself, *Vanity Fair* and the like."

"You researched me?"

"I did."

"I did the same with you. There's not much on you."

"We're new. So you've got an inside track here, Ms. Delaney. Now my advice is, don't be fooled. Someone as clever as you wouldn't be taken in by all the candles and atmosphere, I would expect. But Satan is real. I believe that."

"Do you?"

"Yes. And so do most God-fearing priests, the ones who aren't just filling time. There's too much evil in the world and the evil is too profound to be accidental." He peered deeply into her eyes as he said this, the same technique he used with his congregants. "What is your religion?" he asked.

"I was Catholic once."

"They have you forever, unless, of course, you'd like to come over to me."

"How many people are in your group?"

"About a hundred at services, another thousand via the Internet."

"And how do *they* worship exactly?"

"They receive the minutes of our masses. They can exchange e-mails with me. Buddy up with other congregants."

"And you've been at this two years. Before that? Where did you come from, your basic bio?"

"I'm from Chicago. I taught acting and drama at Macalester. And then there was a turning point in my life. What you heard me tell that woman about her husband's death. That comes from personal experience. My wife, a beautiful woman, kind, generous, was raped and beaten to death. They never found the murderer. You want to talk to me about evil? You want to say to me, there's no Satan?"

She couldn't tell. He had her. He could have been truthful about a wife, or not. She didn't know. And he knew he had her. She could sense it in his expression.

"I'm missing something, Mr. Cummings, in the philosophy here. The connection between the Satan you say exists and the practical means of harnessing Satan's powers, as you put it—"

"I encourage my people to lie, to cheat, to steal, to do nothing other than the big boys on Wall Street do, and the wheeler-dealers in those fancy-ass corporations."

"Lie, cheat, steal, but nothing worse?"

"I don't limit their imaginations."

"You don't seem to encourage them either. As though you're being careful."

"I don't write specific prescriptions, if that's what you mean."

"You seem to be limiting your culpability by not suggesting anything violent. Almost as if you've had benefit of counsel on limits, on being a co-conspirator."

"They can choose their evil."

"It seems to be within limits."

"That was hardly a Sunday sermon. I'm not telling them to run bake sales."

"That thing of sexual freedom. I can see where it can be a big draw. Illicit sexual behavior as a sanctioned activity."

"Whatever works. It's all up to them. Truth is, they need encouragement. They need someone to tell them they can be empowered. And I'm the messenger. They'll be better off for the message, doing unto others before they can be done unto, better off channeling evil, than they'd ever be mired in their helplessness."

"So what all this is, really, is kind of a self-help course with Satan as the hook."

"Oh, you're just too, too sophisticated, aren't you, Ms. Delaney? Our church is growing. People are helped." He had a manila envelope on his desk. "Here are minutes of previous masses. Testimonials from members. Some general background we provide to people who inquire about membership."

"Yes, I logged on to your Web site. It costs a thousand dollars a year to be in the cult, per person, fifteen hundred per family. That's not nothing for people without means."

"It's nothing for the empowerment they get." He handed her the envelope. "Try to go through this with an open mind. Give us the benefit of a fair-minded appraisal, without a 'gotcha' in it, if that's possible. And visit us again if you wish, attend another mass. Call me if you have any other questions."

"I will."

"I'd like to ask you a question: Would you ever go to dinner with a satanic cult leader?" he said wryly.

"Thank you for your time."

"Thank *you*, Ms. Delaney. And I'm serious about the dinner. As you may have noticed I'm very empathetic and supportive."

She prepared to leave. He studied her with his mannered, probing look. She had taken herself to a Black Mass, interviewed the cult leader. She was not intimidated in the least by him, but as she left his office, she was unnerved by his closing remark.

"We might do something about that sadness I see in your eyes."

The dream came again that night. The same elements. The little girl lost in the playground. The shattered glass. Something new this time. Cummings's face. He was peering straight ahead. She awoke, cold and sweating at the same time. She was all right while she was at the church, but she presumed it must have frightened her on some level, the darkness of the place, the violence of the film, the invocations of evil. She was angry with herself. A year since the last time. She thought the dream was gone.

2

For the background research on the piece Ronnie entered the dark tunnel of satanic belief in America. Documented on Web sites and described in articles and speeches accessible on the Internet were the bleak views of people in emotional shadows. They believed in the power of Satan, and in conspiracy theories, that every year across the United States an unknown number of children and adults disappeared completely or for periods of time, kidnapped by satanic cult members, sexually abused or sacrificed in cult rituals, some supposedly murdered, some supposedly returned to their everyday lives with repressed remembrances that could only be unlocked by recovered-memory therapy.

The belief in these abuses had fallen out of favor since the discrediting of such alleged cases in the 1980s, but there were still people holding to the idea of ritual crimes by dark forces. Cults openly invited prospects to join with a fee for membership, as with the Dark Angel Church. Also available on the Internet were the opinions of law enforcement experts debunking the idea of satanic conspiracies, and the pros and cons of satanism were debated in Internet chat rooms. "A gloomy loopiness alive in the land," Ronnie wrote in her notes.

Compared with most satanic Web sites, which featured gothic graphics and dark backgrounds, she found Cummings's Web site to be conservative and well designed, with white space and a clean Bodoni typeface. The Web visitor to Darkangelchurch.org could find the Cummings stump speech, remarks "shared" by congregants, along with a series of images taken from the audio presentation, Cummings's documentation of evil extant. Her overall impression was that Cummings tactically positioned himself as a moderate satanist, if there could be such a thing, nearly New Age in his approach.

On Thursday nights during the public school year Ronnie went to the Thomas Jefferson Recreation Center on 110th Street and Third Avenue to help children from the ages of about twelve to fifteen in creating a recreation center newspaper. Making the rounds of recreation centers was Peter Gibbins, a pediatrician volunteering with a nutrition class for teenagers. Gibbins came upon Ronnie in the lobby and they chatted. He asked her to join him for a hamburger after they were finished for the evening. He, too, was doing good deeds, her social life was dormant, and she accepted. They went to a pub on Third Avenue and Ninety-fourth Street. Gibbins was in his early thirties, five feet seven with soft brown eyes and an innocent, young face, who didn't seem to Ronnie as someone out of college yet, even though he was working at Lenox Hill Hospital in pediatrics.

Ronnie's roommate, Nancy, had been at her boyfriend's apartment for the past three nights. Except for a brief phone conversation with Nancy, and the work with the children at the recreation center, Ronnie really hadn't spoken to anyone for several days. When the conversation with Gibbins moved to her side of the table, her enthusiasm for the article she was working on, and her recent lack of adult contact, encouraged her to describe it all in an outpouring of enthusiasm. Somewhere in the middle of her monologue she became aware that this decent young man was squinting, apparently in distress, listening to her. She didn't know what was causing the reaction—the subject matter, or her—and suddenly she had an uncomfortable feeling about herself, that she was carrying on like a lonely girl with no one she could talk to. But it wasn't that, she told herself, it was as if she were trying out ideas for the piece, using this as a way of organizing the material. However, the squinting, the evident discomfort with her—it certainly wasn't going very well.

"I'm boring you."

"No, it's fascinating. But—odd."

"Odd?"

"You're dealing with such odd people. A person who preaches Satan. Cult followers. Doesn't it scare you?"

"Why would it scare me? It's ludicrous."

"You have to admit, what you're working on, it's not conventional."

"It's just an article I'm writing. *I'm* totally conventional. I don't even have a tattoo."

He didn't smile. Doomed before it began. They went through the motions, small talk about movies they had seen. They both declined coffee or dessert and Ronnie passed on his offer of a taxicab home and went back to her apartment in a taxicab on her own.

"I spooked a young pediatrician," Ronnie reported to Nancy upon arriving home.

"See, that's where we underrated Michael."

"How did we underrate Michael?"

"He's a chef, which isn't a traditional career, so he never had trouble with what you did."

"How do you figure bringing up what was nice about Michael does me any good right now?"

"Sorry, I was just making an observation."

"On the open market I scare guys off. Never occurred to me that a piece on a satanic cult was—odd. *Am* I odd?"

"No, you're single."

———

The concern of every freelance writer was how much time to spend on research before you were overextending yourself on an article. She had been doing the research for two weeks; time spent tracking the satanic noise on the Internet, going through books on satanism in the library, conducting interviews by phone with a priest in San Francisco who had delivered a sermon on God and Satan that appeared on the Internet, and a professor of religion at the University of Michigan, who was an outspoken nonbeliever in Satan. After one more bit of research she was going to begin writing. Richard Smith was the author of *The Many Faces of Satan,* a history of satanic worship she had purchased in paperback. She found it to be a good popular history. On the back cover the author's Web site was listed. Ronnie sent an e-mail to him explaining the nature of her article, asking if he would answer a few questions, and he responded by e-mail that he traveled frequently, but would be in New York that week and he would be glad to meet her for coffee, writer to writer. She e-mailed back and they agreed to meet at a Starbucks on Eighty-seventh Street and Lexington Avenue.

She brought the book along with her; his author photo was on the back cover and she identified him at a table.

"Mr. Smith? I'm Ronnie Delaney."

"A pleasure. I've read some of your things."

"Really? I've read your book."

She judged him to be in his late thirties. He was a trim, athletic-looking man in a blazer, white sports shirt and jeans, black loafers; light brown, wavy hair, pale light blue eyes, high cheekbones; so good-looking he was someone she would have taken for a model or a movie star, not "a noted lecturer on the subject of satanism, who has appeared at colleges and lecture halls throughout the world," as stated on the book jacket.

She told him about her visit to Cummings and his church and he knew about Cummings, that he was a recent starter in the satanic game. Ronnie was largely interested in exploring with someone who had written about satanism where he thought Cummings fit into the over-all pattern. Smith didn't feel Cummings was coming into it "heavy metal," as he put it, more like "easy listening."

This corresponded to Ronnie's sense and she offered that Cummings's approach reminded her of the satanist of the 1960s, Anton LaVey, who had a run for a while as a pop satanist, extolling lust and hedonism.

"Cummings does sound like LaVey. Satanism as a lifestyle. Sort of like being a vegan or smoking grass. Satanism Lite."

A good quote and she checked her tape recorder to see if it was running and jotted it down as backup.

"What do you think of these cults using the Internet? Something as old as satanism being promoted electronically?"

"Just shows the ability of the ideas in persisting."

"Why would you say people are drawn to these cults?"

"Because people believe in Satan."

"Uh-huh," she murmured without enthusiasm.

"Who can prove Satan doesn't exist?" he said.

"Are you talking proof? Who can *prove* he does? By the way, I couldn't tell from your book what you really think."

"You have to draw a distinction between Satan as a literary concept, as a metaphor for evil, and Satan as an actual presence, as an active instrument of evil."

"I don't think Cummings is using metaphors. I think he's talking Satan as an active presence in our lives, intervening, and for his people to follow Satan's lead."

"Well, that's the big leap of faith, isn't it, for people who believe in Satan, that he truly exists as part of our world? I don't think you can run a cult off a literary concept. Cummings would have to weigh in on Satan as a living presence. Like the churches weigh in on God as a living presence."

"And where are you in this?"

"Intelligent people believe some spirit, some force for good, holds things together in the universe. Call that God, if you will. If you accept innate good, couldn't you also be able to accept innate evil? And that would be Satan."

"Satan as a metaphor or Satan as a living presence?"

"If pressed, I'd say both."

"Cummings claims the murder of his wife was a turning point for him."

"That would affect your beliefs. There are very good reasons why people accept Satan."

"His followers seemed so vulnerable. Is he exploiting them?"

"People look for answers. You can ask the same about organized religion."

"Well, if Cummings is the new Anton LaVey, LaVey didn't last."

"Eventually, he died. That'll do it. Clearly, you didn't think much of this Cummings guy."

"He's about as profound as those children's drawings in school windows on Halloween."

They spoke a while longer and as they left the place she wondered if he looked back at her, since she was tempted to look back at him.

Over dinner with Nancy she described the interview with Richard Smith.

"I don't know how much is useful, but he was amazingly good-looking."

"You don't know how much is useful—is about the article. That he was amazingly good-looking is something else."

"I know. I can be into a piece, God, Satan, all that deep stuff, and then what I report back to you—"

"Is that you met an amazingly good-looking guy."

"Interesting how shallow I can be," and they both burst out laughing.

She had a couple of questions for Cummings after speaking to Richard Smith. She called and left a message and he returned the call.

"Ms. Delaney, Randall Cummings."

"Mr. Cummings, thanks for calling back. A couple of things I wanted to pin down. To be clear about it, your Satan, is that Satan as a concept or do you believe it's an in-the-world Satan? A living Satan?"

"Satan *lives,* darling. Watch the news any day of the week."

"Are you familiar with Anton LaVey?"

"Of course."

"Do you see any similarities—"

"None," he said sharply. "LaVey courted celebrities. He was part of the Rock-and-Roll Sixties. I have working people in my congregation and they're well served by their church in their lives."

"Could you tell me again why?"

"For people who feel they've been overlooked in society, who don't live off the spoils of Wall Street or social class, my church gives them safe haven and a level playing field. Did you get that?"

"I did."

"We are who we are and we're proud of it."

She spent another two weeks writing the piece, trying to balance a straight reportorial position describing Cummings, his ritual and philosophy, with her own feelings, that there was something sad in people feeling so besieged and disenfranchised that they were attracted to his church, which was essentially exploitive.

She was responsible for handing in about three thousand words and when she had a workable draft she passed it by Nancy, who liked it very much but thought by saying Cummings was as profound as children's Halloween drawings Ronnie wasn't going to win the Dark Angel Woman of the Year Award.

Importantly, her editor liked it with just a few minor word changes. "Satan on 129th Street" ran in the May 2, 2005, issue of *New York* magazine. Cummings was shown in color on a full page, wearing his black hooded robe, posed at the lectern in the church, his piercing eyes straight ahead in a forceful look that said, I've got The Answer.

Ronnie was careful to get Cummings's quotes straight, but not to sell memberships for the man. She made her comparisons to Anton LaVey, quoted Richard Smith on "Satan Lite," and if the license for sex Cummings offered and the balm for victims appealed to people, so be it. She felt she had done a responsible job.

A few days after the piece appeared she received a note from Father Connolly, her priest when she was a little girl in the Bronx, and who had presided when both her parents died. He wrote, "I saw the article in *New York* magazine and wanted you to know how very proud I am of you and how proud your mother and father would have been." She hadn't come down on the side of the devil and assumed that appealed to a Bronx parish priest, but the note touched her.

Nancy and her boyfriend, Bob, took her to a neighborhood Italian restaurant to celebrate. Bob was a real estate lawyer, a lanky six feet two with brown hair, dark brown eyes, and a hawk-like, intense face. A former distance runner at the University of Michigan, he sometimes jogged with Ronnie and Nancy in Central Park, slowing his Division I pace to accommodate them.

He toasted Ronnie. "To our girl, for a major article."

"And smart," Nancy added. "It's a smart piece."

"I don't imagine Cummings thinks so."

"Hear from him?" Bob asked.

"No, I'm happy to say. He's probably in the school of 'say anything you want about me so long as I get a full-page, full-color shot of myself in print.' "

"What's next?" Bob asked.

"*New York* wants me to do a piece on a bar that's a hangout for European soccer games on TV. How eclectic is this life?"

"This is why that doctor couldn't handle you," Nancy said. "You're a major person. You need more than Mr. Right. You need Mr. Fantastic."

"Then my odds are poor."

"I didn't mean it that way."

"I know. I accept the compliment. We're all major."

Nancy needed to pick up some clothes for the weekend and they went back to the roommates' apartment. Alex, their ancient doorman, was on duty. A frail man, too small for his doorman uniform, Alex was not the most efficient doorman in New York. Perhaps he was one of the oldest. Alex was famous for forgetting to give people packages or for giving people the wrong packages. For most of the tenants Alex was a source of amusement, their Alex, their opportunity to be kind to the working elderly.

"Something for you, Miss Delaney," and he handed over a white box tied with a green ribbon. There wasn't any indication of who sent it, just an index card with Ronnie's name written on it inside the ribbon.

"Do you know who this is from?"

"I didn't see anybody. It was left outside the door."

"Thank you, Alex."

He was pleased. He got the right package to the right person.

They went up to the apartment, Bob took a can of soda from the refrigerator, Nancy went into the bedroom to collect her clothing, and Ronnie sat at the dining table and opened the box. She saw no card on top of the white tissue inside. Her scream brought Bob and Nancy running into the room. Inside the box was a dead black cat.

As Nancy sat literally holding Ronnie's hand, Bob called 911. It took nearly an hour for two police officers to arrive. Bob commented to the women that the leisurely response time was apparently determined by the non-emergency nature of the call; the cat was already deceased. In this period of time Ronnie had moved from fright to something close to rage, positive Randall Cummings sent the box. The police officers asked some preliminary questions, one of them took notes, and the officers went downstairs so that the doorman could be interrogated. He didn't see anyone leave the box. It was outside the front door and he noticed it sitting there with the index card containing Ronnie's name. That was all he saw or knew.

"This is obviously a prank," one of the officers said when they came back into the apartment.

"It's a death threat," Ronnie said flatly.

"I'm an attorney," Bob said, backing her. "Not a criminal attorney, but nonetheless an attorney and I think you gentlemen have to raise the level of concern here."

"I write an article about a satanic cult and I get a dead black cat in a box. I take this very seriously."

The police officers left and an hour and a half later two plainclothes detectives came to the apartment. They were on another level of police work, which was largely dour. Detective Ralph Gomez, in his early forties, was a stocky man of five feet eight with a ruddy complexion, wearing a windbreaker, a checked sports shirt, and jeans. His partner, Detective Fred Santini, in his late thirties, was six feet one and gangly, with a protruding Adam's apple and small, narrow eyes. He also wore a windbreaker, with a sports shirt and cotton slacks.

After taking down the basic information Santini asked, "Is it possible it wasn't this cult guy who sent this?"

"Then one of his people," Ronnie said. "He's got about a thousand of them. For all I know they've got dead black cats stacked up like in a wine cellar."

Santini smiled slightly, Gomez did not.

"May I see the article?" Gomez said.

Ronnie produced a copy of *New York* magazine.

"May we have this?" Gomez asked.

"By all means."

"How long is this going to take?" Nancy said. "We've got a person here somebody tried to terrorize. I mean, are you going to get right on it?"

"We're on it right now, aren't we?" Gomez said.

"I guess we all want to know how this works, what the procedures are," Bob said.

"We'll take the box, determine cause of death of this cat, which conceivably could give us something," Santini said. "Check for prints. Did any of you handle the box?"

"Just me. And the doorman."

"We'll get your prints, if you don't mind," Gomez said. "And your doorman, and see what else is on it. My guess, there won't be anything else. Somebody does this, they don't leave prints."

"How would you know?" Ronnie said. "Have you had any experiences like this?"

"Not precisely the same. But—things go on."

"Ms. Delaney, anyone you're on the outs with? Like an old boyfriend?" Santini asked.

"I did have a boyfriend, but I assure you this is not his style."

The detectives had a fingerprint kit in their car, which they brought up, taking Ronnie's prints and then the doorman's to match against prints they might find on the box. They concurred that Cummings was a prime suspect and were going to pay him a call. Ronnie was eager for that to happen, for Cummings to know the police department was involved. She suggested they also talk to Cummings's assistant, whom she described as having the personality and the pallor for an action of this kind.

"I'm going to say this is nasty, but I'm not sure it's a death threat," Santini said. "If it came from these people, maybe they're just trying out, you know, their way of thinking. To scare you."

"But I wouldn't open any parcels for a while," Gomez added.

"That's very reassuring," Ronnie said.

She was in no mood to sleep alone in the apartment that night and Nancy rearranged her plans. She and Bob stayed there and Ronnie slept fitfully. In the morning Bob suggested a light jog to counter the tension of the previous night and they ran around the Central Park bridle path a couple of times with Cummings as a topic in and out of their conversation. She knew Cummings did it or he ordered it to be done— send the chick a dead black cat.

The lab test revealed no fingerprints on the box other than Ronnie's and the doorman's. Someone had taken care not to leave any. The cat died of rat poison mixed with cat food.

"Grisly, but it doesn't tell us anything," Gomez said to his partner.

Santini reached Cummings by phone and told him they wanted to ask him a few questions related to the recent article about him in *New York* magazine, that the writer received a threatening package, and that he should have his assistant also available.

"No problem," Cummings said smoothly. "One of the things we do in this business is answer questions."

The detectives left the Twenty-sixth Precinct building on West 126th Street and walked the few blocks to the church. The street was quiet, no protesters present across from the church at eleven on this rainy Saturday morning. Cummings told them to come by way of the rear entrance, and the assistant opened the door for them in a black suit, black shirt, black tie, with his chalkish white face, his working outfit.

"Mr. Cummings is expecting you," he said and pointed to Cummings's office.

"Your name is?" Gomez asked.

"Cosmo Pitalis."

"Don't go anywhere, Mr. Pitalis. We want to talk to you."

As they moved on, Gomez said, "We should bring him in. Guy who looks like that must be guilty of something."

Cummings greeted them in his office in a beige cashmere turtleneck and gray slacks, a sporty look for a satanist. He appeared to have left space within his ideology for a touch of personal vanity. He motioned for them to sit.

The detectives set out the circumstance: Veronica Delaney had been sent a dead black cat in an unmarked box and had, in effect, filed a complaint against Cummings, whom she suspected of sending it.

"I'm supposed to have sent it as a thank-you?"

"You have the motivation, Mr. Cummings," Santini said. "I read the article. I wouldn't call it flattering."

"Now why would I do such a thing? Think about it for a minute. I'm working on getting my organization to expand. Why would I try to intimidate the writer of the first major article about us?"

"How about you're the leader of a satanic cult?"

"How about it's not good marketing. I didn't send it."

"One of your people?"

"It wouldn't have been on my say-so. Gentlemen, it makes no sense whatsoever. She served her purpose. She wrote the article. She probably, and I'm guessing, thinks she put me away. But the public is unpredictable. I've actually received a couple of dozen inquiries since it appeared from people looking to sign up."

He wasn't going to admit it, even if he had sent it, and they had nothing linking him to the box. Their presence was principally to show the flag.

"Nothing more like this, Mr. Cummings. Criminal charges on a thing like this expand exponentially," Santini said.

"Absolutely. Nothing more of what I didn't do in the first place."

The detectives stood in the corridor with the assistant, who presented them with a chilly indifference. The Dark Angel Church did not welcome New York City police detectives.

"You saw the article in *New York* magazine?" Gomez said.

"I did."

"The woman who wrote it got sent a dead black cat in a box."

"So?"

"We don't approve of such things," Santini said.

"Do I look like someone who gives a damn?"

"If you sent it, don't do anything like that again, and if you didn't send it, don't do anything like it," Gomez said.

"Let me go inside and write it down so I don't forget."

"Don't get too cute, wiseguy," Gomez said. "You've been warned. We nail you on this, you'll do serious time."

"Noted."

When they were outside, Santini said, "What an operation. They probably did send it, one of them."

"We still don't have anything."

This was a bit of a cartoon now that Ronnie thought about it, a dead black cat. Scary, yes, but also dopey. She tried to put it all out of mind and started to do some work. She compiled printouts on soccer for her next piece. This was hardly her beat and she wasn't even sure there was a good story in the soccer bar; still it was going to allow her to become occupied with something other than this insane reprisal. She was at the computer for the rest of the day. Nancy called in and Ronnie assured her everything was all right. Ronnie watched soccer before going to sleep, a first in her life. The following day she went to the soccer place, located on Third Avenue and Thirty-third Street, and ordered brunch at the bar while various soccer games played on a variety of television screens. She fended off a few guys coming on to her, who were really more interested in the soccer when it came down to it, except for one particularly persistent and obnoxious fellow floating in beer with a burgeoning belly to show for his interests, pressing her on why she was there and whom she was rooting for, and finally she said, "You mean, what's a girl like me doing in a place like this? Writing a piece on blokes like you."

"You're a writer?"

"I'm a writer. Doing it for *New York* magazine. What do you do—"

"Mack. I'm an economist with Merrill Lynch."

She was reminded that you never really knew in bars. She conducted an interview with him—why he came to the place, what the scene was like for him, what he felt about soccer, why it hadn't caught on in the United States with the same passionate fans as in Europe. She bought him a beer as a courtesy for the interview and this seemed to indicate to Mack she was going to have sex with him, imminently, since he began to fill the air with sexual banter. She wondered if his approach ever worked.

"I'm only in this for the quotes," she said.

"What?"

"Never mind. But this is the tough part. For the fact-checkers, I have to ask you for your phone number. Can you give it to me without assuming anything?" He wrote his number on a piece of paper.

"You could call me," he said, sensing it slipping away. "I'm a different guy during the week."

"You're not a bad guy now. I'm just a preoccupied girl and not for you. Thanks for talking to me," and she walked out of the place, returning home to transcribe her tapes. A good day's work, Mr. Cummings. You can't touch me.

Santini and Gomez ran cross-checks on similar unwanted gifts and found nothing relevant. Various perverse actions, largely in the rejected lover category; rotting flowers, cheese, bowel movements sent as "gifts," but no dead black cat purveyor. They visited Ronnie a few days later.

"This would be impossible to prove," Santini said, as they sat in Ronnie's living room. "We suspect it's them. That doesn't do it."

"Cummings said, basically, it isn't in his business interest to do such a thing," Gomez added. "Look, they've been warned. My guess is, they got off on what they did and that'll be the end of it."

"You shouldn't be able to do something like that," Ronnie said, "but journalists, and I'll call myself that, have gone through worse. I'm on to my next piece."

"Good. We're here if you need us," Santini said.

"But it wouldn't hurt—" Gomez started to say.

She finished Gomez's thought, "—to not open any packages I'm not expecting."

She worked for the rest of the morning on the soccer bar piece and then met Nancy for lunch. Ronnie gave her an update on the detectives' findings, that they found nothing, and she was going to proceed as if it never happened.

As she approached the apartment building on the way back from lunch she heard a piercing squeal and hurtling into her path were three black cats. They ran past her, scattering in different directions. The air seemed to go out of her lungs from the shock. They had been thrown from the alleyway adjacent to the building. She ran to the alleyway to see if she could find the perpetrator. No one was there. She ran a few steps and stopped; what was she going to do, confront a crazy person?

In the apartment she called the number the detectives had given her, and within the hour they were sitting in the living room, the detectives writing down the details.

"So much for your theory that this is over," she said.

"We'll ask around. Maybe someone saw something," Santini said.

"And we'll talk to Cummings again."

"Didn't get you anywhere the first time."

"We'll give him the message again," Gomez said.

"Where are we? These people worship Satan. I want to make sure that doesn't get lost here. Am I in danger, or am I just being harassed by truly stupid people?"

"You said it," Gomez responded. "It's stupid. Black cats. I mean, come on."

After they left she went to her computer to work. When she stopped to think about the incident she reminded herself that journalists were known to have been victims of dangerous acts. Throwing cats in her path, or sending her a dead one, was a trivial retaliation. Then she concluded the danger wasn't these acts, rather it was that someone out there was capable of doing such things.

Nancy wouldn't be home for the next couple of nights, she was going with her boss to an awards ceremony in Boston for a client, and Bob would check in, Nancy told her. Ronnie settled into bed and it took her a long time to fall asleep. At some point she didn't even want to check how late it was. Her largest thought was that in the time of these events, interchangeably stupid and frightening, she had no family, her friends had their own lives. She was alone.

3

The unbroken success, the smooth stream of well-praised articles written from college days on through freelance life in New York, the substantial assignments for someone relatively young, hit a goalpost with
the soccer bar piece. Her editor at *New York* magazine sent it back twice
for rewrites, eventually paying her a kill fee and rejecting the piece.
Nancy offered that it was a mismatch of writer with the material, she
didn't have a feel for soccer or a soccer bar. Ronnie agreed, but con-
ceded, unhappily, that she had been thrown off stride by the harassment.
No other incidents occurred in the several weeks since the scrambling
cats. It still lingered in her mind, though—her sense of aloneness at a
time of stress, and the images, those creatures, that somebody would do
such bizarre things to intimidate her.

Determined not to allow further damage, she made queries on a
couple of pieces to *Vanity Fair* and *New York* magazine, and while waiting to hear, accepted a modest assignment from the City section of *The*

Sunday New York Times on upscale retail in the meatpacking district; as she described to Nancy, "Something to keep on trucking."

Ronnie and Nancy brought in pizza for dinner and were catching up— Nancy had been at Bob's apartment the past few nights—when the phone rang and it was Richard Smith.

"I've been out of town and just got back to read your piece on Cummings. Terrific job."

"Thank you."

"And thanks for the mention. I was wondering if I could buy you dinner to celebrate. Are you free Monday night?"

"Well, I really am past celebrating. Somebody was harassing me after it appeared. And I've moved on."

"Are you okay?"

"It stopped, but it put the whole thing out of the celebration mode."

"Let's just call it dinner then. Two professionals. Balthazar at eight?"

She loved Balthazar in SoHo, too pricey under normal circumstances, a special event place for her. But who was this guy, she didn't know anything about him other than his author's credentials.

"Could you hold on a sec?"

She went back inside to Nancy.

"Richard Smith, the amazingly good-looking guy, wants to take me to Balthazar for dinner."

"Is that a problem?" Nancy said.

"Think it's inappropriate to ask for a résumé? I know," answering for herself, "it's just dinner."

She got back on the phone.

"One question. You're not married, are you? We have kind of a house rule around here to not have dinner at Balthazar on Monday nights with married guys."

"Not married. See you at eight."

"See you."

———

He was at the table when she arrived, wearing what seemed to be his signature outfit; blazer, sports shirt, jeans, and loafers; a different sports shirt, beige this time, white the first time—and what did it mean that she remembered the shirts he wore. He *was* amazingly good-looking, she noted, and in a teenage way, rated him as the best-looking guy who had ever sat across a table from her. She wore a simple black dress, but her best black dress, with pearls, a true serious-date outfit.

"Bet you're the prettiest writer to ever expose a satanic cult."

"A narrow field, I'm sure."

"What is this harassment about?"

Over drinks she told him about her travails and he listened thoughtfully.

"You've got the police on it. And Cummings realizes you've got the police on it. My guess is, it isn't Cummings personally. Probably someone in the cult who thinks he's doing him a favor."

"However it evolved, it happened."

"This is probably the level of their acting out. Something like this happened to me about five years ago. I was giving a lecture on cults at the University of Colorado at Boulder and mentioned a group living in a satanic commune nearby, called them 'hippie holdovers,' and the next morning when I went to my car in the motel parking lot, the window was smashed and some kind of blood was splattered on the seat."

"That's ugly."

"But that was it. Nothing else happened. So with Cummings, they may have taken their best shot."

"Who accumulates cats? You think they have a cat wrangler?"

"Main thing is, you wrote a super piece. There are always risks. Write about a powerful person, you might get sued. You'd be better off with stray cats."

They ordered dinner and talked about their respective careers. He described himself as having been at a newspaper in South Dakota originally, where he did a series on a local satanic cult. As he read more about the subject he began to write and then lecture on cults and satanism and found this niche.

She traced her background for him, from college to the present. He offered that she was doing the right thing for her talents, which he could see were in evidence, and she shouldn't be derailed by unworthy people. He was notably at ease with himself. None of the jittery, if I don't get laid in the next hour my entire life is a failure, or how can you be working such an odd side of the street, as with her recent encounters with men. She felt she was in Michael territory, in this person's easy acceptance of her profession. Physically he was not Michael, though, he was dramatic. The hostess came over several times to check on their table, the Brad Pitt treatment.

Richard was interested in the freelance writing life from her perspective. He told her his experience was slanted largely toward the academic side, papers in university publications. His book was published by Excelsior Publications, a small independent press. He was thinking of doing more general-interest writing.

She was conscious about speaking in a rush and tried to answer in measured terms, feeling a little young with him. He was as poised and soft-spoken as he was good-looking, and he stayed alert to her, as though she was the most unusual person for *him* in a long time.

"Something I'd like to show you," and he removed from a black leather attaché case a rare book, wrapped in tissue. "Thought you'd be interested, unless when you're finished with a subject you're finished with it."

She thumbed the pages of a book bound in rich brown leather with gold casing, the pages made of thick parchment paper, the text printed in French.

"It's by an eighteenth-century monk from Rouen. Claimed he dined regularly with Satan and cooked dinners for him. Truly. This is a recipe book of their so-called meals together."

"Fabulous."

"After he wrote the book he committed suicide. Poisoned himself. Or maybe, as legend has it, he was done in by the big guy himself. A cult grew up around it for about twenty-five years or so, people who cooked from the recipes in the hope Satan would drop in on *them* for dinner."

"Wouldn't think he'd be a welcome guest."

"To be in the presence of his power, I suppose. I've got another book, fascinating, too big to carry around. An encyclopedia of Satan, in German, published in 1860. Everything you always wanted to know about Satan but were afraid to ask."

"That's a peppy title for nineteenth-century German."

"Title is simply *Satan,* and it has all known facts about Satan to that point. And personal appearances," he said lightly, "as they were documented up to then."

"Like a celebrity register."

"Something like that," he said, smiling. "Would you like to see it? Now, I mean."

There it was, he was inviting her to his place. She did a quick tally as to how often she went to a man's place this early on. Not often. Hardly ever. She had done so with Michael. It was the nature of their first date, she went to his apartment so he could prepare dinner for her. Richard Smith was such an adult compared to some of the men she had met, she hesitated to even think of this as "a date." The first whatever-it-was and he was inviting her back. Was she actually interested in a Satan encyclopedia published in the nineteenth century after she had already written the piece on a satanic cult? Not exactly. She was a little more interested in seeing where and how this person lived.

After dinner he hailed a taxicab and they went to a brownstone on East Sixty-first Street between First and Second avenues. He led her up the outside steps, through a narrow entrance foyer into the living room, an immaculately designed modern space with high-style Italian furnishings, a stainless steel mantle for the fireplace, and a striking collection of framed Berenice Abbott photographs on the wall.

"This place is wonderful," she said. He guided her past a functional kitchen—we don't cook here—into the second room on the floor, a den/library with floor-to-ceiling bookcases, many rare book bindings on display, and a few more pieces, sofa, chairs, lamps, direct from Milan. "It's like something out of *Architectural Digest.*"

"Thank you."

"Really, all this from lecturing and from one book?"

"I've always been interested in design. As for the building, it's owned by a European corporation. They have the ground floor for offices. Nobody is ever there. I'd like to call them Eurotrash, but why trash a benign landlord."

"Can I bring dates here to hang out?" she said.

He laughed, led her to the sofa, and went to the center bookcase. On the mantle was an unabridged dictionary–size volume he brought over to her and placed on a white marble coffee table.

"Some cognac, another wine?"

She already had two glasses of wine at dinner, her maximum before she fell asleep before their very eyes.

"I'm fine. A Diet Coke, if you have it."

"I'll see."

A Diet Coke. How sophisticated is that? She guessed that right about then he had her down as little more than a teenager.

The Satan encyclopedia contained more than a hundred glossy illustrations, renderings of Satan over the ages, and a detailed history of Satan and satanism, including first-person accounts of interactions with Satan.

"There's a perverse elegance here," she said. "It's a beautiful book."

"Satan's part of religious thought, even if *you* don't take him seriously."

"I'm a modern woman. I drink Diet Cokes," she said, looking to defuse her drink selection. He was drinking cognac, elegantly. "How many copies of this are there, do you think?"

"About three in the world."

"You could probably sell it and buy your *own* brownstone."

"I'll keep that in mind," he said. He had moved from a chair opposite the sofa, sitting next to her as she turned pages of the book.

It was like falling. And fast. He was kissing her, velvet lips, his lips on her neck, his hands confident; and swiftly, as though he would not allow a breath of protest, he had her clothing off, carrying her, kissing her all the way, to a bedroom she never really saw, the lights were out. But for the digital indicator on a clock, the room was dark. His hands and tongue were all over her, above and below.

"You have to wear something," she managed to murmur.

"No problem," he said as he caressed her with hands and tongue until she could barely stand it, he was still not inside her, and he had virtually brought her to orgasm, and then he was there, and it was slow, deep penetration, nearly beyond endurance. They were usually done before her; Michael, in particular, not a long-distance runner; but this man seemed capable of being in control and waiting for her, and then in a gasp, it was there for her, and only then, after her, did she feel as though it was over for him.

In repose, they didn't speak. She didn't know what to say, she was usually in some kind of control, and here she was out of control, played by him, confidently, this is what I can do for you, as though he had given her a drug. That was it, practically drugged by the sex. He was aroused more quickly than anyone she had ever been with, and still he took his time, brought her along with his caresses to the nearly unbearable until she had to have him inside her and then, finally, after his patience, the driving penetration caused her to cry out.

She slept deeply and when she awoke she didn't know for the moment where she was. To add to her disorientation she never really found her bearings the night before, she never saw the room in the light, and now it was morning and the space revealed itself, a large bedroom with more ultra-chic imported Italian furniture, the room silver and white, shimmering silver drapes on the windows, and most notably, no sexual partner in view. The clock on a nightstand next to the bed read 6:53, at least not embarrassingly late, and in the odd modesty of these rituals, she looked around for her undergarments before trying to find him, remembered he had taken her clothes off downstairs, and then saw a neat pile on a chair, all her belongings, as though housekeeping had come in and cleaned up after, and a note sitting on top of the little pile. "Had to make an early flight. Off to Mexico City. Will call. You're great. Richard." Seduced and abandoned, she said to herself. She went into the exquisitely appointed bathroom, used the facility, rubbed some of his toothpaste around her mouth, rinsed, dressed, and left, catching a glimpse of herself in a store window on a street corner waiting for a cab, noting that she looked like the classic girl in a black dress early in the morning, on her way home from a sleepover.

Nancy was standing in the kitchen eating a yogurt for breakfast when Ronnie entered the apartment.

"Yes?" Nancy said, noting the night-before outfit.

"I never got home from Balthazar."

"I see. Was it an intellectually stimulating evening?" she said.

"Best sex I ever had in my life. It was like I was drugged. I could be his sex slave."

"That's great and not great."

"Left me sleeping, with a note."

"A love note?"

"A travel bulletin. Off to Mexico City. What did I do here?"

"It's too soon to tell."

Richard sent a dozen roses, which arrived that morning, serving to ameliorate the cold and impersonal nature of the leave-taking. The card said, "Sorry about the departure. Will catch up when I'm back in town." She jotted down his phone number and address on leaving, but what was she going to do, call when she knew he wasn't there, write him a letter? She had one good way of reaching him and that was by e-mail, her original method of contacting him, and she sent an e-mail after editing it as carefully as if she were working on an article:

Thank you for the flowers. A fascinating night on many levels. I don't usually do what I did but I'm not sorry I did what I did, if that makes sense. What does Mexico City mean, what are you doing there, when will you be back?

She figured he arranged for the flowers before his plane departed. Allowing the travel time to Mexico City, even if he checked his e-mail, and she didn't know if he did, it wouldn't be until evening before she heard back from him. She heard nothing from him for six days and then an e-mail:

Have been doing research in back country. Be back in New York three weeks. Will call when I get there.

Not signed "best" or "love" or "regards" or "stay well" or anything cordial, just "will call when I get there." What was research in the back country? Was he the Indiana Jones of satanic cults, she wondered. It would be a month since their night together before she saw him again, assuming he did call upon arriving.

New York magazine did not hold the lamentable soccer piece against her, the editor acknowledging it wasn't a good fit. They accepted her proposal for another piece about the Public Art Fund, an organization that placed art and sculpture in public places in the city. Almost immediately she found herself in a social quandary. A sculptor, Tony Weston, working on a large aluminum piece that was going in at the edge of Central Park near the Plaza Hotel, turned out to be a nice-looking, curly-haired man in his thirties; sports shirt, chinos, sneakers; prototypical good-looking artist type, articulate, amusing. After Ronnie interviewed him, he asked her to join him for dinner in the park, an offer that couldn't have been more pleasant; they would pick up sandwiches and wine and sit on the grass. She said no. Politely, but no. House rule—she and Nancy were against sleeping with more than one man at one time. But was she sleeping with Richard Smith, was she waiting to sleep with Richard Smith, what was he to her, what was she to him? Trying to elevate their night together to the promise of something else, "on spec," as she defined it, on the chance that it might work out with Richard, she said no to this perfectly acceptable person.

————

"Am I crazy?" she asked Nancy in their dining area. "I have nothing going on with this Richard Smith and I turn down a possibility with someone else?"

"You don't know that. Your Richard—"

"Not *my* Richard—"

"*This* Richard obviously put his sting into you. Play it out. See if he shows up. If not, it won't be the first one-night fling in the history of the five boroughs."

She liked working on the Art Fund piece, enjoyed the people at the organization and the artists, and was motivated to do a good job to compensate for her woeful previous endeavor. Work was in the forefront again, no scary stuff from the cult, that was receding, old news. Not hearing from Richard was integrated into the rest of her life; she would give him another few days, three exactly, and then *she* would call the sculptor, find out if he still had any interest in seeing her.

"Ronnie, it's Richard. Richard Smith."

That was telling for her. He had been intimate with every contour of her body and he had to throw in his last name.

"Yes, well, I'm Ronnie Delaney."

"I really meant to call, but it's been madness. There's this cult, a breakaway from the Catholic Church in Mexico, and I needed to see what they were doing. And they're elusive."

"What is it, a month since that night?"

"Is it? Ronnie, I'm not coming back to New York as I thought I would. I'm in New Orleans. For a conference. And they gave me a really good deal. I can have a guest, free airfare, expenses. How would you like to come down for the weekend?"

"I don't hear from you all this time and you just—emerge—and invite me to New Orleans for a weekend?"

"Ever been here? It's a great city. The Ritz-Carlton, front-line hotel. What do you say?"

They had no house rule covering it. Someone you've already slept
with, whom you've been hoping will call, but were only prepared to
give another couple of days before writing him off, calls within the
time allotted and invites you to New Orleans.

"I don't hear from you, then it's 'jump on a plane and come see
me.' Richard, I have a life."

"I respect that. There's a panel Saturday. Come for that. You could
go back Sunday. It's an open ticket. Good jazz, good eating. Please,
Ronnie. We'll have a great time."

The panel was at Tulane University, "Satan in the Modern Age," featuring Richard, a Catholic priest, and a local journalist who covered religious matters. The moderator was a professor of comparative religion
at the school. The event was being held in a lecture hall with about
three hundred students, faculty, and members of the public in atten-
dance. Ronnie occupied a seat in the rear, fascinated with the discussion, a serious exploration of the possible existence of Satan; the
journalist opposed to the notion, the priest in favor, and Richard taking
a position similar to the attitude in his book, making the arguments and
ultimately coming out in favor of the existence of Satan in a reasoned,
intelligent manner. He was smooth, deft, as confident on stage as he
had been with her.

A student asked a question from the floor following the discussion.
"It doesn't help, does it, when you have the green-eyed-monster version
of Satan? Not very persuasive for someone interested in reality, as I'd
like to think I am."

Richard replied, "You're quite right. Images of Satan, the green
eyes, the horns, the tail, they're artists' conceptions, evolved over time.
They have no more validity than God being a man in a robe with a
white beard. In the modern world we understand God can be a spirit."

The journalist, an intense man in his forties, said, "These spirits, as
you put it, Mr. Smith, God and Satan, do they float around?"

Richard countered, "I wouldn't say 'spirit' in the movie sense, like something you see in some kind of shape or form. Let's think of God as a force, and Satan as a counterforce. In the Bible, Lucifer—Satan, if you will—was a high-ranking angel."

The moderator offered, "Many scholars and laypeople prefer to read the Bible as literature, not fact."

Richard replied, "But people who *do* accept the Bible as a kind of truth do so with a leap of faith. You don't need a leap of faith to recognize evil in history. What I ask us to consider here today is that some acts of evil might not be an intrinsic part of human nature, but the result of an outside force."

"On that note, we're going to bring the discussion to an end. . . ."

Ronnie smiled out of respect for the cool manner in which Richard comported himself. She didn't believe a word he said, but thought he owned the stage.

Back in New York, Nancy and Bob were dining in. Bob had made the dinner, ironically, with a recipe Michael featured on his cooking show, roast pork and beans.

"I liked Michael," Bob said. "Too bad it didn't work out."

"Ronnie and I were in Tower and they were featuring a new album and it was the very Rosetta Dupree. Ronnie sampled the album in the store and here's the bad part, she sings great. A husky, great voice, and you could see Ronnie's face fall. Plus she looked good on the album cover, really glamorous."

"If that's what he was looking for, glamorous. Ronnie's so pretty. Maybe not glamorous, but smart and a terrific writer. Guys are bad news."

"Am I supposed to say not *all* guys?"

"What's she doing this weekend?"

"She's in New Orleans with Richard Smith, who gave her a quote for her piece on the cult, and he took her out, and they got it on, and he disappeared on her for a while, business travel or something, and now he invited her down there."

"Let's Google him."

They went to the computer and found the same material Ronnie originally located, the Web site on the book and a series of listings of lectures and articles on satanic cults.

"Looks like he's smart. Not too much on him personally."

"That seems to be the situation. All she knows, I think, is that he isn't married, or so he says."

Nancy was not going to get into the amazing-in-bed portion, which would lead to a discussion of just what *is* good in bed, and the next thing Bob would be circling around on how he stacked up and you didn't go there.

"Let's keep an eye out. I'm going to want to check this guy out if he's a keeper," Bob said.

"You know, it wasn't like she was in a bad relationship with Michael. He was terrific for her, until the day he wasn't."

"Men *are* bad news."

"Not *all* men, honey," she says, on cue.

After the panel discussion, Ronnie met Richard in the lobby.

"That went very well for you."

"Lively, wasn't it?"

He did not suggest they go directly to the hotel for sex, which she would not have objected to; he offered a little walking tour of the pre-Katrina French Quarter, and they paused along the way to observe street performers on display for the tourist trade. He knew his way around the area and led them to a raffish bar for oysters and beer.

"Wonderful."

"Just an appetizer. This is a great city. Never been here?"

"I'm not the world traveler you are. What is this cult you've been tracking down and how do you do that exactly?"

"A foundation grant. It's a group that adapts Black Mass rituals out of the old satanic playbook combined with Mayan symbols."

"And you do what?"

"Document it. Videos. Interviews."

"You are a true believer, aren't you? 'Outside force.' Really now."

"Just throwing out ideas."

"Throwing out ideas? Are you backing off?"

"Only a little. There's no way to prove anything without that leap of faith."

"Ideologically, you're turning out to be a good-looking Randall Cummings. Not that Randall Cummings isn't good-looking. A better-looking Randall Cummings."

"Let's go back to the hotel," he said. "Relax a little before dinner."

She was ready.

The sex was an intermingling of what she remembered from the first time with him and fantasized since, leaving her searching for the word to describe the state of lovemaking with this man, deciding it was something out of a perfume ad, and the word she settled on was "ecstasy."

They ate dinner at a small Creole restaurant he knew on a side street just off the French Quarter, a brilliant meal, seasoned with his observations about New Orleans, of the early days when the music of churches, spirituals, funeral marches, black brass bands came together in a new musical form that didn't even have a name at first, and then it moved north to Chicago along with the migration of blacks northward, King Oliver looking out for the young Louis Armstrong, at first in New Orleans, then summoning him to play in the Creole Jazz Band in Chicago.

"Who are you? You do God and Satan and Louis Armstrong?"

"I tend to lecture. I apologize."

"Where are you from originally?"

"I was born here. In New Orleans. I was an institutional child."

"Your birth parents?"

"Haven't a clue. The people who adopted me were working people. I wasn't brought up to be religious. They weren't into religion. My father was a carpenter, my mother a seamstress. They died in a fire, visiting her sister. I wasn't there. I was sleeping over at a friend's house."

"That's so sad. How old were you?"

"Ten. I went back into the system, was in four different foster homes through to the end of high school, then after high school I basically self-educated myself, worked at odd jobs, one was with a newspaper in Yankton and there was the cult nearby I wrote about. One thing led to another and I became this expert on satanism."

"So when you said that thing about Cummings, about losing his wife affecting his ideology, it's not a totally benign view of the world *you're* carrying around."

"Can you draw a line from my personal experience to what I believe? More likely, it's that leap of faith."

He was pensive; the waiter came for a dessert order and they allowed the somber mood to dissipate.

He wanted her to hear some jazz in a club he liked and they walked for fifteen minutes through twisting, narrow streets to a part of the city where no one else was walking. Muffled sounds of television sets played in apartments, dogs barked, and notably, cats were squealing in a back alley, an unpleasant reminder. She was beginning to feel uncomfortable on this eerie walk.

"Wouldn't a cab have worked a little better?"

"Walking off the meal. Good for the digestion."

"Is that what this is? Richard, are we lost?"

"I'm leading the way. A few minutes more."

The buildings were shabbier the farther they walked, it was not even 10:00 P.M. and they hadn't seen anyone on the streets for several blocks, and as they turned the corner a half-dozen teenagers in baggy pants, their baseball caps turned around hip-hop style, came swaggering directly toward them, insolent, menacing. She squeezed Richard's hand tightly. Nobody else was on the street, just the two of them and the teenagers drawing closer. He held her tightly by the hand and walked directly into the middle of the group, staring them down, meeting their insolence with his boldness. They parted and he led Ronnie through, around the corner, and the danger was over.

"Street stuff. A thousand stare downs when I was growing up."

"That was dangerous, Richard. What are we doing here?"

"Going to hear some jazz."

They walked another couple of blocks and a neon sign over a doorway announced, BERRY'S JAZZ. He registered no surprise, not a question in his mind that he would find it.

The group in the club was a piano, bass, guitar, and drums, a soft, elegant sound, different from the Dixieland that permeated most of the French Quarter. It took her a while to settle down and absorb the music, ill at ease from the walk there, wondering if he had placed her in danger with his nonchalance. On the other hand, he never gave off the least indication of any danger, and ultimately, there wasn't a problem; they were listening to jazz, as promised.

With the flight down, the long day, the tension of the nightcap portion, she fell asleep shortly after getting into bed. He aroused her in the night and took her, and in the morning the sex seemed dreamlike.

When he informed her he wasn't returning to New York with her, but going to Portland, Oregon, to interview a psychologist who specialized in deprogramming cult members, and then was going to conduct interviews with the people the psychologist treated, she was not surprised.

"Who is this for?" she asked.

"Same foundation as the Mexico work. After that there's a seminar in San Diego. Wish I could be back in New York. Keep working and time will fly, you'll see."

The pattern had revealed itself. At this point he was not someone she would be able to count on for a consistent social life. She could count on him for the sex. Not for a Saturday night movie and hamburgers. Unless he happened to be in New York. Unless there wasn't anyone else. Teasingly, or possibly more than a tease; insistently, she extracted his cell phone number, which she didn't have, Richard warning her he used it for emergencies largely and didn't always check his messages. E-mail was the best way to reach him. She had just slept with a man, again, who traveled, and who didn't answer his phone.

Part of his deal was a car to the airport and they went to the airport together. The driver stopped at her departure area first.

"Richard, a question. How many of me are there?"

"That's too self-deprecating, Ronnie. There aren't any more of you. I do move around a lot. It's the nature of my work. I'll be back in New York in about a week and a half. Call you first thing," which he emphasized with a serious kiss on the lips.

Nancy was at Bob's apartment. Ronnie unpacked from the weekend and went out to buy some ingredients to make an omelet for dinner, her mind drifting; the new article, Richard, the sex, the knowledge that he was not someone you would take home to your parents at this stage of the relationship, if it could indeed be called a relationship, assuming one had parents.

As she left the building she noticed at the alleyway, the same alleyway where the cats were tossed in her path, a man in a black raincoat, chinos, and sneakers, with a deerstalker hat, flaps down, lampblack on his face like a deranged commando. In an underhand motion he tossed something in her direction and darted into the alleyway.

"Hey, you!" she called out, and ran toward the alleyway. When she got there he was gone. She walked back to look on the ground to see what he had thrown. It was a two-inch porcelain death skull with hollow eyes.

4

In a city where violence often led the eleven o'clock local news, these harassments of Ronnie Delaney were insignificant. Ronnie read that in the faces of Detectives Santini and Gomez. She brought the death skull to the precinct and the desk sergeant referred her to the detectives. They took down the information at a desk and kept the object, carefully placing it in a glassine envelope.

"It's Cummings again," she said. "It had to be one of his people. Who else cares?"

"This is going to be very hard to prove," Gomez said.

"If you could see your faces. Why should big-city detectives like us bother with this trivial little case? Why don't we just wait for one of them to kill me and then you'll have something to work with? Do you have a supervisor? Is this like the phone company where I get to say, I'd like to talk to your supervisor?"

"Absolutely," Gomez said.

They withdrew and a few minutes later returned with a ramrod-straight man of six feet four in plainclothes, wearing a blue Dacron suit, white shirt, and blue tie; another cheerless fellow, and that was all right with her, if he turned out to be competent.

"Ms. Delaney—Lieutenant Ed Rourke. I'm in charge of the detective squad here."

"I don't know how much you've been told, but I'm being harassed. In a really scary way."

"Yes, I know all about it. Can I see this latest object?"

Gomez handed him the envelope and Rourke held it up to the light.

"Almost like a Cracker Jacks toy," Gomez said.

"*That* is what's troubling me, the way it's being trivialized around here. I'm being threatened by unhappy people who worship Satan."

"Did the man who menaced you, did he look like someone you might have seen when you were working on your article?" Rourke asked.

"He might have been at the church when I was there, I don't remember seeing him. He looked like a lunatic. Black stuff under his eyes, on some lunatic mission. He might be a member via the Internet. He might be hired for all I know. It's what I'd like you to find out and bring this stupid thing to an end."

"If you're going out of your house to do any shopping, local chores over the next few days, call this number." He wrote it on a pad. "We'll have a police car come by to give you protection. We can't do it forever, but for a while." He turned to the detectives. "Go back and talk to Cummings again. Tell him he's a suspect, that he's aiding and abetting. And we'll go from there."

"Thank you," Ronnie said.

"Detectives Gomez and Santini are from homicide. They've been assigned to us on another matter, but because there was, possibly, a death threat here, they're helping us out. You've got the best of the best, and when Detective Gomez says 'Cracker Jacks,' I understand what he means. It's childish, really. Frightening, I grant you, but childish."

"Except if it's happening to you."

After Ronnie left the station house, Rourke said, "I know. This is impossible. But lean on him. Tell him we'll be questioning him for every violent crime that takes place anywhere in the city for the next five years. He'll get the idea."

"*If* he's involved," Gomez responded. "Could be somebody else."

"Likelihood is it's one of his screwballs. He can get the word out that he doesn't want her harassed. Maybe this'll just go away."

Everybody with whom Ronnie had professional contact during the course of a day or a week or a month would be going to their offices where other people in their offices would be present. She would be home, by herself, unless she called for police protection while she went out to buy a container of milk.

She sent Richard an e-mail:

Came home to find a man outside my building menacing me. Threw a little death skull at me and ran away. It was a good time in New Orleans, but this isn't good.

No instant messaging back. She checked a couple of times before going to sleep. He did not send a reply.

The dream came again that night, the shattered glass, with an added element, a huge death skull filling the screen of her nightmare, jarring her into wakefulness.

She went into the kitchen for a drink of water and when she turned on the light a mouse darted across the floor. Great. New York slices of life. Maybe she should have *owned* a black cat, she pondered. She set out glue traps the superintendent of the building had given her on a previous mouse sighting and went back to bed, falling asleep a second time close to 6:00 A.M. and waking with the alarm at 7:15.

She ate breakfast and went right to her computer for the Public Art Fund piece. Nancy came in from Bob's place to change before going to work and they talked about the weekend. New Orleans with Richard was not the lead, it was the death skull. Nancy suggested that Bob stay over a while; he had spent nights there in the past, and he could just be around in the evenings. Ronnie thought that would be good, as much for the idea of not feeling isolated as for the actual security his being there would provide.

Richard Smith called her Monday morning before nine.

"This is bad stuff. I wish I were there. I'd go right up to Cummings and deck him."

"He's a big guy. I don't think he gets decked easily, but I appreciate the thought."

"The police?"

"They're going to watch out for me. For a while anyway. And talk to him again."

"Good."

"My roommate's boyfriend is going to stay over, too, a few nights, I'd guess. Tell me where you are again?"

"Portland, Oregon. Interviewing people. Are you working?"

"I am."

"Good. Don't let yourself be reduced to the level of this idiocy. I'm going to be back there soon enough."

Detective Santini phoned Ronnie to say they interrogated Cummings to make him feel uncomfortable. He denied involvement. They told Cummings if the harassment didn't stop he was going to bring all kinds of problems on himself; a satanic cult operating in New York City didn't want to be on the wrong side of the authorities.

The first few days after the menacer appeared she was still apprehensive when she went into the street, even with a police car nearby, then she began to feel imprisoned, uneasy with the need to call for protection every time she went out. This was her neighborhood, her city, she didn't want her freedom of movement taken away from her, they weren't going to do that to her. Bob was staying at the apartment and after a few nights without incident, she released Bob of his obligation; she thought it was too disruptive of his life. Rourke called to say they couldn't continue shadowing her, she should let them know if anything untoward occurred. Richard e-mailed a couple of times, saying he was a little off schedule and would be returning to New York imminently.

The Art Fund piece was completed and submitted and she waited to hear about any possible changes. She was eating Chinese food in bed, channel surfing, and on the screen, hooded and glaring, was Randall Cummings. He was being interviewed in a television studio by the same woman reporter who came to the church when Ronnie was there, the peppy Sonya Brill. Why he would be given airtime was answered for Ronnie by the cloyingly friendly manner in which he was being interviewed. Cummings had made a pass at Ronnie, which he didn't seem to expect would work. Something evidently worked there; Sonya Brill had ventured into the occult on a personal basis, Ronnie surmised. The woman was carrying on brightly as if Cummings were an actor in a newly released movie—it was great fun making it, we all had a good time on the set, and we hope the public will really, really like it.

"And you feel people who join your cult are helped?"

"Absolutely. We show results. People are looking for answers in these troubled times, and for many of them, we have the answers."

"And they tell you this?"

For Ronnie it was starting to look like an infomercial.

"Yes, they do. We don't live in an especially moral society. All I'm doing is empowering the little guy with Satan."

Sonya Brill smiled at him warmly. Ronnie could have thrown a shoe at the television set, thinking here was a man who condoned, if he did not actually take part in himself, a series of stupid, loathsome acts designed to retaliate for an article Ronnie had written, and he was being given a forum for his self-promotion.

"A recent article in *New York* magazine was somewhat critical of you and your cult, Mr. Cummings. Did you happen to see it?"

"I glanced at it. The writer came with preconceived notions, a definite bias. Doing some dirty work to further her career."

The compliant Sonya Brill concluded the interview by allowing Cummings to plug his Web site along with the cult's phone number.

New York magazine accepted the Public Art Fund piece and during the editorial process the fact-checker double-checked a quote by calling Tony Weston, the artist Ronnie interviewed for the article. Weston used this as an opening to call Ronnie and invite her to dinner, leaving a message on her answering machine. Richard kept promising he would be back in New York, holding her off with brief, uninformative e-mails. Under house rules, if you didn't sleep with more than one man at a time, did this apply to Richard, since Ronnie was still hard-pressed to define whether they were actually sleeping together? If a tree falls in the forest . . . How could you be sleeping with someone who wasn't there, and if he were there, was he really there if he traveled this much?

"Beats me," Nancy said. They were eating dinner at home on a Monday night. "It has all the contours of just a pure sexual relationship."

"Or a sexual relationship with a married man."

"Think he's married?"

"Maybe. And he comes to New York on business."

"So then he's a liar *and* an adulterer," Nancy said.

"He claims, no. But I'd like to be sure. You can't have an affair with a married man."

"It has been done."

"It's anti-feminist," Ronnie said lightly.

"Ah, I should have known that."

"What I seem to have here is an unreliable sexual relationship. The 'unreliable' is the relationship, not the sexual. You know, this is clarifying," she teased. "I'll give him a little more time. It's not like he doesn't e-mail me—every once in a while."

Richard finally called to say he was in New York, three weeks since New Orleans, nonchalant about the time lag, breezily telling her that he was very eager to get together, he had something exciting to tell her.

"You're getting a divorce."

"What? I'm not married, Ronnie. Where did you get that from? Can we have lunch tomorrow at Aureole? One o'clock. I'd say dinner, but I can't wait."

"Lunch it is."

Proof of marriage, she supposed, was the marriage license, or commonly, the wedding ring. What was proof of not-marriage, the man's word?

He was waiting near the front door of the restaurant in his blazer and jeans.

"Great to see you," he said, kissing her. "I have interesting news," as they were led to a table.

He kept her in a little bit of suspense while they ordered drinks; no alcohol for her in the middle of the day and he also declined, both settling on iced teas.

"Here it is. My publisher, a man named Antoine Burris, very smart, very elegant type of fellow, loved your piece on Cummings, which, of course, I told him to look at."

"Good of you."

"It's really a publisher-editor job he has, small press, interesting projects, good marketing. They took my book and got it onto the trade paperback bestseller list, so they must know something."

"It was a good book."

"Still, there are a lot of good books. So—he has a taste for the off-beat. And what he'd like to do is a book on the history of satanic possession. There isn't a good contemporary one. And he wants you to write it."

"That's very nice of you, Richard. However—"

"It's too soon for a 'however.' This is terrific stuff. You have every-thing from stories of convents in sixteenth- and seventeenth-century France where the Devil swept through possessing nuns like an epi-demic, to the world today where possessions in one form or another are constantly showing up."

"However, I have never written a book."

"Nobody has, until they do."

"And an additional however, I don't believe in satanic possession. Try hysteria. Delusional behavior. I think a shrink would be better suited."

"No, he loved the tone of your piece: bright, appropriately skeptical."

"Do you have any proof you're not married?"

"Would you not jump around?"

"You're really not? You're just inconstant because of the nature of your lecturing, conferencing, researching, et cetera?"

"Absolutely."

"Tell me about this trip."

He gave her an accounting and she said, "The thing about you, is that you seem so smart to me, your beat could be anything. I just don't think you fit, physically, with your subject matter. Great blazer, light salad for lunch, what are you working such a dark side of the street for?"

"Because it's fascinating. And you'd find this book fascinating. Look into it a little. I can recommend some things to read. And—what's this? My publisher just walked in."

"Oh, Richard, this is too obvious."

"Talk to him."

Antoine Burris was a broad-shouldered man in his fifties, five feet eleven, bald, wire-rim glasses; wearing an expensive gray suit, white shirt, and blue tie. After the introductions he occupied a seat at their table.

"An honor, Ms. Delaney. As Richard must have told you, I loved, no, respected your article, which is better than loving it."

"Thank you, Mr. Burris."

"Publishing being what it is, if I put this out with agents, in the morning I'd have two hundred writers recommended. But you're my first choice, based on what I've read; the perfect fit of style with material."

"This is all very flattering—"

"There was a marvelous book years ago, *Possession and Exorcism* by Traugott Oesterreich. William Blatty, when he wrote *The Exorcist,* was an admirer of it. But we don't have anything that's contemporary and smart. I know you can write. What I would need, from my end, is an outline, which we would pay you for, naturally. I don't want you doing any work without being paid. Your agent is . . ."

Nancy's boss, Jenna Hawkins, intervened on fees for a couple of Ronnie's articles. Ronnie assumed Hawkins would handle a book deal for her, should she decide to proceed.

"Jenna Hawkins."

"Excellent. Have her call me. Let's go into business." He shook hands and departed.

"Do you have somebody else coming in, to complete the salesman-ship?

"I think it's a wonderful opportunity. If you could come by at seven tonight, I could get you started on some things to think about."

After she said good-bye to Richard at the restaurant Ronnie went to the Mid-Manhattan Public Library, where the computer indicated far more books in the collections than she ever would have imagined, the material catalogued in library terminology as "demoniac possession." She took notes and was going to return with her laptop since several of the books were noncirculating volumes. She called Nancy and asked if she could drop by the office if her boss had a few minutes to spare.

Jenna Hawkins was in her late sixties, five feet seven, her auburn hair loose around her shoulders. She had been an agent for forty plus years, with a wide-ranging client list from best-selling authors of popular novels to historians of such things as Chinese agricultural practices, a nine-hundred-page book Nancy was obliged to read as her first project

when she went to work there. Ronnie described the lunch and the
guest appearance by Antoine Burris.

"Very professional, to offer to pay for your time on the proposal.
They did do a good job on your friend Richard Smith's book. A little
strange, though, some of their titles. A book on satanic possession is
right in their sweet spot, which tells you something about them. What
really counts here—is this something that interests you?"

"I'm not sure. I can't take possession seriously. What is to be taken
seriously, is that some people do."

"I think that's the crux of it. If you can write a book and tell the
way people have behaved *in* possession and *around* possession, you'd
have something."

"Let me think some more."

"You have to ask yourself if you want to stop writing articles for
a while, lose out on getting the immediate gratification—which we
know you get, everybody who does it gets it—for a longer lead time
with a book."

"Shouldn't we find out the money?" Nancy offered.

"Yes, let's see what we're talking about. Who is this Richard Smith?
Is it serious, Ronnie?"

"I'm not sure who he is, so I wouldn't say it's serious."

"Well, he may have helped put a serious offer on the table, so that's
serious support anyway."

Richard led her into the living room, poured some wine, and brought
out some of the volumes he thought she would be interested in looking
at, as well as a printout of titles she might consider exploring. He
thought they could have a kind of working dinner, going over the material, and he ordered a meal from a French restaurant nearby. This fascinated her. She thought in terms of pizza and Chinese take-out. The
idea of ordering a real meal—salad, lamb chops, dessert—from a restaurant would never have occurred to her.

He managed to prepare hot tea at the conclusion of the meal and
she teased him about his limited expertise in the kitchen. Richard was

lobbying for her to take on the project. She could present an overall picture of satanic possession through the ages within her voice; wry, if need be, skeptical if need be, and respectful. He added "respectful," he said, out of his own beliefs.

The editorial portion of the evening was coming to an end and she was already anticipating. The feeling reminded her of senior year of high school when she was Bobby Muzo's girlfriend and whatever they did, movies, bowling, a Yankee game, at the end of it, the last half hour, the last few innings, she was already thinking ahead, of having his mouth on hers, and his hands on her, and Bobby inside her, with the realization that she wanted him as much as Bobby wanted her; beautiful Bobby, who went into the army when she went off to college, and died in Afghanistan.

"What is it?"

"I was thinking that I'm tired of talking and I'd like to be in bed with you."

"Sounds good to me."

"And I was thinking of a boy I knew who died."

"Were you in love with him?"

"In what love would have been then, yes."

"I'm sorry."

"No more speaking, okay, unless you want to tell me one more time you're really not married."

"You're impossible. Really not."

In bed he was so deliberate and knowing it was the mixture for her of something almost unbearable with something so pleasurable she cried out once again. Did anyone hear? The downstairs Europeans were never there. The next house? She didn't care.

He hadn't left in the morning. She was primed for the note left behind, but she heard him in the bathroom taking a shower. She sat up in bed and he emerged and kissed her on the forehead.

"Would you like to go out to breakfast?"

"I didn't know that was part of the deal."

They went to a neighborhood coffee shop on Second Avenue and that suited her very well; a regular place, not a hotel dining room or a fancy restaurant, something that spoke of normal life. You sleep with someone, you go out for breakfast, and it's natural, what people do. They talked about the book, she was going back to the library to do some more research, he was going to arrange for a couple of volumes to be sent to her. Catching her off stride he asked if she wanted to see a movie that night, a restored print of Ingmar Bergman's *Through a Glass Darkly* was playing downtown. He would be leaving again, that she expected, but not for another day. The thought of a normal people evening, a movie no less, seemed delightful to her.

After the movie and dinner they went back to his place for the sex she had been anticipating, the consuming sex, nothing else existing in the world at the moment.

They went out for breakfast again. She was on the cusp of feeling that it didn't matter if he were married, and that was how, she supposed, women became entrapped in those situations—this is better than anything else I know, and if it's not perfect or not even close to perfect, it's better than what I've had, so it's okay—and yet he was insisting he wasn't married, and when he said she would hear from him in a couple of weeks when he was back from researching a cult in Vancouver for a behavioral studies journal, that was something she could live with. And whether he was a new boyfriend or not, whatever he was—an amazingly good-looking, amazingly good sexual partner, who had given her the opportunity, if she wanted it, to write a book—she was going to wait out the time, closing off all entreaties from the Tony Westons who emerged now and again. The Bergman movie at the Film Forum, the breakfasts, moved them away from the too-precious Ritz-Carlton plateau toward what she considered real life. She was, she announced to herself, in some sort of relationship.

"They're offering five thousand dollars for you to do an outline, for your time researching and organizing the material. Actually, it's crucial work," Hawkins said to her on the phone, "and in a way it's the most important work on the book, but I think it's fair. I'll ask for it all up front so you can have a comfort level. Any feelings?"

"I spent the last three days looking at books. And Richard sent a couple of books to me. It is fascinating. Some of these people in possession-land are looney tunes. But as long as I don't have to sign on to endorsing possession—"

"Burris understands that. He wants your take, but he wants a rounded view."

"Could be fun to do a book."

"Don't say fun. If it's fun, you didn't do a good job. It could be, as you say, fascinating, it could be interesting, it could be challenging; it won't be fun and shouldn't be. It's work. Let me go back and see if I can get a commitment on the actual contract. He was a little cautious there, I guess, because he didn't know if you're interested."

"I'm interested."

"I'll get back to you."

The deal was for a fifty-thousand-dollar advance for hardcover and soft-cover rights. Hawkins described it as a fine offer for a first-time author on a book that was questionable as to whether it could cross over from historic/religious and library interest to general interest. First, Ronnie would need to do the core research and write the outline; the offer was contingent upon acceptance of that outline. Hawkins tried to negotiate the five-thousand-dollar advance for the outline to be separated from the book, but Burris drew the line there—it was fifty thousand for everything. She would receive five thousand for the outline, and when the outline was accepted, ten thousand for the first phase of the book with payouts at intervals in the writing process.

Ronnie was getting intrigued by the material she had been reading and had begun to seriously accumulate notes. For several days she familiarized herself with historic accounts of alleged possessions, which she found to be, by turns, laughable and heartwrenching. She had an exchange of e-mails with Richard and he was very pleased with the events he had set in motion.

So excited at the possibilities for the book. I feel I should be
paying someone a finder's fee, for finding you.

She took it as fairly romantic from a straightforward man.

On a Saturday morning, Bob and Nancy were going for a jog in Central Park and asked Ronnie to join them. Running with Bob, the former college runner, was something the girls particularly enjoyed. There
hadn't been any black cat or death skull incidents since the last and
Ronnie was moving freely around the neighborhood and the city; they
hadn't derailed her with their behavior. She trotted at a light pace to
Central Park West and Ninety-sixth Street where she was meeting her
friends, who were stretching when she arrived.

"Big time today with Big Bob," Ronnie said.

"You ladies make me look good."

"That's what we think about running with you," Ronnie said.

"This new boyfriend of yours—"

"I don't know if we can call him that . . ."

"This new—"

"Squeeze," Nancy said.

"Does he run?" Bob asked.

"I have no idea."

"I would've invited him to join us, to check him out."

"He moves around. He's in Vancouver. Like seeing a hockey
player."

A man in his late twenties wearing running gear and a baseball hat
with a Z on it approached them.

"Interest you in the Zip-Ade Run? Five K. About three miles."

"We're just joggers," Nancy said.

"Free prizes for all participants. Starting in a half hour from
Eighty-sixth Street. You could just amble on over there."

"What prizes?" Bob asked and Nancy threw him a look.

"Free T-shirts for running. Gift certificates from Foot Locker for
the first three men and first three women."

"We might be interested. Ladies?"

"I don't think so," Nancy said.

"Come on," Bob urged, "free T-shirts."

As they headed over at an easy jog, Nancy said, "Ringer. How many of these people do you think are going to be Big Ten three-thousand-meter champions?"

"A lot of serious runners show up around here."

"For the marathon, honey, not for this."

They signed in and received numbers from the crew working the event for Zip-Ade, which was a new electrolyte drink. About two hundred people were assembled in the starting area. Many appeared to be in trim shape, some were less than world-class-looking. Ronnie, Bob, and Nancy lined up together in the middle of the runners. A gun went off and they started out at a smooth, easy pace, Bob controlling it for the trio, letting the other runners settle out in front of them. After a few minutes, Bob's competitive instinct took over and he increased his pace. His friends did not attempt to keep up with him and they let him move forward.

"See you at the end," Nancy called out.

"See you," as he moved gracefully up with the front-runners.

A snakelike formation comprised the pack of runners, Ronnie and Nancy running recreationally with Bob now out of view. In her competitive zeal, a woman runner bumped into Ronnie while getting past her.

"I mean, who cares?" Ronnie said to her as the woman pushed on.

At about the 1.5-mile mark Ronnie and Nancy were cruising along, enjoying the exercise, not having spoken for a couple of minutes when Ronnie began to increase the pace.

"Hey, slow up." She kept increasing the pace, leaving a five-yard, then ten-yard distance between them. "What are you doing?" She didn't appear to hear Nancy. Her face was expressionless as she pressed on faster and faster, passing runners, male and female, oblivious to them as she passed them. Her face was empty, a sleepwalker's, but her eyes were open as she continued passing people, the lithe and athletic among them, her strides fluid as though she were a finely tuned runner. She had passed every one of the women with only a handful of men ahead of her, and she did not appear to be conscious of that, her empty face unchanged as she pushed on.

Bill broke the finish tape first among all runners, ran a few strides to slow his momentum, then turned back. He couldn't believe what he was seeing. Running toward the finish line within a group of trailing men, with not another woman nearby, without a trace of strain or exertion, her eyes strange and unfocused, was Ronnie, the first woman to cross. She kept running, unconcerned with the finish, looking as though she would run right to the end of the park or to the end of the city. He stepped in her path and caught her, breaking her stride and holding her in his arms.

"Ronnie!" She blinked and looked up at him as if he were just coming into focus. "Ronnie, God. Are you all right?"

"Bob!"

"You won!"

"I did?"

"Don't you know?"

"No. I won?"

"Yes, you won. Jesus, you're freaking me out."

A race official came up to them and placed wreaths on their heads, and a photographer took their picture together. They were both stunned.

"How much have you been running?"

"Not much. Guess I didn't know I had it in me."

"You looked so spaced. Did you take anything before?"

"I didn't."

They sat on the curb waiting for Nancy to cross the line, both with hundred-dollar Foot Locker gift certificates in hand. Nancy eventually ambled along with a flock of other recreational runners.

"Ronnie, what were you doing?" Nancy said.

"I won. So did Ronnie," Bob announced.

"What?"

"I don't understand it. I wasn't conscious of anything," Ronnie said.

Her face wasn't empty now, it was filled with concern. How could she possibly win a race that was a total blank to her?

5

"In the zone." Bob offered the concept during the postmortem—the feeling athletes describe of being so "on" that everything in the world seems to vanish and the athlete feels invincible. The word "unconscious" was even used to describe the state. He had experienced it a few times himself when he won races during college meets and he had heard fellow runners describe it as well. In the act of running the mind drifts, much like blacking out, he said, so he could understand how Ronnie could reach that place. But he couldn't reconcile it with her previous running experience. How did Ronnie, an occasional runner, run past people who probably ran regularly?

They were sitting in the Fairway Restaurant on Broadway eating breakfast. Their spoils, the T-shirts, garlands, and winners' gift certificates, were on the table.

"You run around the reservoir a couple of times a week?" Bob asked.

"Couple of times around, if I can."

"Twice around is three miles, twice a week is six miles. What kind of pace?"

"I don't time myself."

"You never ran a race before, did you?" Nancy asked.

"Not a formal race, no."

"So we wouldn't know what she was capable of. Until she did it," Nancy said to Bob.

"I guess. Maybe you're just a natural and didn't know it."

"Maybe. If the writing doesn't work out—" she quipped, and they drifted into the day when Bob won the Big Ten three-thousand-meter championship, which served to direct attention away from Ronnie's race.

The race was over, she didn't want to think about it anymore. She didn't like the out-of-control nature of the experience, wasn't going to join the Road Runners Club or start competing against runners in Central Park. She worked more intensely on the book proposal and could see a huge problem ahead. Even at a fifty-thousand-dollar advance, the book could be quicksand. Any one of the chapters suggested in her outline could nearly be a book unto itself, and in some cases, the material already had been the basis of an entire book. She exchanged a few e-mails with Richard about her concerns.

When he was back in New York, as promised, he called her. He suggested several restaurants for dinner. Ronnie didn't like the idea of any of them; something about seeing someone who could afford to take her to places beyond her lifestyle, in her mind was a little like being kept—if not exactly kept, *influenced.*

"I can see sleeping with him because he's great-looking and great in bed and intelligent and interesting, but I don't like the rich guy thing getting into it," she said to Nancy, the two talking by phone during the day.

"You have standards I don't think have even been invented, but I vaguely know what you mean. He should be judged on who he is, not on his credit cards; although if you took a poll, I don't think you'd come out in the majority on this."

"That's why the evening with the Bergman movie was so good. I could relate to it. I can't relate to dinner that's a couple or three hundred dollars for two, and then I sleep with him and what does that say?"

"I get it, sort of. Where is his money from anyway? The one book? Can't be."

"The articles and the lectures and honorariums for panels, I guess. I'm just happier being a cheap date."

She suggested a bistro on Eighth Avenue and he was comfortable with the idea. She chose not to tell him about the road race victory; she didn't think anything in the story was positive. *I ran a race and don't remember anything about it and won*—that wasn't something she wanted to promote.

The main theme for dinner was her apprehensiveness about the book, of being drawn deeper into the material with all the time required to do the subject justice, so that in terms of economics she would fall behind while working on it. Also she would risk losing her magazine article contacts along the way. Richard said he fully understood her anxiety. He thought she should estimate how long to work on the book and maintain that as a deadline. He also recommended that she could squeeze time out of her week to do a random short piece here and there, for *The New York Times,* for *The Village Voice,* to keep her name in view of the editors who bought articles. During dinner she had held off thinking about sex. Money anxieties, professional responsibility anxieties, will-I-be-able-to-do-the-work anxieties trumped the buzz of imagining herself in bed with him. And then they were in bed, and it was wonderful again for her, and when she woke early in the morning, the anxieties returned.

They went for breakfast at the neighborhood coffee shop.

"Should we talk about my worries about the book again?"

"As I said last night—"

"No, I was just kidding. I don't really mean for us to talk about it nonstop. Let's just say they're healthy anxieties, work connected, as opposed to social life connected, which shows I'm a well-rounded person," she said lightly.

Ronnie asked for a meeting with Jenna Hawkins and Nancy joined them. Hawkins concurred with Richard's thinking. Ronnie should set a legitimate and firm schedule for completing the work. Eighteen months sounded like the outer limit to Ronnie, and Hawkins thought that was the way to proceed, to keep it as a deadline. If she wanted to, she could try to do a random short piece here and there for the exposure.

Ronnie then presented a draft of her proposal. It provided for material on the famous cases of possession through history, some of the lesser known but fascinating incidents, notable exorcists through the ages, the case that led to the fictional *The Exorcist,* a discussion of the impact of *The Exorcist* itself on the culture of possession, the professional exorcists performing exorcisms for a fee, the satanic ritual abuse conspiracy theories, the Protestant ministries specializing in exorcism for a wide range of modern-day manifestations, the current position of the Roman Catholic Church on possession, and the implications of possession—the ways in which belief in possession intersected with contemporary religious views. Hawkins gave her overall approval and Ronnie was going to polish and submit it.

After a six-day stay in New York, including two nights of being together, Richard was headed out of town again, this time to Munich. He had a foundation grant to research a cult that was gaining strength outside the city.

"Munich?" she said to him the morning they said good-bye. "Who goes to Munich?" teasing, but uncomfortable with the continued pattern. "If I stood in the middle of Times Square and yelled, 'Is anyone here going to Munich?' how many people do you think would say '*I* am'?"

"The place to ask is the gate at JFK where I'm boarding," he said, laughing.

The finished proposal went in to Burris and he communicated through Hawkins that he was very pleased. He did have a few questions for Ronnie and asked to see her in his office. Excelsior Publications was located on Fifth Avenue and Twenty-fourth Street, a high corner office with shelves of rare books, resembling one of the special rooms in the Forty-second Street Library rather than a publishing office. Burris sat behind a large oak desk with a library-style lamp. He swiveled in his chair, seemingly a bit high-strung now that she was alone with him.

"We look rarefied here and we publish unusual books, not mass market, but we still need to sell. Now what troubles me about the proposal—and I loved it—but what's a problem for me is that you don't let believers in sufficiently. There are many, many out there. The entire Roman Catholic Church is, so to speak, a believer in Satan, and Catholic priests have performed exorcisms, then and now. There are, as you know by now, hundreds of Protestant ministries today involved in 'deliverance' as they call it, 'exorcism' is the word for it, and that covers a substantial amount of people. You're right on it, in the last chapter, where you're going to talk about the intersection of believers and religion. I'd be looking for you to build that up."

"In that chapter?"

"It might take more than one chapter. Some people do believe in satanic possession. I think you need to give us the reason people believe. What they believe. The Catholic Church position. The delivery ministries' position. Of course, I'm thinking believers will buy the book and may even be the largest market for this book. You don't want to do a book about satanic possession and not give adequate space to explain the reasons the believers believe, and to explain why and how. It doesn't violate your integrity as an author or your personal beliefs. It's a precinct you should be more fully reporting on."

"I hear you. Let me think about that."

Ronnie spoke on the phone with Jenna Hawkins, who agreed with Burris. A book about possession, to be properly rounded, needed to include more material about the true believers. She sent Richard an e-mail describing the meeting and Burris's request. He responded:

Hey, it may even be the prime market for the book, believers
in Satan and satanic possession, but Antoine is right, I think.
It belongs.

She considered the suggestion for a couple of days. The people
who thought they were possessed certainly believed in possession, but
others did also, and she concluded that proper coverage of those beliefs
did belong in a general book on the subject. She knew now that it
wasn't going to be easy to keep within the eighteen-month deadline;
she would need to interview priests, exorcists, perhaps even some of
those people who thought they were possessed, if it was possible to
reach them.

An item on the legal side—would she be responsible for research expenses, travel to places in the United States or elsewhere to talk with exorcists or with "victims" of possession? Hawkins clarified the point.
Burris was prepared to allow for travel expenses up to ten thousand dollars, which Hawkins thought was proof they really were behind the book.

Ronnie amended the proposal to include additional material on
"the believers" and sent it to Burris. Jenna Hawkins called a few days
later to say they were proceeding with a contract, she had a book deal.

Richard was on the phone from Germany, thrilled the contract was going through and offering to throw Ronnie a party in his place to celebrate. He asked her to e-mail a guest list, and this simple request made
her uncomfortable; she didn't know that many people for a party. She
preferred not to admit that, thanked him abundantly for the offer, and
told him she would get back to him.

"If I can invite everyone I ever went out with back to high school," she
said to Nancy and Bob in the apartment, "maybe I'll have a list that
amounts to something, and if they can bring dates."

"It doesn't have to be a big party," Nancy said. "There's us and
Jenna—"

"And the building staff," Ronnie quipped. "And the man in the box."

"And business people, editors at *The Times* and *Vanity Fair* and *The Voice,* those people. It's even a good idea—to let them know you're doing a book."

"If they'll come."

"And I'll invite everyone *I* ever dated," Bob said.

"Thanks, pal," Nancy responded.

"And the publisher, they must have people," Ronnie said, "and Richard. He can bring his wife."

"Ronnie!"

"I'm still not convinced a hundred percent. Anyone who travels that much has to have another port."

"Say yes to the party," Nancy said. "It'll fill up. It'll be fine."

Richard was back in New York. They spoke by phone, she told him her list was a dozen or so people, and he said that would be perfect, cocktails and great hors d'oeuvres, three weeks from next on a Monday, and by then the contract should be signed. The publisher would probably invite people. And Richard, she wondered, would he be inviting anyone? From his end it would just be people he knew at the publishing house. He planned to be in the city for a while, was then going back to Vancouver and would return for Ronnie's party; she needn't worry about the arrangements. He knew a party planner who would take care of it all.

She began working on the book in earnest. Before Richard left the city again, over ten days' time she spent three evenings with him; dinner, sex, a revival of *East of Eden* at the Film Forum, more sex, another dinner, more sex. Three evenings in a ten-day span was about as much contact as she would have with anyone she was going with, short of living together, and she had no complaint about his availability this round. She did wonder what he did the rest of the time. She tried to explore, in dinner talk and pillow talk, the landscape of his life, his early years as a foster child, the loss of his main foster parents, his high school years; did he feel like an outsider, did he have a girlfriend; what kind of jobs did he have after high school, how was it working for a small town newspaper, how long had he been in New York, where did he live before that as an adult, who were his friends, what *did* he do the other nights they weren't together, basic things you would want to know from a man you are sleeping with. Over a several-day period she filtered these essay questions to him and he responded with short answers. He was cordial and either he was totally lacking in introspection about his life or there was a wall he had erected to deal with his childhood and she couldn't get through. His position was clear—I'll be supportive of you, as helpful as I can, but I live a life of professional responsibilities and I really don't like to talk about my personal history. As to some of the specifics, he had reading and writing to do the nights they weren't together, and his closest friend was Antoine Burris. Perhaps one day he would open up, she presumed, or perhaps this was the deal—he was reserved, remote. This still made him more interesting to her than the puppy males with their tongues hanging out of their mouths, panting about themselves. He was intelligent about a truly unusual area of life, and there was the sex. It was so extraordinary, every time, she wondered if this could become like a drug addiction, and counseled herself to keep a balance, to always have the work, now the book, to center herself so that she wasn't just treading water waiting for him to show up.

"The man in the box" Ronnie alluded to as a whimsical possibility for her guest list was a derelict who set up quarters on Broadway and 111th Street in large appliance-sized cardboard boxes, and when rain destroyed the boxes, he sometimes cobbled together his living quarters out of multiple smaller containers. Ronnie guessed he was in his late sixties. He had unkempt graying black hair, a straggly full beard, was gaunt, six feet tall, usually dressed in a flannel shirt too large for him, baggy corduroy pants, and sneakers. In colder weather he wore an army fatigue jacket. He had a rather fine nose and pale brown eyes—a distant look in those eyes suggesting the possibility of another life he had lived, the facts of which would have been impossible to ascertain. He never spoke. He sat in his box staring at people in the street, as if studying them for a book *he* was going to write. A bowl was always in front of the box for people to give money and when they did he never acknowledged them, just as he never spoke. He didn't take up a position in front of a store, rather on the sidewalk along 111th Street so vendors didn't have a complaint he was blocking store traffic. And his silence meant passersby couldn't complain he was insulting them or invading their space. He sat for hours, auditing the movement of people. Periodically, he was swept from view by the police based on the current mood in the department regarding the homeless. Sometimes he slept in his box and was there in the morning when Ronnie or Nancy went out to buy a newspaper. He would stare as they passed with the same flat expression he maintained for everyone. Once, Ronnie was passing when the police took him into a patrol car. He displayed no anger, no resentment. Intermittently the city authorities advocated not giving money to panhandlers on streets and subways, that there were social services for such people, and the giver would only be enabling their drug or alcohol habits. The man in the box seemed to be mentally ill, not an addict or an alcoholic, or that was the rationale Ronny and Nancy settled on, and they would sometimes drop a quarter or two in his bowl when they passed. They wanted to believe he used the money for food. Ronnie adopted her own policy. If she happened to be thinking about work or her career at the moment she passed him, given the disparities in their lives, and for good luck, she dropped a little extra in his bowl; a dollar, or all her loose change.

A couple of days after Richard left town Ronnie was walking to the supermarket and the man was in his place on 111th Street in one of his cobbled-together setups, a couple of cartons that once contained television sets. She was thinking about the book when she saw him, which qualified this to be a bonus contribution, and she took two dollars from her wallet to place in his bowl. He stared at her, not with his usual flat expression. He furrowed his brow and quickly scrambled deeper into the box. Under normal circumstances encounters with the man were odd New York exchanges; out of charity, or guilt, or for luck, or all of these, people gave money and food to him and he offered no acknowledgment. He had reacted to Ronnie with sudden antipathy. The peculiar social compact between the man in the box and people on the street had been broken. He had frightened her.

Richard Smith was a courtly host for the party attended by a couple of dozen people, with employees from Burris's publishing company helping to occupy the space. Richard was dressed in Armani—blue suit, white shirt, light blue silk tie—the standout-looking man in the room. Nancy and Bob came in with Ronnie, and on seeing Richard for the first time, Nancy whispered, "This is *People* magazine stuff. He *is* amazing-looking."

Ronnie made the introductions, Richard declaring he was glad to finally meet Ronnie's friends. Bob was less cheerful than the others, trying to take the measure of this guy, while feeling, in his Brooks Brothers suit, severely out-tailored.

While Richard charmingly concentrated on the guests, Antoine Burris was serving as the co-captain for the event and he made certain everyone's glass was filled and that the hors d'oeuvres were passed properly by the uniformed waitstaff of four people.

Jenna Hawkins arrived with her husband, Jeb, a former Broadway producer; in his seventies, silver haired, with a red W. C. Fields nose and alcohol on his breath, a man now supposedly engaged in writing his memoirs.

"Great place," Jeb said to Richard. "So how do you make your money?"

Nancy and Ronnie exchanged smiles on his directness.

"I write, I lecture."

"On what?"

"Cults, mostly."

"Cults? We talking about the same thing, cults? People following some crackpot?"

"Right."

"What's the most interesting thing about cults?"

"I'd say the way people have a need to be in them."

"And cults gets you a place like this?"

"Jeb—" his wife interceded. "This is supposed to be a nice party for Veronica Delaney and this is our host."

"That's all right, he can handle it."

"I rent, I don't own."

"See, he gave me a good answer. You're a good-looking guy. Ever act?"

"No, I never acted."

"If you did, I'd put you right in a production of *Private Lives.* Know the play?"

"I do."

"Put you right in it. But I'm not active just now."

"Okay, Jeb," and she pulled him away.

Laughing, Richard walked over to Ronnie and said, "I think I just lost my chance at another career."

"Looks to me like you're doing fine."

"I'll say," and he kissed her on the lips, a proprietary kiss.

Richard made a toast thanking everyone for coming and congratulating Ronnie for her book contract. "To the girl of the moment," he said, "and the moment is going to last for a very long time." He introduced Antoine Burris, who told the group he was pleased and honored to be responsible for the first book by an exciting new literary talent. Her inquisitiveness combined with her sophisticated style was refreshing in someone so young, and they were going to do everything they could to put the book on the map.

Ronnie chatted with people from the publishing company as the party rolled on. The art director, a woman in her thirties, brought a date, an advertising account executive in his thirties, aggressive, confident of his own good looks, who took the opportunity when the woman was in the next room to try slipping his business card to Ronnie on the basis of how much he could help her with the book when it came out. He knew everything there was to know about advertising, and might they get together, he was really ending his other relationship.

"I'm flattered, but I'm not available. Richard Smith and I . . ."

He got the message although she couldn't finish the thought. Richard Smith and I . . . "sleep together" was the best she came up with for herself.

They didn't have a plan for dinner after the party and as people began to leave Richard took Ronnie aside and said, "If it doesn't violate your sense of appropriateness, I'd like to take you to dinner. An Italian place. More expensive than our coffee shop, but it is a special occasion."

"You got it, but let's not make a habit of it," she teased.

"How about every time you start a new book?"

Her face was glowing, with everything, and on the other side of the room watching them, decidedly not glowing, was Bob.

Ronnie came over to Nancy and Bob, who were ready to leave.

"I feel like that guy in *My Fair Lady,* what was his name?" Bob said to them.

"Professor Higgins," Nancy said.

"Not him. The villain."

"Kaparthy," Ronnie responded. "And why do you feel like Kaparthy?"

"Where did Richard say he's from?"

"New Orleans."

"I was in law school with a guy from New Orleans and he didn't sound like this guy."

"He traveled around a lot when he was younger so he can sound like anything."

"Something I don't trust about the guy, I'm sorry to say after two vodkas. And he better treat you right."

"I appreciate the concern. He steered me to this book, so that's pretty right."

"Come on, Kaparthy," Nancy said. "Beautiful party, Ronnie."

"Thanks, guys."

———

Unable to shake his concerns and fueled by the two vodkas, Bob doubled back to find Richard alone.

"Ask you something? You're from New Orleans?"

"I am."

"Where did you go to high school?"

"Loranger."

"And then you kind of moved around, different places, and became a writer and a lecturer on cults?"

"Roughly."

"Pretty unusual background. Only, I know a New Orleans accent and you don't have one."

"Assuming there is one."

"In my area of the law, real estate, you meet a lot of off-center characters, and you seem a little off-center to me. Like Ronnie was speculating whether you were married—"

"You're telling *me.*"

"Are you? Assuming you're not using an alias, I could find out, you know."

"Not married. What's this about?"

"I like her a lot. Kind of a kid sister to me. I don't want to see her get hurt."

"Neither do I. Loranger, 1985. As Casey Stengel used to say, you could look it up."

On a Tuesday at 7:12 A.M., a woman in shorts, T-shirt, and running shoes, twenty-eight years old, jogging from her apartment building on 115th Street, crossed Riverside Drive on her way into Riverside Park when a car that was double-parked lurched toward her at full speed, slamming into her and sending her flying several feet. The woman crashed headfirst into the side of a parked car, killed by the driver, who sped off. The hit-and-run incident was front page news in the *Daily News* and the *New York Post* and the first page of *The New York Times*

Metro section, abetted by an eyewitness account from an elderly woman, a dog walker out on the street at the time, who told police and the media, "It looked like he aimed at her."

For the police, the elderly woman's account was important; it didn't sound like an accident. Unfortunately the woman could offer no further details as to model of car or license plate number and couldn't describe the driver. She thought it was a man, hence, "*He* aimed at her."

Public interest was high on the case, people saw themselves as a possible victim in a similar incident. The police department issued statements on the progress of the investigation to the media and it was a running story in the New York newspapers and on the local television news. Detectives Gomez and Santini were among those assigned to the case, and through typical detective work, the peeling of the onion, aspects of the woman's life began to reveal themselves. The victim was Jane Claxton, single, a travel agent for Arden Travel on Broadway, a graduate of SUNY Albany who came to New York after college and lived alone. Neighbors remembered a boyfriend recently, and various boyfriends over the years, but descriptions of the most recent one were unclear. Her parents were divorced, her father a car salesman in Schenectady, her mother a waitress in Albany. She was an only child. Her address book was a source of leads and the detectives fanned out, contacting people in the book, many of whom turned out to be clients at the travel agency. The owner of the agency, a woman in her forties, said she was a "good worker," somewhat shy, and not open to discussing personal matters.

A friend came forward, a woman pharmacist in a local Rite-Aid store, who struck up a friendship with her several years before and they met for dinner about once a week. The woman did identify the most recent boyfriend. She knew they had broken up and he had not been around for two months. He was a clerk in a video store and would-be movie producer. He quit the job without notice three weeks earlier and had not been seen at his apartment on the Lower East Side. Instantly he was the prime suspect in the case. His picture, obtained from a drawer in the victim's apartment, appeared in the tabloids—Have you seen this man? The friend revealed the victim was a volunteer in a Literacy

Partners program at a local library, adding to the mix for the media and for the police, the senseless death of a decent person.

"We're going all out to find this boyfriend," Rourke said to the half-dozen detectives in his office. "But let's not get snookered here. It might not be him. Look for disgruntled customers, did anyone think they were supposed to get a refund or something for a trip they didn't take kind of thing. You know, somebody who might've gone postal. But let's nail this."

For Rourke, the case had an additional resonance; his daughter was a couple of years younger than the victim and had just taken an apartment in Brooklyn, living alone, teaching school. It was one of the deaths that gets through to people.

Ronnie and Nancy talked about it. Nancy had parents in Wilton whom she saw about once a month; either she went there or they came into New York; she had an older sister in New Jersey, who had two little girls, three and four, Nancy's star nieces, and she saw them all at least once a month. Ronnie, on the other hand, only had Nancy and Bob, and she didn't know in which ledger to enter Richard Smith. She identified with the victim, too—Ronnie, someone on her own, just trying to make it in New York.

Richard was gone again, having left the day after the party, to Edinburgh this time, an international conference: "Cults, Superstitions, and the Fear of the Unknown." Ronnie thought it an overripe name for what he claimed was going to be a serious conference. From Edinburgh he was going back to Munich.

She wrote an e-mail to him expressing her uneasiness about the death of the hit-and-run victim and he wrote back:

> Read about it here. A random act. You can't take anything from it. It's endemic to life itself.

She replied:

That's a bit grim. Something like that is inevitable?

He replied in turn:

Dark things sometimes happen. It's one reason why some people turn to religion for reassurance. And when their needs are very acute, they lean too heavily on religion and become enveloped by it, *possessed* by it. So here's the thought for you. When they are possessed, and you can put possessed in quotes if you'd like, are they imagining the possession or are they people especially sensitive to the angel of darkness by their need, and therefore open to the possession? This is a longwinded way of saying to you, the woman's death is terrible, I don't mean to minimize it, but it is part of the overall, sometimes dark, yes, sometimes inevitable rhythms of life, and that relates to the relevance of the wonderful book you're going to write.

What the hell was he talking about, she wondered. A perfectly decent woman was murdered by a psychopath and Ronnie identified with the woman for obvious reasons of geography and social class and singledom. Richard was intelligent, no question; however, all those conferences and lectures had taken *him* over, she decided. The man certainly could be overly academic. A "don't worry, honey, it's not about you," would have been fine. She e-mailed back:

Thanks. Enjoy your time.

There was no immediate reply and that was all right. She preferred having him in bed to having his e-mail.

Two days later, on a Saturday morning, she went for a jog around the reservoir, a test, her first time since the race, checking herself along the way to stay alert, conscious, and wondering if you do black out, how do you possibly know that you blacked out if you *are* blacked out. She played with that puzzler while giving herself signposts, now I'm passing the pump house, now I'm passing the tennis courts, I'm fine, I'm running normally. Another time around and she jogged back to the building.

She picked up the mail, a few bills, flyers, and in the batch was an envelope with her name and address and no return address. She sat at the dining room table and opened the envelope. It contained the author's portrait of her from the article she wrote in *Vanity Fair.* The picture was cut in two pieces. The head had been decapitated.

6

The Twenty-sixth Precinct was on a war footing with a high-profile hit-and-run death, its detectives emotionally invested in solving the crime. The bereaved, people who knew the woman, or those who read or heard about her, were leaving flowers at the sidewalk in front of her building, a little shrine. And then came a setback for the police. The main suspect, the former boyfriend, was in Los Angeles and had been at the time of death, documented by eyewitnesses. He had been in plain view working as a production assistant on an independent movie being shot in Venice, California. The police had nothing now, no substantial leads; no one else apparently saw anything that morning and they were starting over, running the list of people whom the victim knew.

In this atmosphere, Ronnie Delaney walked into the police station with her cut-up head shot, something so unrelated to the immediate concerns of these detectives that Santini and Gomez, and even the more politic Rourke, looking over his detectives' shoulders, barely reacted.

"This is unfortunate," Rourke said.

"These aren't isolated pranks, it's a campaign. I want you to arrest Randall Cummings."

"We don't have enough to do that, Ms. Delaney," Rourke said.

"We'll check this for prints, interrogate him again, quiz some of the cult members, send a message, let it be known this is serious activity," Santini said.

"If you arrest him, that'll send a message."

"This is all completely circumstantial," Gomez said.

"I write about them, it isn't complimentary, and I get death threats."

"It's harassment. It's a form of menacing. Whether or not it's a death threat, that's harder to say," Rourke told her. With the false start on the hit-and-run case in his immediate experience, Rourke was inclined to think of other possibilities. "Why don't you provide us a list of anyone other than Cummings who might have taken umbrage with something you wrote, or something you did, or something you said, people like that."

"Honestly, it's Cummings, it's his people."

"Would you give us a list, please?"

"I will."

"This feels very temporary to me, Ms. Delaney. No disrespect intended, but your article is going to become old news and my sense is, in time, this is just going to go away."

"And if it doesn't?"

They were silent for a moment or two after she left, knowing they hadn't been much help.

"We'll talk to Cummings again," Gomez said. "Thing is, he isn't a creep and he's not easily intimidated. He's pretty smooth."

"He's got like a thousand followers. It could be any one of them," Santini said. "Do we really have time for this now?"

"No," Rourke responded. "But maybe by letting them know we're still on it, we'll discourage them. Or it could be somebody she might think of. More likely, it's what I said, this is just going to go away."

Ronnie, Nancy, and Bob convened at Bob's apartment. Bob's first suggestion was that for protection he move back into Ronnie and Nancy's apartment for a while, or that Ronnie stay in his place, she could sleep on the couch—except none of them could figure out what it would accomplish. The threats were variously dropped off, thrown in her path, and mailed to her. Bob's physical presence wouldn't necessarily deter these insanities. She could go away for a while; Nancy offered her parents' home as a way station. Ronnie didn't like the idea of hiding, of allowing Cummings and his cult to drive her out of her place, and how long could she stay away? Eventually she would come back, or even if she didn't, if she moved, she couldn't disappear. People this deranged would eventually find her if they intended to do her harm. Or perhaps she wasn't in danger. They all wanted to believe in that possibility, that these people would harass her until they grew bored or found another target for their hostility.

They agreed Ronnie would remain in Bob's apartment for the next couple of nights. Ronnie would work at Bob's place and then they would rotate, Bob staying at the other apartment for a few days. Nancy went to retrieve some of Ronnie's clothing and her laptop. The arrangement they decided upon threw into relief the absence of Richard, in Edinburgh or Munich, working on his career. To be involved with someone who was so impossibly unavailable at a time of crisis like this did not fit her definition of a meaningful relationship. She sent him an e-mail describing the threat and she heard nothing from him for several days. She was back in her apartment, Bob installed there, when she finally received a reply:

My e-mail was down, sorry. This sounds like more of the same petty stuff. Bluntly, if they haven't harmed you, they're not going to harm you. I'm sending someone to see you, a private investigator at my expense, Paul Stone. And don't say no. This isn't like a too-expensive restaurant. Just talk to him, please.

On 118th Street a woman jogger, thirty-two years old, was heading for Riverside Drive a few minutes after seven in the morning when a double-parked car suddenly accelerated toward her. She was able to see it coming and leaped out of the way as it was about to strike her. She tripped and fell to the ground as the driver momentarily lost control, scraped a parked SUV, and sped away. The near victim was able to see that the car was driven by a Caucasian male. His face, though, was never in full view and she could not describe him. In her shock she was unable to identify the make of car or the license plate. As to the color, at first she said dark blue, then wasn't sure and thought it might have been black. The incident raised questions within the police department and the media. The first hit-and-run victim may not have been killed by someone who knew her, it may have been someone picking off women. A SECOND MADMAN OR THE SAME? was the headline in the *New York Post*.

In the dream a car hurtled toward her. She was in her jogging attire. She leaped to get out of the way, as in the news descriptions of the second incident. Ronnie awoke, upset with herself for the dream, for converting her feelings into such mayhem.

In the flow of activity at the station house, the rush to reorder priorities and question anyone in the vicinity of the second incident, Ronnie's predicament was overlooked. She called the precinct and the next day Gomez returned her call. They hadn't spoken to Cummings yet, they fully intended to, and given the time delay between her previous incidents, he didn't think anything unusual was imminent. She had her own personal madman, he just wasn't one the police were interested in at the moment.

―――――

Richard's private investigator, Paul Stone, a man with a high, thin voice, contacted her. In the absence of any commitment from the police she consented to see him. After several days Ronnie had resumed normal living arrangements, back in the apartment with Nancy except for the times when Nancy stayed with Bob. Ronnie arranged to meet Stone at four in the afternoon at a nearby Starbucks. He would be wearing a beige suit and a yellow tie.

He looked like a jockey, a small, muscular man in his forties, no more than 125 pounds, five feet five, and she assumed his appearance must have helped him in his work if he did any surveillance; he could disappear in a room if you weren't looking for him. She was interested in how he knew Richard. Stone told her they first met when he was doing work on a missing person who disappeared into a cult in Utica, New York, a cult Richard was researching.

If Nancy were present she would have laughed out loud at what Ronnie said next; Ronnie couldn't help taking a stab at it.

"And do you know his wife?" she said, supposedly innocent.

"Richard Smith isn't married."

"Oh, I thought he was. The way he's always out of New York."

"He does travel a lot, but no. Not as far as I know."

"And he lives permanently—"

"In New York."

"In New York, right."

Richard had given him the general outline, Stone asked her to fill in the details and she gave him an accounting, including her last inadequate exchanges with the police.

"They're all caught up in this hit-and-run business," he said.

"That's clear."

"Ms. Delaney, may I call you Veronica?"

"Ronnie."

"Ronnie, I've been a private investigator for over twenty years. And here's what my experience tells me. People who would do things like this, they're crazy." She thought, That's a major insight? "From my perspective," he continued, "it's a good news, bad news thing."

"The bad news I know. I've been on the receiving end."

"The good news, as I see it, the likelihood is—this is basically what they do."

"I'm a writer, and the word 'likelihood' is the word I worry about."

"I understand. These things are designed to frighten you. My guess, because they want to get back at you for what you wrote."

"So you think it *is* the cult."

"I do. But they only frighten you if you're frightened."

"Who wouldn't be?"

"Somebody who recognizes this is their act. I can provide you with security, up to twenty-four hours a day with rotating people, but the way they've tried to come at you, somebody even standing right next to you isn't going to stop them. Maybe I could've run after the person who tossed the cats in your path, or the trinket thing, but this time they didn't do anything like that, they sent something by mail, so a security person wouldn't have stopped it."

"Personal security can't help, is what you're saying."

"I don't think so. I'll provide it if you wish, at no expense to you, but no. The biggest problem, and this is where they're clever, is that it's practically impossible to pin pranks like this on anybody."

"Cummings. His people."

"No evidence. Not like a gun you can trace, or fingerprints, or someone you can ID. That's why the cops are dragging their feet, also they're preoccupied."

"So you're saying it's practically impossible to get the person who's doing this to me. Why exactly are we talking?"

"Well, I am offering security—"

"Which you're telling me is useless."

"*And* I'm telling you all this can only frighten you if you allow yourself to be frightened. You could put your mind in the place of— this is stupid and I won't let it get to me."

An unprotectable, unprovable harassment was directed at her, and these experts, the police and now this private investigator, were telling her to ignore it and eventually she would be left alone.

"I'm not going to let my life be turned upside down by some snake oil salesman in a hood. Thank you. I'll let you know if I need anything from you."

She was going to cut this off at the source.

On 129th Street across from the Dark Angel Church the protest group assembled, sometimes two or three of them, five at the maximum, holding placards for the benefit of passing motorists, pedestrians, or the occasional people in and out of the church during the day. The wording of their signs proclaimed, GO TO HELL, DOWN WITH SATAN, SATAN WORSHIPPERS GO HOME, and WHO BELIEVES IN THE DEVIL BELIEVES IN EVIL. The last, more biblical than the rest, missed the point as far as the cult members were concerned; they wanted to believe in evil. The protesters were middle-class whites who knew each other from the First Calvary Roman Catholic Church in Staten Island and they commuted by public transportation, ferry and subway, taking up their positions according to a sign-up schedule maintained by the group leader, John Wilson. He was six feet one, gawky, and wore too-short chinos and inexpensive checked sport shirts. His brown hair was thinning to baldness, his face sallow. A bachelor of forty-six, he was a dealer in religious artifacts he sold from home, a two-bedroom apartment he rented in the rear of a private house. His place was a kind of religious shrine, but with shipping boxes. He had neither female nor male relationships of a sexual nature, seldom went to the movies because he deemed them immoral, and devoted himself to his work and his Catholicism. He sold, by a combination of Internet and mail order, crucifixes, statuettes of Jesus Christ and the Virgin Mary, and religious paintings imported from a wholesaler in Rome. He first became aware of Cummings and the Dark Angel Church while surfing the Internet. He attended a mass to see the Devil's handiwork firsthand and was outraged. Wilson reported back to a couple of the churchgoers and the idea was born to create a protest vigil.

Alice Bayers, a stout woman of five feet two, forty-eight, a widow, was the self-proclaimed strategist. She had worked as a volunteer on behalf of local politicians and was a regular viewer of *Meet the Press,* which she lorded over the others in promoting her intelligence. She devised the concept of a vigil during the day, when they would most likely be seen, and in order to be economic restricted night protests to Saturday nights, the church's time for mass. Wilson would have liked a more vigorous union-on-strike schedule, the others objected, and it was agreed they would take up their positions for a few hours during the day and on Saturday nights, provided the weather was dry and not too cold.

Beattie Ryan, sixty-five, a retired mail carrier, a beefy woman of five feet six, and a horse player, was designated weather marshal. She liked to boast she could stand on the street for long hours because of her powerful leg muscles developed in her work and from long days at the track. Lacking her physical abilities, the others carried lightweight folding chairs to the site and, although she claimed not to need one, Beattie Ryan brought one with her, as well.

Peter Askew, fifty-three, a recent alcoholic, and Martin Beale, fifty-eight, his mentor in Sunburst, the recovery group at the church, were two of the other loyalists, both army veterans from Vietnam on disability. Askew was five feet eleven, with a belly over his belt, currently unemployed, which freed him up for standing his post. Beale, five feet seven, did odd jobs in carpentry, and came and went as a protester according to his available work.

Discussions between the police and the protesters established ground rules: no use of hand-held public address speakers, no physical contact with cult members; the right to protest, but not to impede people from entering and leaving the church. Their position was across the street from the front entrance to the church, they were able to use the restroom in a nearby gas station, and the police left them on their own during the day, save for a periodic drive-by from officers on duty. When the church was in session and the interactions between cult members and the protesters might escalate, two police officers were assigned to the protest site. Apart from shouting matches between opposing parties, which had become routinized street theater, violence did not occur.

Cummings lived in Yonkers and drove in each day, parking at a designated spot behind the building, out of the sightline of the protesters.

When he did appear in front at the conclusion of a mass he was greeted by insistent booing, the protesters unaware that they were unwittingly bestowing a form of celebrity status on their enemy.

"We need literature," Alice Bayers, the political strategist, declared one day when they were in their spot. "Something we can give out to people who pass by." The group at the time consisted of Wilson, Askew, and Beale.

"We also need a name," Wilson said, looking to assert his position in the group. He was the leader, he organized it, and he didn't want Alice Bayers usurping his position in the bureaucracy. "How about the Anti–Dark Angel Church Group."

"Why would we want to name ourselves after them?" Bayers said. "It gives them publicity."

They nodded in agreement. Power was slipping away from him quickly, Wilson felt, and he needed to come up with another name fast.

"How about the Anti-Satanist Group?"

"I think it's good," Bayers said and the others agreed.

"So we have it, the Anti-Satanist Group," Wilson said. "Praised be the Lord."

Bayers and Wilson collaborated on the flyer, which included, "This Randall Cummings and his so-called church advocate more evil at a time when the world needs less evil. . . . This evil-spewing church and its teachings oppose everything God-fearing, good people believe in. . . . This evil-spewing church is opposed to all organized religion. . . . This evil-spewing church and its members and their possible actions are a threat to everyone outside their church." Wilson contributed, "This evil-spewing church's members should go to hell since they admire its gatekeeper so much." He was proud of that. In summation they called for local, state, and federal authorities to shut the church down.

After her meeting with the private investigator, convinced of the course of action she needed to take, Ronnie called Cummings.

"Randall Cummings."

"Veronica Delaney."

"Ah, Ms. Delaney, calling me to make a dinner date?"

"Don't leave your office, Mr. Cummings. Don't go anywhere. I'm coming there."

"It will be the highlight of my day."

Wilson wasn't doing very well distributing flyers on a humid May afternoon, the temperature in the nineties. Beattie Ryan was his only colleague on this sticky day and few people were interested in taking the literature. The sight of Ronnie walking toward the building aroused them—someone was actually there—and they began raising their banners and shouting, "Down with Satan, down with Satan." She glanced over at them, not slowing her step. Wilson hurried over to Ronnie as she was about to head toward the side entrance of the building.

"I'm John Wilson of the Anti-Satanist Group," he said, trying to behave in a leaderly fashion.

Under other circumstances she might have evidenced curiosity. She just wanted to get at Cummings.

"Okay."

She turned away from him and he glared at her, offended.

"Our literature," and he handed her a flyer.

She took the flyer without looking at it and folded it into a pocket of her jeans as she resumed walking.

Wilson was extremely disappointed in her reaction. He wanted her to read the flyer in its entirety in front of him so he could answer questions. Her indifference was an affront to him and he suddenly went from calm to seething at her behavior.

"I do the Lord's work!" he said. "Do you work for the Devil?"

"No," she answered. "I'm freelance."

Ronnie rang the bell at the side door and Cummings's assistant appeared.

"I spoke to Mr. Cummings. He knows I'm coming."

He looked at her with contempt, stepped aside for her, and continued out of the building. She entered Cummings's office and by contrast he was veritably sunny.

"Ah, the beautiful and talented Veronica Delaney."

"Mr. Cummings."

"I should add, and the egregiously misinformed Veronica Delaney."

"Mr. Cummings, since I wrote the article I've been sent a dead black cat, black cats were thrown in my path, a death skull trinket was tossed at me by someone weird who ran off, and the latest is, I received in the mail a head shot of me, cut, with the head separated from the body."

"Now what would any of that have to do with me?"

"Retaliation?"

"For what? I have more members since the article appeared than I had before. Surprise you? You probably thought you were putting me out of business."

"Nobody else would care about me. It's you or that assistant of yours or another one of your people."

"Cosmo? He may be a little—socially challenged. But he wouldn't do anything I didn't tell him to do, and I didn't tell him to do anything. As I said to the police more than once and I'll say to you, it isn't in my business interest to badger you. Now you got a good article out of me. I *am* good copy, let's face it. Nice byline in a major magazine. Good for your career and a chance to get your *vivid* writing on display. By the way, you're a very good writer for somebody so young. You *could* use more objectivity."

"About someone who takes advantage of people?"

"I read your piece, darling. Anyway, we both got something out of it; you helped your reputation, I got the exposure."

"But the exposure of the way you've been harassing me, if I wrote about that, it wouldn't be so good for you, would it?"

"No, it wouldn't. The media likes to protect their own and if it got to be a big deal, that isn't the kind of coverage I'm looking for."

"So let's come to an agreement here. I don't write the follow-up piece telling how you harassed me and you don't follow up with any more of these harassments."

"I can't say yes to that."

"And why is that, Mr. Mephistopheles?"

"Because, as I keep telling you, which you don't want to hear, I had nothing to do with it. Here, want me to e-mail my people telling them to cease and desist? You can write it yourself." He turned to his computer, did some typing, and read aloud, " 'To all members. It has come to our attention . . .' What would you like to say?"

"You say it. They're your people."

" 'The writer, Veronica Delaney, who wrote an article about the Dark Angel Church for *New York* magazine, has been receiving unpleasant . . .' "

"Make that 'has been receiving threats.' "

" 'Has been receiving threats.' " He composed aloud as he typed, " 'These are not the wishes of your leader, and anyone involved must cease and desist, effective immediately. Noncompliance will result in expulsion from the church.' There. They've been told."

"All right. But it doesn't cover *you*."

"It doesn't have to cover me. I would never do anything like that. Use your logic. Why would I? I don't need you here, threatening me with bad publicity. On some level, all publicity is good publicity, we've seen that, but I don't need that kind of story. I didn't do it. Repeat, I didn't do it. Nobody under my instructions did it. You think there's some rogue member of my cult, acting on his own, making the assumption it's what I wanted? I truly doubt it. And if it's so, and I do truly doubt it, with that e-mail, it's over."

She began to become dizzy, something about the tension of this encounter, she presumed, and Cummings began to blur in her vision. She vaguely heard him saying, ". . . it becomes me being the one harassed . . . the police . . . the time dealing with it . . ."

She made an effort to rise from the chair, ". . . get you something . . . water . . . call a car for you?"

She was aware of saying, "It's over then," and she made her way out of his office, holding her hand against the walls of the corridor for balance, and walked shakily into the street. She squinted from the sun, everything blurry, the group across the way chanting when they saw her, "Down with Satan, down with Satan," a car horn blasting, someone yelling, "Watch where you're walking!"

Her fingers brushed the sides of buildings for balance. If she could only sit for a minute she would be all right, in the shade somewhere, she couldn't just sit on the sidewalk in the sun. With her blurry vision she saw something in the distance as if it were a mirage, benches beneath trees, and she sat on a bench and closed her eyes, and passed out.

She regained consciousness, a headache pushing in on her eyes. She checked her watch, 3:49. She had been up there an hour and a half. Her sight was clear now and she saw that she was on a bench outside an apartment building in a housing project two blocks from the Dark Angel Church. People were going in and out of the building and whoever she was who nodded off, a junkie, or a drunk from downtown, they were indifferent to her. She walked to 125th Street, hailed a cab, and closed her eyes until they reached her building. She was shivering from the strangeness.

7

Another black hole, no consciousness, a blank. She remembered talking to Cummings to a point and then nothing. She couldn't trace a memory from the moment her vision began to blur to the time when she awoke on the bench. She lay on her bed with the lights off. She had been tense, it was a hot day, perhaps she had become dehydrated, but mainly the tension, she believed, the cumulative effect caused her to become faint, and Cummings, the tension of dealing with him, arrogant and blameless—and for all his protestations she still had no assurance some other awful object wouldn't be sent her way.

No way around it. She needed to see a doctor. Her gynecologist worked in a medical group with other doctors and Ronnie prevailed upon her to arrange for an appointment with an internist.

By evening, after rest and a couple of aspirin, she was feeling more stable. She scanned her e-mail; Richard had written to her.

Paul Stone says you are gorgeous and smart. I didn't need a
P.I. to tell me that, but apparently he thinks as I do, wait it
out and the bad guys will go away. Back in New York in
about two weeks.

An e-mail from Nancy:

Straight to business thing for Bob, then his place. See you in
the a.m.

A break for Ronnie in television programming; *Roman Holiday* was on
cable. She made an omelet for dinner, ate in bed watching the movie,
then went to sleep.

Cummings made an appearance in her dreams, he was her taxicab
driver and drove her into a black hole. She awoke and fell back to sleep.
The clock radio went off at seven. Her intention was to try restoring
herself physically with a jog in the park. She was getting into her jogging clothes when Nancy entered after spending the night at Bob's
apartment and called out a hello to Ronnie. Nancy went into her bedroom and turned on the television set to the news. The announcer's
tease for the next item after a commercial break startled her.

"Ronnie, get in here right away!"

Ronnie hurried into the room.

"Coming up, you're not going to believe this," Nancy said.

The female announcer appeared with an insert behind her on the
screen, a shot of Randall Cummings.

"Satanic cult leader Randall Cummings is dead. The head of the
Dark Angel Church, located on 129th Street, was apparently strangled
to death in his church yesterday."

"What?" Ronnie said, and her insides tightened with this shock to
her system.

"He was found by an employee of the church. Police officials report a motive for the slaying is unknown. The Dark Angel Church ad-
vocates worship of Satan; the cult said to number over a thousand in the

Manhattan-based congregation and via the Internet. Cummings was forty-five years old."

The announcer started her next report and Nancy clicked off the television set.

"My God, I was there. Yesterday. In the afternoon."

"You know how lucky you are nothing happened to you? You might have just missed the killer."

"I went there to tell him to stop harassing me. I was *in* his office."

"Strangled to death. Whew."

"He sent an e-mail to his congregation to leave me alone. I think he was going to cooperate. I can't believe it. He's dead."

Nancy eventually went to work. Ronnie took a long bath, contemplating the nearly incomprehensible events of the previous day. She went to see Cummings to confront him, she blacked out, she couldn't even remember much of her time up there, and he was murdered. What if she *had* been present when the killer arrived? She might be dead, too.

A few minutes after 11:00 A.M. she pushed herself to her desk to coordinate notes on the book. She worked unevenly. If she had never written about Cummings, she contemplated, would attention not have been directed toward him and would he still be alive? Did she contribute to the death of someone? It was a hard way for the harassment to stop, with his death, but she assumed it would stop now.

The original call to the police about Cummings came the previous afternoon from the assistant, Cosmo Pitalis. When Santini and Gomez arrived he was sitting on a step to the rear door, weeping. After observing the editing of a new film for the Web site, Pitalis returned to the church from the production studio at about 4:30 P.M. and found the body, he told the detectives. Beginning to build a time line on suspects, they asked if he could remember when he left the building. A few minutes after 2:00. His appointment at the video studio was for 2:15. This was later confirmed by three different people at the production house, located on

125th Street. Pitalis arrived there at 2:15 and departed from the studio at 4:20. He originally left "when that woman arrived," he said.

"What woman was that?" Gomez asked. The detectives were kneeling next to the overwrought assistant.

"The Delaney woman. That so-called writer."

"She was here?" Gomez said. He and Santini were taken aback by the information. "What was she doing here?"

"I have no idea."

"And she came just after two. What time did she leave?" Santini asked.

"I couldn't tell you. I was gone. Why did they kill him? His mission was to help people," and he began weeping again.

"How do people get in and out?" Gomez asked.

"Front door, locked during the week. Side door, when I open it. This door is for deliveries and it leads to parking."

"Can you just open a door and walk in?"

"Can't get in unless a door is opened for you."

"So you found the body—"

"In the corridor."

"Near this door?" Santini said.

"Yes."

"Did you see anyone entering the building at any other time when you were here or anything suspicious when you left the building?" Gomez asked.

"Nobody. Except the assholes."

"What assholes might that be?" Santini said.

"With the signs."

"The protesters," Santini said. "They were there when you left the building?"

"Yes."

"And when you came back?"

"Yes."

"How many were there?"

"Just two, I think."

"All right, sir, we thank you for talking to us. We're going to want to talk to you some more. To help things along, we'd appreciate it if you don't leave town for the next period of time."

Pitalis moved away from the building past the police, the area taped off as a crime scene. Santini and Gomez remained there a moment.

"What the hell was she doing, complaining about the guy, then she comes here," Gomez said.

"Maybe she didn't like the pace we were moving at. Can't blame her for that."

"I guess. Let's talk to the crazies."

John Wilson and Beattie Ryan left their spot to join the dozen people outside the building observing the police. They carried their banners and their chairs, worried someone might steal their possessions if they left them across the street.

"Could we speak to you folks?" Gomez said and motioned them to move away from the others and they walked a few feet from the onlookers.

"What happened here?" Wilson asked.

"A crime was committed," Gomez answered.

"What crime?"

"We're not at liberty to divulge. Now who are you exactly?"

"The Anti-Satanist Group," Wilson replied.

"Why have you been out here?" Santini asked.

"It's in our literature. Praised be the Lord," and he handed them each a flyer. The detectives read the material, which thrilled Wilson. "Do you have any questions?" Wilson said, referring to the flyer.

"We have a lot of questions," Santini said, and took down their names, addresses, and phone numbers and asked for the same on any other members of the group.

Santini and Gomez asked to see where they had been positioned. Standing where Wilson and Ryan had been, the detectives noted the protesters had a clear view of the front door of the building and the side door, but no view of the rear door.

"I want you to think very hard about whoever you saw going in and out of the building while you were out here," Santini said.

"The weird guy," Ryan answered. "He went out and then he went in."

"Do you remember when?"

"We got here about noon, so he must have gone in before. Then he came out, what time was it?" she said to Wilson.

"Maybe two or so," Wilson said. "After we ate lunch. Around when the girl came. She went in, he came out. Then he went back in around four thirty."

"Could you describe this girl?" Santini said.

"Pretty. A brunette. John talked to her."

"A slut. The devil's slut," Wilson said.

"How's that?" Gomez asked.

"He had his way with her, that Cummings."

"He had his way with her?" Gomez said.

"When she came out, she was weaving, like, you know, he entered her with his Devil's staff."

"She was weaving and that tells you he entered her with his Devil's staff?" Santini said.

Ryan offered on Wilson's behalf, "People follow him, evidently. Could be he stiffed her. She *was* walking funny."

"She went in around two, you say, and came out when?" Gomez asked.

"She was in there about an hour and a half, servicing the Devil's lust," Wilson said.

"Is that how you remember it?" he asked Ryan.

"That's right."

"And you people, where were you from noon when you say you got here?"

"Right here," Wilson replied.

"You never left the spot? Neither of you?"

"Not until the police came," Wilson said. "Then we went across the street to look."

"You were right here, never left?"

"Right here. Don't you think we're entitled to know what happened?" Wilson asked.

"I'm sure you'll hear about it on the news. Don't either of you leave town. You're potential witnesses. Anything else occurs to you that you saw, anyone in or out, anything, give us a call," Santini said and handed each of them a business card.

Ronnie gave up her attempts to work and tried to learn more information about the death of Cummings on the radio and the Internet. The information was the same and she set out for her doctor's appointment.

In detail she described the blacking-out episodes to the internist, Dr. Emma Lawson, a thoughtful woman in her forties, deliberate and thorough in her medical Q and A. She also asked about any changes in Ronnie's social life that might have had a bearing on her emotional state.

"I was with someone and we broke up. That was a few months ago. I've been kind of seeing someone since. He travels a lot."

"Does that cause you stress?"

"I doubt seeing this guy has caused stress, over and above the New York usual. Maybe more, but not significant. I'd say the death threats I've been receiving—"

"Death threats?"

Ronnie recounted the incidents since the article appeared. The doctor somberly took notes.

"That would cause stress in anyone. You said you lost consciousness in the race you ran, but you were able to keep running?"

"Yes."

"Were you aware of anything in your surroundings, the path of the race, the runners?"

"No."

"So you were physically intact, but it was your consciousness that was affected?"

"Yes."

"And before that day, can you recall similar incidents?"

"No."

"And it happened again yesterday. Except yesterday was somewhat different. You lost consciousness *and* you were feeling faint. You actually passed out."

"Yes. Some ways it was worse. Everything was worse. He was murdered, the man I went to see, sometime after I saw him."

"Murdered?"

"A man named Randall Cummings."

"I saw something about it. You have some heavy traffic in your life."

"I'm very upset. I didn't like him. I knew he was behind the harassment, but not to the extent that I'd want to see him dead. I even thought we worked it out yesterday."

"Being upset about his death doesn't account for what happened yesterday or that race you ran. Our medical puzzle is why you're going into these fogs."

The tests the doctor ordered were the most extensive Ronnie had ever taken; blood was drawn, she was administered an EKG, chest X-ray, stress test on a treadmill, and, finally, a CAT scan. Ronnie was there all afternoon and the doctor met with her once more.

"We'll have to wait for the test results. Give us a week or so on that, but from what I can see here, you're in excellent shape. Now for the stress, I can offer you some medication to round out the edges for you."

"I'm a writer and I'm writing a book. I'd be afraid to take anything to round out the edges."

"If you change your mind, it's there for you. Let me know if there are any other episodes. And, Ms. Delaney, if those threats were causing you stress and they're over, then that's hopeful, isn't it?"

"It is. But there's also the guilt. I wrote about the man, I brought attention to him, and he was murdered."

"Why guilt?"

"Why not guilt? I was Catholic as a little girl."

At New York City police headquarters Rourke met with the department's chief of detectives, the chief of Manhattan North Homicide, and the police commissioner. The meeting focused on the headline-making cases of late, the Cummings murder and the hit-and-run case. The mood in the room was somber, the feeling among the participants that, based on the initial evidence, these were going to be difficult cases, and they could still be unsolved well after the news stories faded.

To augment Rourke's detective squad, two more homicide detectives were assigned. Tom Carter was an African American in his late thirties, a muscular, six-foot-tall former baseball player for Fordham University. Bill Greenberg, five feet seven, in his midthirties, was a stocky Jewish boy from Brooklyn, the first detective ever from his Crown Heights congregation.

"Coroner says Cummings died by strangulation, approximately three o'clock. A frontal assault. What does that give us?" Rourke asked his detectives at the station house.

"We have these religious nuts across the street," Gomez said, reading from his pad. "Man named Wilson, woman named Ryan. They were protesting the cult. They alibi each other. Claim they never left their spot across the street, so they would have been there time of death. As possible witnesses, they were in a position to see who comes in and out, but not for the rear door of the church. Anybody came in and out that way and didn't come around to the street, they wouldn't have known it."

"We have Cummings's assistant. He says he leaves the building around two, is back around four thirty," Santini said, "and he's got a production studio where he went confirming he was at the studio the whole time."

"The only other person seen going into the building around that time is Veronica Delaney," Gomez told them.

"Really?" Rourke said.

"Yes." For the benefit of the other detectives Santini said, "She got all kinds of stupid pranks played on her after she wrote an article about Cummings, like a dead black cat, decapitated picture of her, and she was sure Cummings or his people did it. Anyway, she goes into the building at two, according to the assistant and the religiosos across the street. The assistant isn't there, so he doesn't know when she comes out. The religiosos say she comes out, walking funny, hour and a half later."

"Walking funny?" Carter asked.

"So says this guy, that Cummings entered her with his Devil's staff."

"Brother!" Carter said.

"She's there time of death then," Greenberg offered.

"If you can believe these people and their powers of observation," Santini said. "They're pretty strange. Plus she's little, probably doesn't weigh a lot more than a hundred pounds, and he was—"

"Six two, two forty," Rourke said from his notes.

"Be a real long shot that she strangled him," Santini said.

"She's your account," Rourke said, gesturing at Santini and Gomez. He turned to Carter and Greenberg. "Check out the religiosos."

"They were protesting the cult?" Greenberg said.

"The Anti-Satanist Group, they call themselves," Gomez responded.

"Well, with this guy dead maybe they don't have so much to protest anymore," Greenberg remarked.

"We're going to have to get a list of who was in this cult and work through it," Rourke said. "And we're going to have to find out if he had enemies, rivals. We've got wackos inside and out—and a goddamn strangler walking around."

Ronnie sent an e-mail to Richard:

> Cummings strangled to death. I feel badly about it. Like if I
> didn't write about him he wouldn't be dead.

He did not immediately respond.

Santini and Gomez revisited the crime scene with Carter and Greenberg. Carter downloaded the files on Cummings's computer, found a list of names, addresses, and e-mail addresses of congregants and printed it out, more than a thousand names; a daunting task ahead if they needed to interrogate these people. With his confirmed alibi for the time of death Pitalis was not a prime suspect. He was a valuable source of information about the cult, though. Carter and Greenberg went to his apartment on Dyckman Street where he gave them two hours of background on the cult. He was of the opinion that Cummings had no rivals in the field and said, "No one in the congregation would have wished our leader any harm."

Ronnie was watching the eleven o'clock news. Two people identified as the parents of Randall Cummings were shown coming out of the Twenty-sixth Precinct house, the father a tall, bald man, his face ashen, the mother a thin woman wearing dark glasses. They stopped for a moment in front of cameras and microphones and he spoke, a father's public opportunity to redeem his son and salvage a legacy for him.

"We would like him remembered, our son, Randall, as a person who found a way, unconventional as it may have been, of helping people get hold of their lives."

That was all he was going to say, a dignified, succinct epitaph, and the parents started to move on. An aggressive, no-sympathy-for-the-grieving reporter shouted out, "But he was a satanist, wasn't he? He promoted evil."

"He was originally an actor," the father said in an even tone that effectively diminished the reporter. "He was creating theater."

"Creating theater." On hearing this, Ronnie felt even guiltier about the possibility that she was a journalistic accomplice in his death.

Ronnie knew Cummings's assistant would tell the police she was there that day and she would have to deal with that eventually. She did not want to precipitate the upsetting admission that she couldn't account for part of the time. If she had a reliable male friend she would have been with him these evenings, to confide in him and deal with a crisis the way she imagined people together behaved.

Richard finally sent an e-mail back.

This Cummings murder has nothing to do with you. It's the madness of the world.

"The madness of the world" was rather grim for encouragement, she thought.

In the hit-and-run case, in an effort to explore all possibilities, a fax had been sent from police headquarters to auto repair and body shops in the city advising the establishments to report instances of body work on the driver's side. Someone was looking for such work on his car at an auto repair shop in the Bronx, and the man seemed so peculiar his behavior attracted the shop owner's attention and he called the police.

Santini and Gomez went to see the owner, Joe Drennan, at Elite Auto Repair. The car was a 1998 Buick and a dent ran along the driver's side. Drennan saw a lot of dents, he explained, but the owner of the car seemed extremely odd and Drennan immediately thought about the hit-and-run killer. The customer's oddness took the form of rapid mumbling. He would talk in complete sentences and where the normal pauses in conversation would be, he mumbled. The customer also complained of a problem with the steering. Drennan told the detectives the steering problem was consistent with that type of body damage; the car obviously had struck something that affected the steering and the wheel alignment. The detectives checked, and according to the registration the car belonged to an Alfonse Batrak of 138 West 118th Street, the same name and phone number he gave Drennan. Santini and Gomez thanked him for his help and immediately impounded the car.

Lab tests indicated that the dented side bore paint residue that matched the paint of the parked SUV that was damaged in the near-miss of the second female jogger. And fabric strands snagged in the headlamp portion of the Buick were an identical match with the fabric of the cotton running shorts worn by the jogger who was killed. They had the vehicle that was used in the crime.

———————

Santini and Gomez went to the address on 118th Street, a few blocks from where the victim was killed. Sitting on a step of a five-story building was a Hispanic woman in her fifties in a housedress.

"We're looking for Alfonse Batrak," Gomez said. "He lives here, doesn't he?" and he flashed his badge.

She smiled, taking satisfaction, it seemed, from the moment.

"He in some kind of trouble?"

"Remains to be seen," Gomez said. "Do you know him?"

"Sure, I know him. I live here. My husband's the super. What did he do?"

"Is he in?" Santini asked.

"Gets home from work soon."

"What kind of work is that?" Santini said.

"Painter."

"And he went to work, far as you know?"

"Saw him leave."

The partners looked at each other, instinctively knowing what the other was thinking. Unless someone else had been driving the car, this Batrak person undoubtedly killed someone and attempted to kill someone else and he went to work. He painted walls somewhere, his life went on in pure banality. People didn't necessarily flee after a murder, sometimes they watched television, sometimes they went to the office, sometimes they painted walls.

The woman established for the detectives that Batrak had lived there for two years, and that his wife, "good-looking," left him a month previously. One day she just walked out the door; long overdue, by the woman's estimation. They had screaming fights at night everyone complained about. The wife cursed him in Spanish, people heard through the apartments, and she did it in public when people were nearby. Batrak, "some kind of pollock," didn't know what the hell she was yelling, a source of amusement to the Spanish-speaking people within earshot. She would scream about the smell of paint on him, and the way he talked, the way he looked. The detectives asked if the wife had any boyfriends. She said it was just the two of them, as far as she knew.

The detectives sat in their unmarked car and waited for Batrak to return home.

"The clues match up, beautiful, and motive drops right in our laps," Santini said. "Rage against his wife for leaving equals rage against women. And there it is."

"Can't be this simple. Maybe he was framed," Gomez said.

"By who?"

"The wife. The wife's lover. Could be she had one."

"She doesn't have to frame him. She's out the door."

"She does it to be vindictive."

"And gets someone killed she doesn't know?"

"It's someone she *does* know. The woman who died was someone she wanted dead, and she frames her husband," Gomez said, playing with the possibilities.

"She gets somebody to drive his car and figures out that if he scrapes another car it'll leave paint samples and if the car hits someone it'll leave a fabric trace to frame him? You kidding me?"

Gomez said, "I'm done. He did it."

"Right."

"But why doesn't he just go after the wife?" Gomez asked.

"That's why it *isn't* that simple. He moves over one space and kills someone else."

Alfonse Batrak walked up the street, a strong-looking man of five feet ten, in neatly pressed dark slacks and a striped sports shirt, carrying a small zipper bag, fastidious enough to have changed out of his work clothes after finishing work. As he neared the building, the superintendent's wife, trying out her adopted role as an undercover agent for the police department, nodded in the direction of the detectives. Santini and Gomez emerged from the car.

"Mr. Batrak?" Santini said.

"Yes."

"Police department."

He flashed his badge.

"We need you to come with us," Gomez said.

"I'm walking. I'm walking home. I'm not bothering anyone."

"We have your car—the damage. You know what we're talking about," Santini said.

"Not bothering anyone. Step in front of me. Stopping me. Not stopping someone bothering someone. Stopping *me*." The next was incomprehensible to the detectives, between spoken language and a child's gibberish, but angry, an angry undertone to the mumbling. And then, "Out of my way. Going home. Shower, I'm going to shower. Watch TV. Not coming with them. Not bothering anyone."

"Mr. Batrak," Gomez said and moved closer to him. They were about to handcuff him when Batrak suddenly pulled a metal putty knife out of his back pocket and lashed at Gomez's face. Gomez, the portlier and less athletic-looking of the two, was a softball player, a serious hitter with a serious hitter's reflexes. He ducked the weapon, much as he might duck an errant pitch, and now lower than Batrak's head, in a near crouch, he swung up and hard with his fist into Batrak's stomach, knocking the wind out of him as the man crumpled, gasping, to the ground. A few seconds and they had handcuffs on him and pushed him into the rear of the car, Batrak mumbling in a fury.

Tabloid headlines followed and then trailed off, the rest of the case relatively routine, bureaucratic, his court-appointed lawyer staking out an insanity defense, resulting eventually in Batrak being remanded to a psychiatric facility.

For Santini and Gomez the case was unchallenging; a good tip, and a direct line to the perpetrator. They would take them all like this; not for the ease of the work, rather for the certainty, the chance to get a psychopath off the streets.

Rourke complimented them and several of their colleagues gave them good wishes, as well. They did not celebrate, not together, or with others, or individually. This is what they did. The man was not going to run down any more women.

Santini gave his wife a report in the dining area of his apartment the night of the arrest after the children went to sleep. They lived in a two-bedroom on Second Avenue and Ninety-fifth Street, their girls, seven and ten, sharing one of the bedrooms. Santini's wife, Alice, was a nurse at Mt. Sinai Hospital, a petite woman, pale, usually harried trying to keep up, juggling the children's after-school activities, grateful when her husband's erratic hours fell in their favor and he could take over with the children. He was matter-of-fact about the arrest, a relatively easy case, a tip from a concerned citizen, a blowup by the suspect. She did not see it quite as casually as he did. Here was his very reason for being—partly hers, too, the wife of a New York City detective—the constant anxiety, young children who needed a father, the tragedy if they all would lose him. This was the justification for the fear and hardships, this thing he did, that he did on this day.

"Someone driving around targeting women. You boys did well."

"I guess."

"You did. Ralph this nonchalant about it?"

"He knows it wasn't exactly the *Times* crossword puzzle."

"I'm proud of you," which she needed to say for both of them, for their life.

"Yeah, he could've killed somebody else."

"Could've."

Gomez lived in Co-op City in the Bronx. His son, a nineteen-year-old, was a junior at SUNY Stonybrook, where he played on the soccer team. He planned to be a physical education teacher and was working as a counselor in a soccer camp in Connecticut. Gomez's wife died four years earlier, random insanity, a brick thrown from an overpass on the Grand Central Parkway. The person was never found. The window of the car was open because the air conditioner was broken and they were waiting for Gomez's next paycheck to get it fixed, and she was struck and killed. He was cynical about human behavior before the crime; her death did not improve his worldview.

He called his boy, Eddie, at the camp that night.

"How are you, son?"

"Good, Dad. Good day here."

"Here, too. That hit-and-run. Broke wide open. Guy practically tumbled into our arms."

"Dad, that's terrific."

"A psycho, but he's done."

"Mom would've been real happy."

Gomez bit his lip. A sweet boy, to invoke his mother's memory and in this context.

The hit-and-run case was over and now they would be able to focus again on the Randall Cummings murder. The hit-and-run victim was an innocent, Cummings was not, he was a satanic cult leader murdered in his church. Gomez supposed some people would make a distinction about these two victims. For him there was a basic overriding fact: You shouldn't be able to kill people.

The Dark Angel Church had no plan in place for a successor. Cummings ran the operation with Pitalis serving as his office manager. With Cummings's death, the church was out of business. Cummings's father brought a lawyer in from Chicago, where the parents lived, and the lawyer teamed up with a New York accounting firm to see what could be learned from the books and to determine the church's assets. They were limited; not even the real estate of the church itself was an asset, the building was rented space. Pitalis was advised by the lawyer to shut it down and Pitalis sent an e-mail to all congregants that the church no longer existed.

With Cummings and his followers gone, the Anti-Satanist Group disbanded. They were still under scrutiny, were interrogated; they were of little help and little value to the investigation. Wilson seemed primarily interested in having the detectives ask him questions about his flyer, losing the theme, that it was no longer relevant.

When the media coverage of the hit-and-run case marginalized the Cummings murder, Ronnie presumed she was of no further interest to the police concerning her blackout afternoon. This was a miscalculation.

8

Epidemics of satanic possession in sixteenth- and seventeenth-century European convents, the Devil supposedly sweeping through bedrooms, possessing nuns like a vampire in the night, was delicious material to Ronnie. Her strategy was to start the book with a description of these serial possessions, and she began writing the text. She loved the language in the early work by Traugott Oesterreich, "The epidemic spread like a patch of oil . . ."

A writer couldn't do a book on this subject, she decided, without giving attention to the most famous of these incidents, the serial possession at the convent at Loudun, France, commencing in 1632. Several nuns were afflicted, the epidemic escaped to the town, the local priest, a sexually freewheeling man, was blamed for being the Devil's vehicle and burned at the stake, and one of the exorcists brought in for disaster control claimed he himself was possessed. To modern eyes, to her eyes, the events were casebook mass hysteria combined with manipulations by the presiding officials.

Ronnie was working on the material at her computer when the doorman buzzed up to say, "Two men here to see you, Miss Delaney." She wanted to be immersed in seventeenth-century France, in the world of nuns and hysteria and Catholic tribal rites, and now reality was intruding. She knew the police had caught up with her about that day.

She offered Santini and Gomez bottled water, which she herself needed, and they sat in the living room.

"Ms. Delaney, first of all, have you received any unwanted packages or mail lately?" Santini asked.

"Nothing."

"That's good. Obviously, we need to know your movements on the day Randall Cummings was murdered. You *were* there?" Santini said.

"Yes, I went there."

"Why?" Gomez asked.

"I didn't think the police department was doing anything."

"And what did you have in mind?" Gomez said. "To be a vigilante?"

"To negotiate with him. If he stopped harassing me, I wouldn't write a piece about the way he was harassing me."

"And you told him that?"

"I did. And he seemed to agree. He sent a cease and desist to his congregation."

"Yes, we saw that in his computer files," Santini said.

She thought, if you knew it, why are you asking; but then these were detectives, they had to ask or they wouldn't be detectives. She was feeling very uneasy. Eventually, they were going to ask her to account for time she couldn't account for.

"You went to his office about?" Gomez asked.

"Two-ish."

"And came out?"

"Also two-ish. I wasn't there long. A few minutes."

"Who did you see when you were there?" Santini asked.

"His assistant. He let me in."

"No one else was on the premises?"

"Not as far as I know, just Cummings."

"And outside the building, on your way in, anyone suspicious?" he continued.

"Nobody suspicious. A couple of people protesting across the street."

"Those people, they say they observed you going into the building at two or so, but that you came out much later, an hour and a half later, and that you were walking peculiarly when you came out," Gomez said.

"I was only there a few minutes."

"Did he make any sexual advances toward you?" Gomez said.

"What?"

"He didn't come on to you and you had to fight him off?"

"He came on to me, an earlier time, but it was about dinner, Detective. There was no physical contact between us."

"Here's the thing, the protesters, they say you were in there all that time, and according to the coroner's report, he died around three, so they place you in the building at the time of death," Santini said.

"Not true. I had long left. Let me ask you something—would you trust those people, with their insane literature, standing out there for hours on end with their dopey banners, to be reliable about anything? I've told you really all I know. I hated that Cummings was harassing me, but I never wished him dead. I'm actually pretty concerned about it, that maybe by writing about him, I encouraged some lunatic to go after him, but I don't know any more than I've told you."

"This is what we do," Gomez said. "We ask a lot of questions, see a lot of people, poke around. We didn't want to see Cummings dead either. We don't want to see anybody dead, and there's a killer out there, a very bad person, and our job is to find that person and make sure that person doesn't kill somebody else."

"I don't know any more than what I've told you," which was strictly true; she didn't know any more than what she had told them.

"If anything else occurs to you—" Santini said.

The detectives sat in their car and went over their notes.

"Too bad the coroner didn't find semen," Gomez said, "or I'd take a shot at this: they had sex, he went for asphyxiation ecstasy, it went too far, and she choked him to death. Accidentally."

"Man, that is reaching."

"He was a Satan guy, he could've been into kinky sex."

"With her? She thought he was messing up her life."

"So they didn't have sex and she's too small to just walk up to him and strangle him, but there's the Mariano Rivera factor."

"Mariano Rivera strangled him?"

"Mariano's just a wiry guy, not too big," Gomez said. "No way, if you saw him on the street, would you say he can throw ninety-five-mile-an-hour fastballs and break people's bats with his splitter. Concealed strength. If she was in a rage enough, she might've been able to do it. I mean, she *is* placed there time of death."

"That's if the coroner is dead-on accurate and these jerks can be relied on."

"I wouldn't dismiss her as a suspect. She seemed really jumpy to me, *and* they've got her there time of death."

"If you had to put all the people we've seen so far in a line, she wouldn't be the one I'd pick."

"You know what I know? You never know."

Ronnie called Nancy at work, could they go to a movie that night, do something, she didn't want to be alone. Nancy and Bob gathered her up and they went to a neighborhood Chinese restaurant. Nancy and Bob were present the first time she blacked out, but she never told them about the second time, with Cummings. If she told them now and the police at a later date got around to questioning them, it might come out she couldn't account for her time. The doctor knew and it was in Ronnie's medical file. The detectives probably wouldn't know about the doctor, so that area seemed safe. She realized she was making sure her tracks were covered when she couldn't remember the tracks in the first place. She didn't think she was failing in any civic or moral duty. She had observed nothing that would be of help to the detectives. If she confessed she blacked out she would walk right into becoming a suspect in the case. Even if she were a dubious suspect, did she really want the police barreling into her life? Then, too, she was mortally embarrassed by her inability to be conscious of all her waking hours. The goal, as she saw it, was to keep the police at a distance so she could concentrate on work, write the book, and this would pass, they would find the person who murdered Cummings.

At dinner Bob brought up Cummings's murder.

"Here's the tough question," Ronnie said. "If I had the choice of his still being alive and my still getting horrible things sent to me, versus his being dead and horrible things not getting sent to me—and they aren't, they seemed to have stopped—which would I choose?"

"It's no question," Bob said.

"It's beyond a non sequitur," Nancy added.

"It is a question if you think my writing about him contributed to his death."

"You mean like, oh, here's an interesting article. I think I'll kill this person. Ronnie, for a smart girl, you can be a real dumbbell," Bob said.

"I love you guys."

"And we love you. Does Richard Smith? Where is he?" Bob asked.

"Europe."

"He's not much good to you traveling, is he?"

"That's very subversive," Nancy reprimanded.

"He's just trying to be helpful," Ronnie said. "Old wounds—his father traveling so much, his mother patient, and then for her patience, he rewards her by upping and leaving."

"What did you say? How do you know that?"

"Which? About your father traveling? You told me."

"I never did."

"One night at the apartment, you had some wine, and you told me."

"Never."

"Maybe you don't remember, Nancy was in the other room and we were talking, you had some wine, absolutely."

"I never said a word. Nancy, did you know my folks broke up over my father's absences, and he suddenly left?"

"I knew they were divorced."

"But not those particular details. I never told you, Ronnie."

"Yes. You did."

They were all uncomfortable and eased into safer conversation, work-related conversation. But Ronnie was positive Bob told her about his father; that he had too much to drink that night, which was why he couldn't recall.

Richard arrived bearing gray pearl earrings, which triggered an immediate reaction from Ronnie, of caution, I don't know if I can accept these, they're beautiful, but too expensive. He had chosen a middle-range Italian restaurant on the East Side, and offered the gift. As she sipped a glass of wine and appraised the handsomest man in the place, she wondered about her priorities. She danced around what was appropriate and not appropriate in a sexual relationship; that's what it was primarily, certainly not an intimate relationship in a talking-about-intimate-things sense; and yet she was willing to conceal from the police that she was unable to account for an hour and a half on the day when Randall Cummings was murdered. She wasn't going to tell Richard, By the way I've developed a little habit of blacking out and sometimes I don't know what I'm doing or where I've been.

"I can't accept these."

"I knew it. Here's the receipt."

"Why do I want the receipt?"

"Look at it."

"A place in Munich."

"Sixty-four dollars, American. Sixty-four dollars, Ronnie, that's less than a dinner in most places. They're pretty, it was a steal, please accept them."

She could hear Nancy telling her to lighten up, just accept a gift from the guy, you can accept a gift from someone you're sleeping with if he travels around the world and decides to pick something up for you.

"They're beautiful. I'll accept them on one condition."

"Which is."

"We go bowling."

"Bowling?"

"When you were away, I had this fantasy. That the man I'd be with would be the kind of person who I could do normal things with, like bowling, and we would also have sex in some kind of order."

"You give new meaning to high maintenance."

"I know. Aren't I interesting?"

"Bowling. Sure. The whole time, dealing with these cult people in Germany building primitive altars to Satan, sacrificing farm animals, I thought, when I get out of here, I'm going bowling with Ronnie."

"Somewhere in there is the point—that it's so ordinary it's good."

She accepted the earrings, they were going to make plans for bowling, she was even going to get to invite her friends to come along, Richard consented to that, a bowling double date.

Back at his apartment, the sex was as she fantasized it, the best sex she ever had, except for the last time with him, that was the best sex she ever had. Afterward she thought holding on with this transient man was the right thing to do, to not bolt because of his inconstant behavior. Being here with him at this place at this time had the power to obliterate, if only for these moments, the disquieting events in her life.

In the morning they went to their breakfast place. He was going to be in New York for a couple of weeks and then he needed to return to Munich. He described the cult, an atavistic group that favored ancient satanic rituals, that somehow was attracting young people from the city. The cult leader was a man in his sixties who wore farmer's clothes for his mystique, there was always a mystique, he explained, and the dogma was a return to the land and simple pursuits, the cult members joining a working farm, with a nearly medieval worship of Satan. Antoine Burris thought there was a book in it; Richard wasn't so sure, but he needed to go back. This was clearly the deal, which she fully recognized: Richard was there when he was there, and then he was gone.

"What do you do with all your frequent flyer mileage, get luggage?"

"Maybe I should use it for bowling lessons. Is there such a thing?"

"Richard, there's something we need to talk about."

"Still not married, Ronnie. You'll be the first to know. Maybe not the first."

"It's about Cummings. I can't get rid of the idea that if I just left him in obscurity, he'd be alive today. If I never wrote about him—"

"Wait just a minute. He had over a thousand members. He was rolling along. If you didn't write about him, somebody else would have, me even. Someone somewhere was going to write a piece on him."

"But *I* did. And he's dead."

"And? Where's the connection?"

"I put him in the spotlight."

"You're a professional journalist and you wrote a professional journalist's piece. You wrote the piece that needed to be written."

"It wasn't a rave review, Richard."

"Appropriately."

"His father was on TV. He said Cummings was—creating theater."

"That was his problem."

"What do you mean?"

"Look at enough of these—he was a dabbler, Ronnie. He probably *was* creating theater. He wasn't a true believer like this German guy. It wasn't well thought out. Be evil, but not *too* evil. You picked it up in your piece."

"Then he wasn't that harmful. Makes it even worse."

"You did a terrific job. Stop. You can't beat yourself up over it."

"Still—"

"His death had nothing to do with what you wrote. What you have to do is focus on this book, put every bit of your energy and intelligence into the book, make it as good as it can be. I was watching tennis on television and the announcer said something very interesting. Not all points have the same value. Some you *have to* win. It's like this book. It doesn't have the same value as an article. It's your chance to win, to do something really substantial. All of you should go into it. And you can do it."

He leaned over, took her hands in his, and kissed them. For all his sexual athleticism, he was not a particularly physically affectionate person, no light touches on the hand or on the waist, and this was as intimate a gesture outside of sex as he had made toward her.

"Thank you, Richard. I hope I hear you."

Just when she wasn't expecting much, his latest time in New York turned out to be better than she would have thought. They went to the theater to see *Doubt,* and to a New York Philharmonic Concert in Central Park—bona fide New York activities.

An oddity, but she noticed that when she was at his place the phone never rang. She wondered if he had a telephone system that screened calls, and yet the phone in his bedroom was connected to an ordinary answering machine. He had told her he didn't have any relatives and that Antoine Burris was his closest friend. Apparently he had no other friends, and when she was there Burris didn't call, nobody called. This had the effect of making their time together unique, it was just the two of them. However, she found it strange to never hear a phone ring in someone's apartment because there was no one else in his life to call him, apparently. At the least this did damage to theories about a wife, or other women.

On his last night in New York they went bowling. Ronnie arranged it and booked an alley at Chelsea Piers. Ronnie was not a particularly good bowler. Her idea was people leading regular lives go bowling and that is why they were there. Nancy was a little better than Ronnie, Richard slightly better than both of them. Bob, the runner and athlete and someone who did bowl frequently when he was growing up, was fairly competent.

"I don't think off this performance we should get club jackets," Ronnie joked as they were leaving.

The women went to the ladies' room and Bob excused himself to go off to a hallway so he could make a business call on his cell phone. Richard was left alone at the lane. He looked at the pins set up and with sudden seriousness, picked up a ball and, with perfect form, threw a strike. Bob came back into the area and happened to observe this. Richard hadn't thrown a single strike while they were playing and had a couple of gutter balls. As Richard walked away from the lane, Bob stepped toward him.

"What was that, you were dumping when you played with us?"

"Nothing to think about. Lucky, that's all."

"That was perfect, like you could bowl a perfect game if you wanted to."

"Bob, really, a lucky toss."

"You were patronizing us. Why would you? I don't get it."

"Nothing to get."

"And now you're off again, right, big guy? And Ronnie sits around, seeing nobody, basically waiting for you to show up."

"Is this really your business? She seems to be happy."

"I saw an interview with Sting and he said some people have as their song, 'I'll Be Watching You,' which he said was strange since it's a paranoid statement. Paranoid this may be, but whoever you are, buddy, I'll be watching you."

Bob couldn't get over the image of Richard, after a spotty bowling performance, throwing a perfect strike. At his apartment, before they went to sleep, he described it to Nancy.

"Maybe he was just being social, he's a good bowler and he didn't want to outshine us."

"Customer bowling?"

"That's the effect it had, we were all sort of on the same level, except maybe for you, and you're no champion, and we had a good time."

"Here are the possibilities—"

"Bob, please, let's go to bed."

"He was being social, like you say, holding back for the group. Or it's an indication of something duplicitous about him, he's not always who he seems. Or, and this is interesting, that the last strike was for *me,* that he wanted *me* to see it, a little dig at me: You thought I was just like you, but I'm not, buddy-boy, I'm so much better than you."

"So this is really about you, in competition with him."

"If it is that, he's still not who he pretends to be and he was still duplicitous with us."

"I'm saying good night now. Call Oliver Stone."

"Ms. Delaney, Doctor Lawson here—"

"Yes, Doctor."

"You're in excellent health. The blood test, the CAT scan, everything is normal."

"Really? Excellent."

"Sometimes simple medical advice is the best. When it's warm, drink plenty of fluids. If you exercise, do it at cool times of the day. Not too much alcohol or wine at night, it can disturb sleep. A hat when you go out in the sun. Call me if you have any more problems. We detected absolutely nothing, Ms. Delaney."

"Thank you, Doctor."

Relieved, she happily consigned the episodes to not taking sufficient care of herself in warm weather. Richard was off to Munich. She went back into seventeenth-century France, loving it.

A consultant to police departments in New York State, Charles Larkin, a bookish, slightly built man in his forties, came in to talk with the detective squad at the Twenty-sixth Precinct. His expertise began ten years earlier with Satan's Hand, a satanic cult in Watertown, New York, whose members were committing crimes in the community. While working as a detective on the case, Larkin became interested in cults and eventually became a police expert in the field. He told the detectives he doubted Cummings would be murdered by anyone from a rival cult; there weren't substantial rivalries between cults. As to a competition for Internet members, he suggested there were enough odd people to go around and doubted anyone in another cult would be so antagonized by Cummings's operation as to kill him. Rourke also questioned whether it was likely for one of his cult members to be a suspect, since they were, after all, his followers. Larkin didn't rule out jealousy as a motive, or someone who felt they received bad advice, but he thought a cult member would be extremely unlikely to murder Cummings. His general feeling was that it would be more productive to concentrate on this as a murder by someone with a grievance: the Anti-Satanist Group, who were public in their objections; someone in his personal life, a lover, a lover who might have hired an assassin; or it might have been a thief, an intruder. Simply because nothing was stolen didn't preclude its having been a robbery gone awry.

Santini and Gomez sat in their unmarked car as Ronnie went to the recreation center for volunteer time with the youngsters. She didn't work on the newspaper project at this time of year, she merely went to encourage any of the young people who were hanging around to develop their computer skills. The detectives ate dinner in the car, pizza from Patsy's on First Avenue, and waited until she emerged an hour later. She was standing on the sidewalk with two teenage girls, joking with them, then made her way over to Second Avenue to take a bus downtown, and a crosstown bus to the West Side. They trailed her to the point where she entered her apartment building.

"Excellent pizza is what I get out of the night," Santini said.

"So she's doing ordinary things. So was Batrak."

"We're wasting our time with this girl."

"Placed at the scene of the crime, at the time of death, with a grievance against the victim."

"You see that show on the comedy channel last night, the old comics?"

"No."

"They had Don Adams from *Get Smart* and his routine was a take-off on old courtroom dramas and this defense attorney has a thing for the defendant and he says, 'I ask you, ladies and gentlemen of the jury, are those the knees of a homicidal murderer?'"

"Very funny. But she was still there."

"Let's go home."

———

Detectives Carter and Greenberg went to Staten Island to work their way through the Anti-Satanist Group. Peter Askew, the unemployed recovering alcoholic, was not present the day of the murder, according to his colleagues, John Wilson and Beattie Ryan. The detectives found him at Staten Island Hospital, where he was recovering from a heart attack. He was sitting up in bed, playing cards with his mentor in the church recovery group, Martin Beale, another member of the Anti-Satanists.

"I'm Detective Carter, this is Detective Greenberg. We're here about the Randall Cummings murder."

"Right," Askew said.

"We read about it," Beale added.

"And *your* name, sir?" Carter asked.

"Martin Beale."

"You were in the group, too."

"When I could."

"I'd like to ask why you guys were interested," Greenberg said.

"Because he was a dangerous individual," Askew answered. "He encouraged people against God's ways."

"The kind of person it was a good idea to eliminate?" Carter asked.

"I didn't say that. I wouldn't have killed him to get him out of business. I'm not sorry he's out of business."

"And you, Mr. Beale?"

"I'm not sorry either. They were looking to do evil. Somebody did it to him."

"Why would you *care*?" Greenberg asked, intrigued. "To come all the way from Staten Island—"

"Somebody had to . . . to stand up to those people. Wilson told us what he was doing and it seemed like a good idea to us," Askew said.

"Tuesday, May twentieth, you recall where you were that day?"

"I was here. First time I had problems."

"You were admitted—"

"Day before. I would've been there with them, but I couldn't."

"And you, Mr. Beale?" Carter asked. "Can you account for your whereabouts that day?"

"I was here, too. The nurses saw me, if it's an alibi I'm needing. We didn't like Cummings or what he stood for, but we didn't murder him. We were right here."

"All right," Greenberg said, on the complete strikeout. "It's still a lot of energy to expend, to go all the way to Upper Manhattan from Staten Island just to protest somebody."

"It was something to do," Askew said.

Beattie Ryan was seated on a chaise in the small patio behind her garden apartment going over the *Daily Racing Form*. The detectives questioned her and she talked to them while reading the handicap charts. She repeated the account that Santini and Gomez were given on the day of Cummings's murder: Her arrival was after twelve o'clock with John Wilson and they were in their position until the police cars arrived at the building close to five when they went over to observe. She saw the strange guy come out of the building at about the time the girl went in. The girl came out about an hour and a half later, then the strange guy returned an hour or so after that. Nobody else went in or out of the building that they could see, and she and Wilson were there the entire time from noon to the arrival of the police.

They found Wilson at home. He was packing orders into boxes when they arrived.

"We'd like to talk to you about the events of Tuesday, May twentieth," Carter said, showing his badge.

"I already spoke to the police. I can't spare much time. I'm very busy."

They stood while he sat in a chair in his living room/storage room.

"We're trying to reconstruct the events of the day of the murder and we need your help," Carter said.

"God has already given his help, removing this evildoer from the world, praised be the Lord. I don't know what help I can provide."

"Your colleague, Ms. Ryan, has you at the site where you were protesting that day. When was that?" Greenberg asked.

"We got there about noon and we left after your other detectives talked to us. We already talked to you people, you know?"

"We're *other* people. And who went in and out of the building?"

"The man who worked there. And the girl."

"She was there how long?" Carter asked.

"About an hour and a half."

"She says a few minutes," Carter said.

" 'She says.' She's the Devil's mistress. He entered her with his evil staff," Wilson declared.

"Was that something you observed from an open window?" Greenberg could not resist asking.

"The Lord had a hand in his death, I'm certain. Not directly, but it was His will."

"And who, in your opinion, acted on his will?" Carter asked.

"Maybe the man who worked for him, maybe the whore, maybe somebody else."

"In any case, you couldn't see the rear door from where you were standing?"

"No."

Wilson did not add anything to the detectives' knowledge and after a while they concluded with him. Ryan and Wilson were not identified by anyone as being anywhere other than at the protest spot. They said they were there at what was established by the coroner as the time of death, remaining until the police arrived. Interviews with a few of the onlookers at the crime scene had been unproductive. Nobody else had come forth or had been found who could contradict Ryan's and Wilson's account. They were each other's alibi.

Alice Bayers, the last of the Anti-Satanist Group, was working at a storefront Republican Party office, the detectives directed there by a neighbor. She was unable to contribute anything about the murder. Her alibi for the day of Cummings's death could have been upheld by as many as six other people; she was working in the office. She seemed a reasonably intelligent person, making phone calls for campaign contributions.

"Why did you ever join up in this protest against Randall Cummings?" Greenberg asked.

"My fellow church members. We saw it as taking a stand for God and against evil. They're always saying people should get involved."

"I think they mean involved politically," Greenberg said.

"Thank you, Ms. Bayers," Carter added and he pulled his partner away.

As they walked to their car, Carter said, "What are you doing getting philosophic with this person?"

"Sorry, but she's totally screwed up on church and state."

"They're all screwed up, if you ask me. I think it's a mixed blessing for these people, Cummings going down. It took away their fun."

The man in the box had not made any appearances in the neighborhood of late, and he was back, in his place on 111th Street off Broadway, sitting in one of his favorites, a corrugated container from a refrigerator. With Ronnie's idiosyncratic standard for determining the amount of money she gave him based on whether or not she happened to be thinking about work when she passed, he was in a good recipient's position; she was thinking about the book much of the time. She took all her change from her wallet, about four dollars' worth, and glanced at the man as she dropped it in his bowl. He was sitting while looking at his feet, indifferent to the world; he couldn't be bothered with people's need to give him money. He noticed it was Ronnie. He did not recoil as the last time, rather he stared at her, studying her, as if he were reacquainting himself with her, then he shook his head negatively, and turned over the bowl, spilling her change onto the sidewalk.

"Why did you do that?" she said.

He did not answer and drew himself into the box. Ronnie walked on, upset. She knew he was mentally unbalanced, still, his hostility was disturbing.

She was alone in the apartment that night and made herself warm milk before she went to sleep, second-guessing herself about not accepting medication from the doctor to "round out the edges." Everything was edges. She watched the local news, realized she had already fallen asleep for a moment, turned off the set, and retired for the night.

The dream had the customary element, broken glass. This time the glass was from her bedroom window breaking and through it came Satan, a dark angel, winged, with human facial features; a profoundly evil face, black eyes, lascivious lips. He stood at the foot of her bed, smiling. Her being in the bed, her bed, in her bedroom, was part of the dream. She looked at him in the dream as Satan smiled at her. Within everything horrible of the dream, this was more horrible, that his being in the room while she was in the bed was so real. In the dream, she screamed. She awoke, screaming.

9

From the artistic renderings of Satan in the books she had been re-searching, Ronnie dreamed a composite Satan, much as police artists create a composite drawing out of an eyewitness account. She came to this realization the following morning when she leafed through a few of the books and photocopies of pages she was using as reference and saw some of the same visual elements of Satan she had incorporated into her nightmare.

Wondering if anyone else had a similar dream, she entered a chat room on kindred spirits of Satan, hoping it was a commonplace type of dream, rather than the uniquely haunting dream it seemed to be.

Anyone have a dream of Satan, winged, evil, with human features, standing at the foot of your bed?

She sat for a while, received no response, then entered the same question on two online message boards on satanic Web sites. She took the day's newspapers, read them in the chair at her desk, looking at the screen periodically, receiving no response. She checked on and off during the day, read some magazines, and began work in the late afternoon.

The next day, a Sunday morning, she read *The New York Times,* declined an invitation to join Bob and Nancy for brunch since she was back in a writing mood. She worked for the rest of the day and went online once more. She found a response to her inquiry from someone signed CR.

I know that dream. Horrible. He stands at the foot of my bed. Superior. Like a father superior.

Ronnie was caught off stride. After nearly two days she assumed no one would weigh in, and this was so specific. She wrote:

Does he do anything in the dream?

CR was still there, and sent Ronnie an instant message:

> **CR:** He just smiles.
> **RONNIE:** And the surroundings, are they supernatural like he is?
> **CR:** No, that's what's horrible. Everything is so real. He's right at the foot of my bed. And I'm there. I see myself lying there. It's a dream, but it's like it's really happening.
> **RONNIE:** Are you sure? You're not just thinking this was your dream?
> **CR:** I know my dreams. Satan has been in them for about as long as I've been here.
> **RONNIE:** Where is that?
> **CR:** Empire State Psychiatric Facility.

Someone had a dream exactly like hers and the person was institutionalized. Ronnie signed off, got under the covers, channel surfed on the television set for a while to try distracting herself, and eventually turned off the set and fell asleep.

She dreamed that she was dreaming, that she was in bed, dreaming, and the dream was of Satan, who stood at her bed again, smiling, the dream of a dream, like a trick drawing of someone who is holding a picture of himself holding a picture, which is a picture of himself holding a picture.

"You said to contact you if I had any problems. I've had a couple of really disturbing nightmares, Doctor. I really need to see a shrink."

"I think that would be a good idea."

"Is there someone you'd recommend?"

"Best I know in the world is Martha Kaufman."

Ronnie was familiar with the name. Martha Kaufman wrote a book about social hierarchies in a Brooklyn high school, which Ronnie had read, and was one of the psychotherapists whose names regularly appeared in the media.

"I couldn't afford anyone like that. I don't have coverage in my insurance."

"I'll suggest she see you in the clinic. I'll have her call you. I'm sure she will. She's my aunt."

"Really? Thank you, Doctor."

"We've got to get you well."

She noted the pointed nature of the doctor's remark, blacking out in random circumstances and experiencing disturbing nightmares was not being "well." Martha Kaufman called a few hours later. She offered Ronnie time when she was in the clinic. Her normal rate was three hundred dollars an hour. If Ronnie would allow their time together to be recorded and ultimately used anonymously for research, under a grant at New York University Medical Center, Kaufman would see her at no charge. Ronnie was scheduled for 6:00 P.M. the following day and tried to apply a writer's approach to the consultation, writing down an outline of her recent experiences to make a proper presentation.

———

Martha Kaufman was sixty-four, five feet six, slender, with gray hair cut short, wearing a stylish black suit and white silk blouse, looking like someone who did indeed work for two hundred an hour when she was not in this clinic. The room was spare, impersonal; a desk, a couple of chairs, white metal file cabinets; a place used by rotating psychotherapists.

"You said on the phone you were a writer."

They sat in chairs opposite one another. Her voice and manner were distinguished. Ronnie thought she could have been an actress.

"I freelance. I'm doing a book on satanic possession. What got it for me was a piece I did for *New York* magazine on a satanic cult leader, Randall Cummings."

"That was yours? I read it. Very good."

"He was murdered, as you may know. I was there the day he was murdered." Nothing to conceal here, she thought, this was the place you tried to find out what was going on. "I blacked out at some point when I was talking to him, and woke up, or came to, I guess you would say, a few blocks away on a park bench over an hour later. It was the second time I blacked out. Which is why I went to see your niece. During a race in Central Park, I just went sort of unconscious, and kept running, and incredibly, I won the race. She said I was physically fine."

Ronnie checked the index card to see if she had been making the points in the order she intended.

"Ms. Delaney, you needn't work from notes. There's no 'getting it right' in here. What matters is how you, with your particular emotional DNA, respond to the world around you. Now, is it important for you to get it right?"

"I suppose. I never thought of it that way."

"That's what we have to do in here, get you to think of what you never thought of that way. Were you a good student?"

"Yes."

"Where did you go to school?"

"Bronx Science. Brown."

"Anything you feel you haven't gotten right lately?"

Ronnie virtually sighed.

"What?"

"This Cummings, I didn't see eye-to-eye with him. I got a dead black cat sent to me after I did the article, and someone was stalking me, threw black cats in my path on the street, and a little death skull. And a picture of me came in an envelope, my head cut off—"

"How terrible!"

"I'm sure it was him, or somebody from him. It all stopped when he died. I had no—partiality toward him, but here's the thing that troubles me. His father, he said something about Cummings, that he was just creating theater. And maybe I missed something there, came down too hard on him."

"You didn't get it right."

"Maybe. And maybe somebody saw what I wrote and killed him."

"You're taking quite a lot on yourself there."

Kaufman asked questions about Ronnie's childhood, parents, her current day-to-day experiences, and Ronnie described those aspects of her life. Then she was asked about her social life and described the relationship with Nancy and Bob, and then Richard, his sexual attractiveness combined with his general unavailability, which Kaufman offered might be what made him desirable; for Ronnie to be passionate while not getting too intimate. Time was up and there were items on Ronnie's index card they hadn't touched.

"The bad dreams I've been having, they're what made me realize I had to see someone."

"If you choose to come back, we can deal with it."

"I would like to."

"My general observation—you're entitled to come back not merely for the dreams. There are violent acts here for you to process. Not for a long time have I seen anyone, except for perhaps adolescents in the middle of a gang war, under as much stress."

They were scheduled for another session in a week. Nancy and Rob went off for a two-week vacation to Canada and Ronnie filled herself up with the book. At seven in the morning, as she was about to get out of bed, the phone rang and it was Richard.

"Hi. How's it going?"

"To answer you in Hemingway terms, the work, it goes well. The social life, that's you, sir, it does not go so well."

"The earth does not move for you."

"Not if the one who can help move it is in Germany."

"Then how's this? Don't say no until I make my speech. I rehearsed in front of a mirror."

"You did not."

"No, I did not, but I thought of rehearsing. There's a conference next week in Paris, international players in the behavioral field. As part of my participating, the deal was a round-trip air ticket, business class, from New York. I am already in Europe, as we know. And we just got into the details, and they still owe me the ticket—Ronnie, how would you like to come to Paris this weekend?"

"What?"

"Come Friday night. We'll have Saturday and Sunday, you can fly back Monday, take your laptop if you're feeling driven and work on the plane going back. All expenses paid, not by me. There's no morality involved, just for you to make the weekend available. Say yes."

"Richard—"

"It's Paris, Ronnie. Paris for a weekend, what could be a better change of pace?"

"I've never been to Paris."

"You must do this. You must."

He met her flight and they took a cab to the hotel on the left bank, the Hotel Lutetia, her very idea of what a Paris hotel would be, with a view of the Eiffel Tower from the room. She was tired from the lack of sleep on the plane and she did not require much coaxing for him to suggest she rest for a while, and then he was undressing her, and then he was inside her, she could have nearly passed out from the pleasure. She awoke, Paris outside the window. He left a note on the pillow; he had a meeting at a bookstore at 22 Rue Mazarine, a short taxi ride or a ten-minute walk from the hotel. He would see her there at one. He had left a wake-up call for noon. She was awake before the call. She showered, changed, and decided to walk, nearly disbelieving—a few days ago I was in a nightmare and now I'm in Paris.

Ronnie browsed store windows on her way over and reached the store before one. She looked in the window, a classic rare book store, vintage books throughout. Richard was dressed in his blazer, sports shirt, and jeans, talking with an elderly man wearing a bookseller's apron, and another man, lean, with close-cropped hair, wearing a dark suit, dark sports shirt, and sunglasses. They appeared to be in an intense discussion. Ronnie entered the store.

"Sorry. I was early and thought I'd just come."

"Perfect. Ronnie Delaney, this is Pierre Frateau." As Richard made the introduction the man in the dark suit started out.

"Monsieur—" Frateau said, acknowledging his departure. The man was out the door, not waiting for an introduction. Ronnie watched him as he walked out of view, then turned back to take in the store.

"Your first time in Paris, I hear," Frateau said.

"Yes."

"How marvelous."

"I wanted you to meet me here because Monsieur Frateau has something wonderful to show you."

Frateau placed a leather-bound book with gilt-edged pages on a counter. He wore white gloves to open it for her.

"This is very rare," Frateau said. "*Possessions of the Heart,* it's called. From 1832. A visual history of a ten-year-long possession, of Sister Anna Marie, in the convent at Notre-Dame-de-Veniers. She described the various shapes Satan took in possessing her, man, demons, animals, fish, birds. An artist in the town, Michel Martray, we don't know anything about him, drew these according to her descriptions. As far as we know, this is the only edition that has ever been found."

He turned the pages for her, each black-and-white plate covered with linen paper; twenty-six plates, the renderings detailed, phantasmagoric, consistent in their madness. The possessing spirits flowed out of the head of the innocent-looking nun portrayed, her eyes closed, hands uplifted as if worshipping the Prince of Darkness in his various incarnations.

"Richard says you are writing a book on possession. If you would like, you may use any of this for illustration. We can photograph the images."

"That's very nice of you. We haven't discussed illustrations, or if there's a budget for it."

"Antoine has to know it's required in a book like this," Richard said.

"It's fantastic work, monsieur. Very kind of you."

"A pleasure."

Frateau showed her around the shop, then Richard suggested lunch, and they said their good-byes. As they walked along, Richard said, "Café de Flore on Saint Germain? Touristy, but fundamental Paris."

"I'm game. So, Richard, who was that other man?"

"Works for a collector, a very rich old guy who's interested in buying the book."

"He was so extreme he looked comical, like a CIA agent in a movie."

"Just the way he dresses. He's in the security business. He wants you to know that. Helps him maintain order, I would suppose."

"Richard, are *you* CIA?" He laughed heartily. He had chuckled in the past, laughed a little, this was the biggest laugh she had ever heard from him. "To be around such a villainous-looking guy," she said. "All your comings and goings. Flights here, flights there. I think this cult stuff is your cover and you're a CIA agent."

"I am not a CIA agent," and he laughed again. "You've lost your category. You're in nonfiction, not fiction."

The next two days had a dreamlike quality of their own; long walks through what Richard described as "the greatest walking city in the world," visits to the Musèe d'Orsay, Musèe Picasso, the Louvre, meals in his favorite Paris bistros. He was connected, alert to her, seemingly thrilled at her delight in everything, and the sex in a bed with the Eiffel Tower out the window was incomparable, movie magic. She was twenty-four, in October she would be twenty-five, and she had never been to Paris, never made love in Paris, and to have him so responsive to her being there made it feel like she was falling in love with him; not really love the way she understood what love should be, not when he already announced he was going back to Munich, and after that he might have to go to Rio, but close to love, like a song she heard on the radio a while back, "The Next Best Thing to Love." Richard took her to the airport and they kissed good-bye, a long kiss, and she thought they looked like the couple in the Robert Doisneau photograph of the lovers kissing in Paris.

When she returned to New York her dreams were uneventful, no signs of dizziness during the day, and, feeling better than she had in weeks, she went back to see Martha Kaufman for her next session. Ronnie was eager to get on to the subject of her nightmares. She described the earlier dreams, the recurring element of the broken glass and lost little girl, and went on to the dreams with Satan, and the shock of discovering that a person with the same dream ended up in Empire State Psychiatric Facility.

"You and this woman shared an image in a dream. But Veronica, Satan is a very common symbol. And you're working on a book that involves people imagining Satan. I don't find this such a thunderous coincidence."

"With me in the dream and Satan standing at my bed?"

"What goes on in a bed?"

"You sleep."

"And?"

"You have sex."

"You're currently in a sexual relationship, you said."

"I just came back from Paris. Very romantic. Very sexy. I suppose I should say it's the best sex of my life."

"Is it important for you to say it?"

"Maybe it is. Growing up with my father, he was pretty repressive."

"You were eleven when your mother died?"

"Yes."

"And your father—"

"I was out on my own when he died, a heart attack."

"So it was not a cheerful time, living with your father?"

"Cheerful? No. He was very smart, a botanist. As far as I know he never dated after my mother died. We'd exchange a few words over dinner and he'd go to his room to read or whatever. Now and then on the weekend he'd take me to a movie. Mostly, it was schoolwork for me as I remember those years."

"Sounds like it was an awkward relationship, the two of you."

"Awkward, yes. He'd question me about boys sometimes. I think he believed if I didn't get pregnant when I was living with him, then it was a victory."

"This sex with Richard, it's not what your father would have approved of, then, a relationship where sex is important and pleasurable for you?"

"He would not have approved."

"And do you have a religious upbringing?"

"We went to a Catholic church in the neighborhood."

"Veronica, we dream in code, in symbols. What does Satan symbolize to you?"

"Evil, I would say. Evil in the world."

"What about evil in you? Do you believe you're evil? You did an article about Randall Cummings, maybe you went too far, you told me, and he was killed. You're in a sexual relationship with a man that wouldn't have been approved of by your father or the church of your childhood. Could be that makes you a bad girl, an evil girl? So you summon the clearest image of evil we know of, Satan, and bring him into your dreams as a reprimand. And it's a symbol of evil you have easy access to in your work. Probably that woman also thought of herself as bad, as evil. We don't know. What we do know is that you dream a symbol of evil, and my sense, based on doing this for thirty-five years, is that if we can get you beyond thinking that you did something bad with Cummings or bad with this man you're seeing, your symbol of evil will vanish."

Ronnie thought hard about Kaufman's appraisal, then said lightly, "Then I'm done here."

Kaufman smiled in response and said, "If only. Something else is there, I don't know what it is yet. See you next time."

Homicides by strangulation did not rank high on the list of causes of death at the Twenty-sixth Precinct, or anywhere in the city, ranking far below stabbings and gun-related crimes, and the investigation was not gaining traction. The MO was rare; they recalled the Boston Strangler at the precinct, nobody could recall anything similar locally in recent years. The break in the hit-and-run case was straightforward; the nature of the crime indicated the assailant's car was damaged, the fax went to car repair shops where someone might bring a damaged car, and Batrak, through his damaged vehicle and his peculiarity, drew attention to himself. Cummings would have been facing the assailant, and the strangling to death of a man, six feet two, weighing 240 pounds, set physical requirements for the perpetrator. The assailant needed to be powerful enough to commit the crime, accounting for Santini's reluctance to consider Ronnie a true suspect. Cummings would have towered over her. Gomez, however, brought his worldview to bear so that anyone was a suspect, and on a couple of mornings he still insisted on parking at a distance from her building in an unmarked car to observe. They knew she went out for the newspaper or jogged, they trailed after her to the extent that they could, and then she went back into the building a while later; innocent activity.

In Staten Island, Carter and Greenberg spent time similarly shadowing the former members of the Anti-Satanist Group, which quickly seemed a waste. The easy breakthrough was not going to be forthcoming, like a false move by the perpetrator in an attempt to sell something valuable stolen at the crime scene. Nothing was stolen. A man was strangled, period.

———

Cummings's father called Rourke and the police commissioner every day from Chicago and they had little to offer him. They were going nowhere. With empathy, Rourke said to his detectives, "Cummings was an adult, a forty-two-year-old man, and for his father, his son is like any child who went to the big city to make his name—and got killed."

In the next session, Kaufman tried to make her patient understand that writing an article about someone who was marketing himself, created his own Web site, lobbied for congregants for his misguided cult, was not the same as outing an innocent who wanted to be anonymous. Ronnie still thought the world was not a better place for her having written about Cummings, that there were many pieces to be written, it didn't have to be hers. The guilt was fascinating to Kaufman and she pursued it.

"What's the source of this highly refined guilt, Veronica? Church? How religious were you at home?"

"Sunday churchgoers."

"Were you in parochial school?"

"No."

"Not even that. Do you still go to church?"

"No."

"When was the last time you went?"

Ronnie didn't answer right away, her eyes momentarily distant. Kaufman noticed the pause.

"When I was eleven."

"Eleven. And that's when your parents stopped going to church?" Kaufman caught herself, remembering the biography, and rerouted the question. "Veronica, you told me your mother *died* when you were eleven."

A longer pause now, significant to the patient, as well. Dark waters.

"I stopped going when my mother died."

"Yes?"

"I wouldn't go again. My father did, but I wouldn't."

"Is there more you should be saying here?"

"We were on our way to church and afterward we were going to Pelham Bay Park, something my father had to do there, so we took the car. My father was driving, my mother was in the front seat, I was in the back. We'd just pulled out and I was fussing about a magazine I wanted them to buy for me. My father turned to tell me to settle down. He took his eyes off the wheel. When he looked back, somebody stepped off the curb. He pulled wide to avoid the person, hit a truck to his side, we spun around and a car hit us head-on. My mother went through the windshield. She died that night." Ronnie began to weep. "My father blamed me."

"He told you that?"

"I knew it. He was an internalized, reserved man, and she was beautiful and gregarious, and she chose him, and she was the love of his life, and I took her from him, and he always resented me."

"An accident. It wasn't your fault. It was an accident. Did you talk to anyone, see a therapist? To be present at the death of your mother!"

"A priest tried to help. Father Connolly. A good man. He came to see us a few times, and he talked to me privately in my room. He tried, I know he did. He told me my mother was in heaven and her dying had nothing to do with me. But I got into my head that I was going to hell for what I did."

"This is the guilt of all guilts."

"I told him my mother's death was Satan's work, that Satan won over God. I never set foot in a church again."

"Satan. Veronica, Satan. It's so clearly your symbol of evil."

"My mother was an elementary school nurse, but she was more than that, a counselor for the children, a confidante for them, a wonderfully good person. My father died on an ordinary day, without any prior heart problems. Like he went as far as he could go, and any private pact he may have made in his heart for her, to look out for me as I was growing up, to keep a roof over my head, wasn't needed any longer. I was an adult, on my own, and he couldn't go on another day of this life without her, and three years ago, he just expired."

"If I look a little, I can even see you folding your father's death into this somewhere, that you were somehow responsible. It's not far to go, someone who carries these feelings around, to think that you had something to do with Randall Cummings' death, too. You didn't. You had nothing to do with any of these events. Your mother's death—so many things had to happen in succession. You were one element and not even the most important one."

"But still an element."

"The broken glass in your dreams. The broken glass of the car? The shattering of your life?" Ronnie did not respond, trying to absorb the thought. "Do you know the term 'magic thinking,' as regards children?"

"A child conceives of itself as the center of the universe."

"Exactly. So if the parents fight, or get a divorce, or one of them dies, the child believes it's the child's fault. This is what you did, classic magical thinking."

"There may be a term for it, but the child still feels it."

"Veronica, there's no medical cause the doctors could discover for your blacking out. My sense is, when you're under serious stress, and you have been, you react as a traumatized child would, which is what you were when your mother died. You recreate, as an adult, your childhood behavior."

"I regress?"

"You regress. You were helpless then, so in stress, this blacking out, this fog you go into, could be a way of acting out the feeling of being helpless again."

"I don't know if it works that way."

"I don't either. It's my best sense."

Nancy was back from vacation and Ronnie sat with her and Bob at the dining room table, the friends dissecting the therapist's observations.

"One night *Spellbound* was on television and Michael wanted me to see it. Ever see it, the Hitchcock movie?"

"I don't think so," Nancy said, and Bob shook his head, no.

"With Gregory Peck and Ingrid Bergman. He's a really screwed-up guy. And suddenly, the shrink figures everything out about him, like in one burst, 'There's your secret repressed experience!' Bingo. That's how I feel. This shrink is saying, Aha! You're blacking out because you're guilty over your mother's death and you're regressing!"

"Why can't that be true?" Bob asked.

"It can. It's possible. Acting on the knowledge is another matter."

"See, *you're* looking for bingo. It's a process. Give it time," Nancy said.

"There's something I can't keep from you anymore. The day I went to see Cummings, the day he died, I blacked out then, too. I was in his office, I don't remember leaving it. The next thing I know I was on a bench a few blocks away, and during that time, according to the police, Cummings was murdered."

"What are you saying?" Bob asked.

"That I blacked out that day."

"Yes, now we know why," Nancy said. "Being in the room with the man, a really stupid thing to do by the way, probably upset you a lot, and as the shrink says, when you're really upset you feel helpless all over again, like you can't cope, and you black out."

"I can't account for myself when Cummings was murdered."

"You don't have to," Bob said. "*You* didn't murder him. He was a big galoot. If he wanted, he could've strangled *you*. Consider yourself one lucky girl you got out of there before the murderer showed up."

"I didn't tell the police. I didn't want *them* harassing me."

"I don't blame you," Bob offered.

"Should I tell them?"

"No!" Bob said. "You haven't been yourself. You want to go into a room with the police and tell them you weren't fully conscious around the time Cummings was murdered? They'll grill you. They'll stress you out, for which you are the ideal candidate, and you'll end up admitting what you didn't do. It wouldn't be the first time."

"That's a little fantastic," Ronnie said.

"It's realistic. Do your book. Work on your therapy."

"It is work, the therapy."

"I didn't know about the way your mother died. I'm very sorry," Nancy said.

"She was a wonderful person."

"So are you," Nancy told her.

Richard surprised her, he was in New York, he did have to fly to Rio, but he arranged a one-night stopover so he could see her. "Going there on CIA business?" she teased.

"A conference," he answered, " 'Ritual Behaviors in Modern Societies.' "

Did they really have these things around the world, and so many of them to keep him occupied? Skeptical, before she met him for dinner, she checked online and the Rio de Janeiro Conference of Behavioral Science did feature Richard Smith as "a renowned expert on cults," along with a psychiatrist and an anthropologist appearing in a workshop on ritual behaviors.

Taking into consideration her feelings about choices of restaurants, he suggested a moderately priced Greek restaurant on the West Side. They went back to his apartment for sex, no Eiffel Tower, still blissful, and in a reversal it was she who couldn't dally the next day; she needed to get back to the apartment so she could work on the book.

"I'm thrilled you're so into it."

"Seems like I want to get it right."

"You will. I spoke to Antoine. He's open to some illustrative material. So, as you're going through, think about it. See you in a couple of weeks."

"See you," and she kissed *him* good-bye.

Two days later she received a package from Pierre Frateau. He sent the material at Richard's request. Enclosed were twenty-six immaculately photographed 9×12 black-and-white images of the drawings from the book in the shop, the fantastic delusions of a nineteenth-century nun, as interpreted by a gifted, unknown artist. She looked through the images, taking more time to examine them than in the shop when the others were looking on. The overall effect reminded her of the naive asylum drawings and paintings she once had seen at the Outsider Art Show in SoHo.

The demon had bulging eyes in a savage bird's face with a long serpent's tongue extended, and talons, stretched and grasping, a hideous creature. Ronnie awoke, frightened into wakefulness. She had seamlessly transferred into her sleep one of the more violent images from a nineteenth-century delusional nun.

10

The balance between cynicism and commitment was significant for the man—when to let it go, the hell with it, there's always another psychopath, and anyway I'm not going any further in the department than this, I'm no good at the politics, too much like my father, a cop on the beat, I can't do the politics. And then there was the other side of it, his father's sense of duty, and his, so Ed Rourke couldn't slide the Cummings folder farther down on his desk or into a drawer. It stayed on top and every day he took the call. Never "How is the case going?" or "Any leads?" Always the same question, "Anything new on my son?" Cummings's father always said "my son," and it tore at Rourke. And he had little to tell him.

Rourke's wife was a secretary in a midtown law office, forty-three, petite; long, loose red hair; their daughter, the teacher who lived in Brooklyn, had the mother's hair, the daughter he worried about living on her own now. Another balance—to be the civilized husband and father, although his work often brought him in touch with the uncivilized. The way it was troubling him, he needed to bring this case home. They were in the bedroom of their apartment on East Twenty-eighth Street.

"The Cummings case, we have nothing."

"He wasn't a saint. He actually encouraged violence, didn't he?" his wife said.

"I don't know if he did. I can't find it. We did a lot of checking. A couple of people in the cult were caught for things like shoplifting, and that's it. The father calls, I haven't got a thing for him. I don't see us ever solving this case."

"No?"

"The people who were protesting Cummings, they alibi each other. The guy who worked there has his alibi. The girl who wrote an article, who was also there, is no bigger than you are, she couldn't strangle someone that size. What do I keep telling the father?"

"That you're doing your best."

"Are we?"

He had to consider the implausible: Someone came in from the outside with a delivery, someone who snapped, offended by what Cummings stood for, or the size of his tip, or some other imagined offense. Pitalis gave them a list of everyone who conceivably could appear at the church during the day. The detectives checked, nobody in the area, at take-out places, or at the post office, or Federal Express, confirmed a delivery made at the time of the crime.

They began working on the idea of a crime of passion: Somebody, a woman, a man perhaps, a person Cummings would have known and allowed to enter the building, who caught him by surprise and before he could react, overpowered him. The father had given the detectives a list of names of everyone Cummings knew on a personal level whom the father was aware of, and they had found an address book in the drawer of his desk and were working through those names.

As part of the process, they called a Beth Colette, Santini telling her she was in Randall Cummings's book and they needed to speak with her in connection with his murder. Santini and Gomez went to see her in an apartment in the West Village. She was an artist working in wire sculpture, abstract pieces filled her loft apartment. Beth was thirty-eight, six feet tall, thin, in a blouse, jeans, and sneakers, a striking woman, with a countenance that was serious verging on morose. She motioned them to a sofa in a living room area.

"Could you tell us please what your relationship was with Randall Cummings?" Gomez asked.

"We were together for about a year. Living here mostly. We broke up three years ago."

"And breaking up, whose idea was that?" Gomez asked.

"Mine. You reach a point where it goes one way or it goes the other."

"You were in his address book," Santini said.

"We talked now and then."

"When was the last time?" Gomez said.

"About a year ago."

"Is this where you work?" he continued.

"My sculpture, yes. I'm an art therapist. I work at Roosevelt Hospital."

"What are your hours?" Gomez asked.

"Monday to Friday, ten to six."

"And on Tuesday, May twentieth? Can you recall that day?"

"This is too funny. The day Randall was murdered? I was working. You can check."

"We have to check everything."

"I understand. I didn't kill Randall."

"Any opinions on who might have?" Santini said.

"None. He was Icarus. He flew too close to the sun. Or the dark side of the moon." From a calm demeanor, she began to cry. "The fool. The stupid fool. What was he doing? A satanic cult. Stupidest thing I ever heard. He had no beliefs like that. Too smart for his own goddamn good."

"What do you mean, too smart?" Santini said.

"The entire conceit, it was like some New Age theater project he was trying to pull off. Ridiculous. He would've been better off just selling out, working on some soap opera."

"Was he straight?" Gomez asked.

"Totally straight. If you're done with me . . ."

They reported back to Rourke, Cummings was likely straight, so a male lover of sufficient strength to commit a crime of passion was the remotest possibility. And although it had no bearing on the identity of the assailant, as general information, his former girlfriend was of the opinion he didn't really have the convictions for his calling.

"Makes it even worse," Rourke said, wearily. "Made a wrong career decision and got himself killed."

Ronnie, back from food shopping, played her messages, startled to hear the voice of Michael, celebrity chef and three-star cad.

"Ronnie, it's me, Michael, remember me?" he said in a puckish voice. With more urgency he added, "It's very important that you call me. Please, Ronnie."

At her desk she contemplated Michael—and Richard. She missed Richard. Paris couldn't alter the reality; he was away more than he was there. This *must* be what it's like to be involved with a CIA agent, she speculated, and from there she went to the possibility that he *was* a CIA agent, really, something like that, but then there was his book, and the articles, and his public appearances; yet you could be both, perhaps he was both, an expert on cults *and* a CIA agent, or someone working in the substrata of a government agency, the kind in *The Bourne Identity* or *Mission: Impossible* type of movies. His being away more than he was present—was that the appeal, was the shrink on to something, his appeal was in his very absences? Had she become a New York career girl who didn't want to be held back by a relationship, things to write, a ladder to climb; or was she just wary of getting involved, you get involved and you get hurt. Michael was her longest relationship and it contained a cautious quality, they weren't actually living together. Did it go back to the Bronx, did all roads lead back to the Bronx, the remote, distant father-daughter relationship, the man holds himself away from you, and you do the same, you love your mother and she dies, so don't get too close to anyone.

This material, along with the hideous demon of her dream, was what she brought into her next session.

"Implications of your social life—I like you thinking about that, Veronica."

"Instead of horrible dreams?"

"Seems to me this latest one is still another variation of Satan, just as the nun imagined her variations."

"My omnipresent Satan."

"Your omnipresent feeling of being bad, or evil. If you could only see yourself."

"Meaning?"

"You're a beautiful woman. And talented."

"So *am* I attracted to Richard because he's the man that isn't there?"

"Are you?"

"He's other things. Sexy. Supportive. He could be funnier. Not all that much humor there. Also there's the vanity of it, it feels great to walk into public places with him."

"Then the good features *could* be the reason you're attracted to him."

"Am I allowed to ask if you think I should call back my previous boyfriend? He left a message."

"Do you want to call him?"

"I liked him very much. I was very hurt."

"My opinion, anything that makes you feel good about yourself is what you should be doing these days."

"Strange. This takes on some of what I would imagine a mother-daughter dialogue would be. I never had one in my adult life, or my teenage life, even. All the conversations I never had with my mother, the things she would never know, that Bobby Muzo kissed me in ninth grade on the stairway and said I was pretty, that I got into Science, that I went to Brown, that I got my first bylines, that I became a writer."

Tears formed in her eyes and as they trickled onto her cheeks she didn't wipe them away, she needed to feel herself crying.

"When you were a little girl you must have had many conversations you can't remember with her, and in part the person you are, and the successes you've had, come from her." Ronnie was pensive and Kaufman studied her. "What you've had to be is your own mother and your own father. It's a burden and another kind of strain, so that when you're thrown off balance, such as by those terrible threats, you're shaken more than other people would be, because you need to maintain such tight control."

"And when I lose it, I lose it."

"Yes. You've been frightened. Who wouldn't be? And given your background, when you're frightened you're particularly vulnerable, therefore, the blacking out. Your way of saying, 'I can't do it all myself, I can't handle it anymore.' And instead of the adult woman, we get the helpless little girl."

"This is deep," she quipped.

"You're doing a service," Kaufman said, smiling, "good material for our research."

She decided she would call Michael. As Kaufman said, "Anything that makes you feel good about yourself." Swimming in the anger wasn't going to put her in a good place.

"I thought we'd end up playing telephone tag, Michael."

"How are you?"

How was she? Emotionally troubled, under siege, recently in therapy for the state she was in.

"Coping."

"Name of the game. Can I see you, please? It's really important. Tomorrow, my night off, dinner, a drink, you name it."

"We can meet for a drink."

"Come to the restaurant. It'll be quiet. Seven?"

"Seven it is."

Stars and Stripes was located on Ninth Avenue and Forty-eighth Street. In a feature on American homestyle cooking, the *New York Times* writer said, "Celebrity chefs such as Michael Ruppert, with his cooking show on cable, sometimes stumble under the weight of their celebrity. Mr. Ruppert is doing fine, thank you. Please pass the meat loaf." Ronnie didn't watch Michael's program. With the book and Richard occupying her, he had moved outside her field of vision.

The restaurant was closed on Mondays during the summer and it was Michael who greeted her when she tapped on the door. He was much slimmer than the last time she had seen him, markedly so, wearing a cotton sports shirt that showed off his new clothing size.

"Look at you."

"Changes," he said, leading her inside.

He threw a light switch. The decor was tasteful: simple white tablecloths, recessed lighting, beige walls adorned by large-format black-and-white photographs of American roadside restaurants.

"Do you have a reservation? We're pretty full tonight," he joked.

"This is fine," and she sat at one of the tables.

"Would you like me to make something for you to eat?"

"No, thank you. A drink is what we said. A Diet Coke would be good."

"You can do better than that."

"That's all I want."

He brought the soda for her, a glass of white wine for himself, and sat at the table.

"So what's going on with you?" she asked. "You look fantastic."

"I have a trainer. I'm on a new diet. I'm in therapy."

"Seems to be working."

"*You* come up a lot."

"Oh."

"The way I behaved. Why I did that. By the way, I'm not seeing Rosetta anymore."

"Her album is selling really well and she dropped you for Emeril?"

"I ended it. We were stage props for each other."

"Isn't that what you wanted?"

"It was a mistake. With therapy I've gained some insights."

"Michael, people *not* in therapy don't talk that way, 'gained some insights.'"

"It's true, though."

"Were your insights about fear of commitment and love of celebrity?"

"Some of that, all of that. Ronnie, I was in love with you and I couldn't deal with it."

His voice trembled as he said it.

"I see. Too bad we both didn't know that," her voice uneven, as well. "But I can't say if it ever would've worked out with us. Your hours—"

"Lots of chefs have relationships."

"Seems to me, when you're not married, all you have is the commitment you make to each other."

"I would now. It's a new me."

She had cared for him and now he was asking to come back. The timing was off.

"Maybe I'm not the girl you think I am. I've been seeing a therapist, too. For bad dreams and bad memories and some bad experiences. So I'm not much of a bargain these days."

"You just said it. You were a bargain beyond my imagining and I let you get away. I'm the one to see you through a bad time. I'm your man."

"If you're that person now, then that's good for you and you'll be all right, Michael. Problem is, I'm sort of in a relationship. Or I'm in sort of a relationship, which might be more accurate."

"I'm really stupid. How could I assume you'd be available?"

"You look wonderful. Keep it up. And thank you. I'm touched.

And sad. We both lost out from the timing of all this." She kissed him on the nose. "Maybe some sweet angel will look out for us both."

Ronnie remembered reading in an article somewhere a quote from an interior decorator who said cynically about his clients, "When they're paralyzed about making a decision and they can't buy a dish towel without you, is when you have them." Was she becoming dependent in that manner on Kaufman, she wondered, or was this the therapeutic process? She discussed the meeting with Michael at her next session. Kaufman was interested to know if Ronnie felt guilty about her decision not to resume with Michael. Ronnie said she did.

"Because you assume guilt so easily," Kaufman said.

"I seem to, don't I?"

"You would do well to recognize that. Guilt over things you shouldn't feel guilty about."

"I also feel guilty because he looked so contrite and I really did care for him."

"Richard Smith, do you really care for him?"

"I miss him when he's not here. Am I becoming some kind of sex slave?"

"I don't know what that means. Sex can be an expression of love or a form of love, if you will, pleasurable, a release of tension, a way of feeling alive—or for you, not what your background dictated, and therefore rebellious. If any of it keeps you in a bad relationship, or keeps you from a better relationship, it could be enslaving, to use that term. Is this a bad relationship?"

"Is that a judgment?"

"It's a question."

"I'd say it's an unusual relationship—and interesting."

"Your move then, Veronica."

In Kansas City for a business meeting, Bob was going to pick up food from Arthur Bryant's famous barbecue place, have them wrap it, carry it with him on the plane, and serve the long-distance take-out at Nancy and Ronnie's apartment. He was also inviting one of his colleagues from the office, who was bringing his girlfriend. The roommates, excited, stocked up on wine and beer and prepared the apartment. The phone rang and they thought it might be Bob, he was about to land. It was Richard. He just came back into town, he told Ronnie, and wanted to take her to dinner that night. She thought you could overdo the element of surprise, which he apparently thrived on.

"And for how long exactly did you know you were arriving?"

"I was just going to have another airport stopover and we wouldn't get to see each other, but I rearranged things."

"Stopover for?"

"Stockholm."

"You're cracking an international cult that smuggles Volvos."

"Ronnie—"

"How long is the Stockholm portion?"

"A couple of weeks."

"Will I see you then?"

"You can see me now, I'm going to be here overnight. I did rearrange things."

"I can't see you tonight. We're having a food binge from Arthur Bryant's, Kansas City. Would you possibly like to come?"

"Absolutely."

"You would?"

"Hey, Ronnie, I'm a regular fella."

Bob arrived bearing his treats, cheerful. He was momentarily deflated when Nancy informed him Ronnie invited Richard Smith. Bob recovered and said, "I'm not going to let that iceman ruin the evening."

His friends arrived, Mitch Karras, thirty-two, a belly-out, there-is-never-enough-beer guy, five feet eight, in jeans, with Sally Burns, a secretary in the law office where the men worked, thirty, a round, five-foot-three brunette with bangs, a substantial bosom, and a chronic giggle. She came to a dead stop when Richard entered in his blazer, white sports shirt, jeans, loafers. Bob wanted to help Nancy and Ronnie in the kitchen, reheating the food, setting everything out, so he didn't have to deal with Richard and make small talk, a task left to Mitch and Sally in the living room. Richard asked what they did for a living. Sally defined herself as working in Mitch's office. Mitch declared he was a bankruptcy lawyer specializing in real estate entities.

"I've never met anyone who did that kind of work. What are you working on just now?" Richard asked with the suggestion in his voice that indicated he hadn't the least interest in the answer.

"A mall in Utica that went south," Mitch said, and, rather than risk that he was being put down by this good-looking man whom his girl-friend was staring at with an I-can-dump-this-guy-in-no-time look, chose to get the spotlight off himself.

"And you?"

"I'm a writer and a lecturer on cults and on satanism."

"You are?" Sally said. "Wow!"

"Why don't you help the ladies?" and Mitch nudged her to get up and she left the room reluctantly.

Mitch determined the man had no interest in him and he had no interest in Richard and they just sat silently until something else happened, the serving of the food.

They feasted on the chicken and ribs, Sally sufficiently diverted that she stopped ogling Richard and resumed giggling. Bob asked them to rate the barbecue with other barbecue and they agreed the barbecue wasn't very good in New York. Mitch once ordered some mail-order from Georgia that was outstanding and he ate it in New York; that didn't make it New York barbecue. This was at the top. "Surely the best *take-out* chicken and ribs," Bob said brightly.

Ronnie observed the way people were eating. Despite their care, food stains were getting on clothing; not so with Richard, who ate without a mishap. Richard Smith, refined in every setting, even while eating barbecue, recalled to her the unflappable WASPs in the John Cheever short stories she read in college.

They went from the merits of their barbecue to general small talk and eventually to the war in Iraq and the left versus the right, all the

while Richard choosing not to contribute. He didn't ignore the participants, his eyes followed the speakers, he had nothing to say. At one
point Ronnie asked, "What do you think, Richard?" to include him
and also curious as to what he did think and he answered, "I'm just interested in what the others are saying."

Not an admirer of Richard's, Bob was feeling competitive with
him because of Richard's very silence; it appeared he wasn't participating because the talk was beneath his consideration.

"Richard, you've been pretty quiet," Bob said.

"I enjoy hearing you all."

"This isn't exactly for your enjoyment."

"Bob!" Ronnie said in a reprimand.

"Nothing here appeals to your intellect?" Bob continued, undeterred.

"I'm not looking for an argument."

Richard had a slight smile on his face and this had been his expression for some time, infuriating Bob, certain Richard was patronizing
them.

"Waiting for more information to reach you up there? Did I get
that right?" Bob said, contentiously.

The smile on Richard's face vanished.

"There's a trivial quality to your little discussion, as though it really
matters," Richard said in a superior tone of voice and continued in that
tone. "The expression 'permanent government' comes to mind, the
idea that whatever the party in power, a standing bureaucracy still exists;
the functionaries in governmental agencies, the countless decisions
made by people you never hear of, sometimes small decisions in the
governmental scheme of things that affect some people's lives more
than anything accomplished by elected officials on the left or the right,
the grinding, relentless, compartmentalized apparatus, sitting there
beneath whoever is president like a disembodied heart pumping, and
here's what you don't accommodate in your sincere discussion of the
political scene," he said with bite verging on contempt. "If you step
back far enough so that you're not looking at an individual election or
even the time of a party in power, you would see this landscape that so
interests you is nothing more than the 'permanent politics' of a nation,

and it grinds on, whoever the players, with overlapping alliances and allegiances so that you get individual companies and individuals at companies contributing to both parties at the same time, and doesn't that tell you something about the sameness of the so-called opposing forces? And you get cyclical wars that fall on the watch of either of the major parties—Vietnam was an elective war and that was the Democrats, Iraq is an elective war and that's the Republicans. But there's another vantage point, out there, farther out, the perspective you might have if you were in space observing the essence of the blue, milky orb sitting in the vast universe, and you might, if you happened to have the imagination, recognize the larger, fundamental issue is not who is president of the United States, or which party is in power, but the larger, infinitely larger, conflict between God and Satan, the one a prior power, the other a counterpower, both creating consequences from the belief of people in their powers, and that conflict is what determines ultimately lives lived, the quality of those lives, the fate of those lives, neighborhood to neighborhood, city to city, nation to nation, with people more affected by the great, nearly unimaginable conflict between the light of God and countervailing darkness of Satan than by your banal politics. God and Satan. Now there's a conflict that interests me, pal."

Seething, Bob went into the kitchen and Mitch also went in to help as people scurried about, ill at ease with the tension. Nancy took Ronnie aside in Ronnie's bedroom.

"We were supposed to have a fun evening. That was almost violent, what he did to Bob. Bob was foolish, he baited him. Still—"

"I know. Could you bring Bob in? I want to apologize."

Nancy retrieved Bob, who was still furious.

"I'm very sorry. He talks . . . professionally. He's an authority and it looks like he doesn't have that integrated into his personal life very well."

"I'll say. Ronnie, only my affection for you, and possible criminal proceedings, prevented me from punching him out."

Mitch and Sally left, Nancy and Bob withdrew to Nancy's room, and Ronnie came in to Richard in the living room.

"That was astonishingly rude. Are you so undersocialized you have to obliterate somebody like that?"

"I should've just kept quiet."

"Keeping quiet is how we got there. Not participating is condescension and people were feeling it."

"I'm like a racehorse. Put me on the track and I run. He got into me, the bell went off, and I ran. I hope I didn't get you in trouble with these people."

"These people are my friends. Nancy and Bob love me. I'm willing to bet they don't love *you*."

"I was making a point that seemed to have gotten lost in the personal drama. I believe there is a greater struggle than anything on the political scene."

"I got the point, Richard. With people in a room, you don't have to lecture. There's something called being conversational if you're in a conversation."

"You're absolutely right."

"I sure am, Professor."

She was inclined to cap the night, send him home. Richard's superior, competitive attitude was a pin in the balloon of Bob's party, and yet Richard would be gone the following day, she had not seen him in a while, she wouldn't see him for another two weeks, and she left with him. She had to have his hands, his lips on her, she had to have him inside her.

11

If he rearranged his schedule to include seeing her when he was going to be between cities, if he exhibited concern for her, to not allow gaps of time to intrude so blatantly on their relationship that they reached a tip point, if he wanted, perhaps needed, to be with her and would be back in New York in a couple of weeks and this was a bonus, a chance to steal time together that he went out of his way to arrange, then this was probably not the time for a major confrontation, not after they went back to his apartment and she spent the night followed by break- fast in their place, in their little morning-after ritual. She could see an argument being made that having a place that was theirs for breakfast was romantic, even an ordinary coffee shop, the idea of it was romantic; except he was so impossible with Bob that she was still annoyed with him the next day and not inclined to let him go off to Stockholm with his smile and his blazer without extracting some solid information.

"You'll be back—"

"In two weeks."

"And why exactly are you going?"

"There's a new Internet magazine called *Behavior*. Doing a piece on a man named Piers Larssen, a behavioral scientist. He's been studying whether there might be a genetic predilection toward cult participation, examining people who gravitated to cults, their ancestors, and the ancestors' behavior. Sounds a little dicey to me, but he has a lot of data, and wants me to meet with people—"

"And after that, you'll be traveling to where, for how long? Just curious. I would like to book my fall season, figure out how available I am."

"I would never presume, given the way I travel, to expect an exclusive relationship, Ronnie."

"You'd expect me to sleep around?"

"I don't mean that."

"Oh, then it's about *you* sleeping around? Should we talk about that, whether my sleeping with you in any way means you should only be sleeping with me. Or is that something I shouldn't presume?"

"You're still angry about last night."

"I don't see where last night is what we're talking about."

"What I'm saying is I just wouldn't presume anything for myself about your exclusivity to me—at least until now."

"And what does 'at least until now' mean?"

"This is a little premature, but when I'm done with this piece, which should be a little after Labor Day, I'm pretty sure I'm doing a new book for Antoine. Not on the Munich cult. Something else entirely. It would need some travel, here and there around the States, but I'd be writing it *in* New York and I'd just be here much, much more of the time."

"Really? Richard Smith settles down, more or less."

"That's right."

"And what's the subject of this book?"

"Satanic ritual abuse. The conspiracy theories. The known facts. Is there a network? What does exist? There's a slight, only a slight bit of an overlap with material you might cover, but this is the whole ball of wax on whether people are out there, or under there, allied in secret groups, looking to take over our children, sexually abusing them in cult rituals, spreading their word, looking to move in on our institutions, as some of these theories claim."

"A little sensational for you, isn't it?"

"Let's say it's a bit more box office than I usually go for, but if the conspiracy theorists are sizable in number, and I suspect they are, then it's a major subject that's been operating sub rosa. And if there's nothing there, then I get to write about why the conspiracy theories got started in the first place, what need it fulfilled, what kind of people believed in them."

"Sounds like you have it either way; a conspiracy exists and this is it, or it doesn't, and this is why people thought it did. I do like the writing in New York part."

"So do I. By the way, I'm sending Bob a bottle of excellent cognac with an apology."

"Okay."

"I may turn out to be an all-around good guy, after all," and he smiled, handsomely; the best-looking man in any restaurant he walked into was the best-looking man in a neighborhood coffee shop at nine in the morning.

The detectives continued to work the list of cult members, looking for any possibility that could possibly lead to a possibility. Mike Gabler, a former cult member who lived on West 139th Street, had been arrested on a charge of spousal abuse. His wife claimed he tried to choke her in the middle of an argument, a charge she later dropped. This was a flag to the detectives; Cummings was strangled, this member of the cult choked his wife; they weren't getting any better connections to the crime.

Carter and Greenberg buzzed on the intercom of a three-story walk-up and after an unintelligible exchange over broken wires, walked up to the top floor. A hulking man, late thirties, six feet tall, nearly three hundred pounds, in a filthy Belle's Auto Repair work shirt and filthier jeans, with unruly blond hair, massive neck, tattoos up and down his arms, was standing at the door when they came to the landing.

"You buzz me?"

"Mr. Gabler?"

"Who wants to know?"

"Police department," and Carter flashed his badge.

"She dropped the charges. Don't you people check?"

"This isn't about your wife," Carter said.

"Ex-wife. We're getting a divorce."

"This is about Randall Cummings."

"I didn't kill him, so get lost."

"We can talk here, pleasant," Greenberg said, "or you can come down, and we'll talk at the station house."

Gabler left the door open for them to enter. The dark rear studio apartment reeked with urine from an unclean bathroom and beer from opened cans scattered about. The bed was unmade. Surfaces in the room—a bridge table, chest of drawers, an end table—were covered with soiled underwear, socks, tossed shirts, items that would be put away somewhere under normal living conditions. The television set was tuned to the Cartoon Network and in a move toward self-respect Gabler turned it off. He stood, back to the wall, not offering the detectives a place to sit, and the only chair in the room was being used for dirty laundry.

"I gave the maid the day off," he said.

"You were a member of the Dark Angel Church?" Greenberg asked.

"For a couple of minutes."

"Why did you join?"

"I was looking to improve my station in life," he said acidly.

"Your wife, she didn't join?"

"No, just me."

"Got another reason why you joined?" Carter asked.

"Sounded interesting, like I could get something out of it. Lost my job and figured what the hell."

"What was your job?"

"Security in a club called Horizon in SoHo. Some guy wanted to get in, had to wait, called me a bozo. You don't call me a bozo. Got a little rough, they sided with him."

"Your wife, did she call you a bozo?" Carter asked.

"My wife is garbage. Ex-wife."

"You had an argument, so you choked her."

"Wouldn't call it an argument exactly. I told her she might get off her ass and look for a job and she kicked me in the balls."

"So you choked her," Greenberg said.

"If I punched her, I would've killed her."

"A lot of logic there," Greenberg offered.

"But she dropped the charges. Why was that?" Carter asked.

"Part of our predivorce agreement," and he laughed for his own enjoyment.

"What happened at the church, why did you quit?" Carter asked.

"Was a sham. One night after a mass I say to Cummings, 'I'd like to throw my wife out the window. Do I have Satan's permission?' I mean, I didn't need Satan's permission, but I thought I'd ask, see what he'd say, whether he was just conning us, which is what I was getting. And he says, 'What's the problem?' And I say, 'I got fired and she won't get a job to help out. She watches TV all day.' And he says, 'Maybe you should get some help,' and he tries to give me a number of somebody at a goddamn health services place. Health services! I'm in a satanic cult and this guy is telling me to get help from some health services? 'Take Satan into your heart. Do something evil.' It was a joke."

"Sounds like you had a lot of anger for Cummings," Greenberg said.

"Sounds like you had a lot of anger for Cummings," he repeated in singsong, mockingly. "I got a lot of anger for a lot of people. What else is new?"

"May twentieth, Tuesday, in the afternoon. Where were you?" Carter asked.

"You want to book me for the murder of Cummings? What's your evidence? Monday, Thursday, any day, I play cards at Farrell's Bar on 136th."

"That's your alibi?" Carter said.

"No, that's my goddamn life. I drink some beer, I play some cards. My pal scores tickets for a ball game, maybe I go. You got nothing here, guys."

"Don't book any trips to exotic places," Greenberg said. "We're going to want to talk to you some more."

He gave them an I-could-care-less look, and didn't hold the door open for them to leave.

The detectives went to Farrell's, a long, narrow, musty bar, the only occupants an elderly man at one end, and a burly bartender in his forties with a toothpick in his mouth watching stock car racing on television. To the side were a couple of booths with torn red cushioning. Posters from beer promotions were peeling off the walls. Carter flashed his badge at the bartender, who nodded, expressionless.

"What's your name?" Carter said.

"Jim Meehan."

"Jim, know Mike Gabler?"

"He's a friend of mine."

"And he comes in here?" Carter asked.

"Every day now he's not working. We play cards, watch a game, he has a few beers. What's the problem?"

"Every day?"

"Yeah. Hey, Sal—how often Mike come in?"

Sal was at a barstool; a gaunt man in his forties who did not look up, using the bar counter as a pillow.

"All the time."

"We're thinking specifically the afternoon of Tuesday, May twentieth," Greenberg said to Meehan.

"Hey, man, I don't know if I can remember one day from the next. Tuesdays, though, that's easier. Tuesdays, I open. I would've been here."

"What time did he come in, can you remember that?" Greenberg said.

"He always comes in around noon. He would've come in around noon. Sal—"

"What time Mike comes in?"

"Whatever you say."

"Around noon."

"And you remember him here on Tuesday, May twentieth from two until . . ."

"Five, when I got off. End of story."

The detectives went around again, getting the same answers to the same questions.

Carter and Greenberg met with Rourke and reported on this round of interviews. Gabler was physically capable of performing the crime. He was known to Cummings so it might have enabled him to gain entrance to the church. Cummings could have let him in. And he resented Cummings. The elements were closer to fitting the profile of a crime than anything they had thus far. He was a big, angry man, probably angry at Cummings, and he was someone who had used his hands in violence. However, nothing directly linked him to the murder. Gabler had someone providing an alibi for the time the crime was committed and possibly Sal would be a second person vouching for Gabler being in the bar. They brought Gabler in for further questioning, a lawyer was provided; he never wavered from his basic story, he was in Farrell's all that afternoon. This wasn't anything they could begin legal proceedings on and when Rourke discussed it with the district attorney and with the police commissioner, they were in agreement. Gabler was the definition of unindictable circumstantiality.

They added Gabler to Ronnie as people they were keeping an eye out for, although Ronnie was a special case; "Gomez's Folly," Santini called the random surveillance.

Gabler's anger over his exchange with Cummings fascinated Rourke, Cummings looking more and more to Rourke like having been the wrong person for the wrong work. The next day when Mr. Cummings phoned to ask, "Anything new on my son?" Rourke said, "We're still working on it," thinking the murder victim, despite his public presentation of himself as a man extolling the powers of evil, was oddly, and sadly, an innocent who played with fire.

In writing the Cummings piece, Ronnie had been interested in getting a representative from the Roman Catholic Archdiocese of New York on the record as to the presence of a satanic cult in the area. She played telephone tag with someone for a few days, her deadline was closing in on her, and she finished the piece without a quote from anyone. She suspected they preferred not to go near the subject and not give Cummings the dignity of a comment. She considered the Catholic Church the prime authority on Satan matters, they had been at it for so long, and she sent a letter with her bona fides to the archdiocese, looking to give herself some lead time on what she thought was essential for the book, the church position on possession and exorcism. She received a reply from Father John G. McElene, suggesting they talk in his office. She arranged the meeting with his secretary and brought her notebook and tape recorder to the archdiocese offices on First Avenue and Fifty-third Street.

Father McElene was a fit sixty-four, white hair, six feet one, and as the framed photographs on the walls indicated, a former army chaplain. Other images showed him with church luminaries, Pope John Paul II, Cardinal O'Connor, Cardinal Egan, photographs with civilians and with children in several settings, and there were several framed awards for public service.

"An impressive life," Ronnie said.

"A life in service of the Lord. Impressive isn't in my reference, Ms. Delaney."

"My apology. So you understand, I'm trying to give an overview of satanic possession in this book and somewhere along the line I'm obliged to deal with where the Catholic Church stands on the subject and on exorcism."

"I don't speak for the entire, worldwide church. I can give you a sense of some of the current thinking around here, in this archdiocese. Right now, I'm what you might call our spokesperson on church matters. So I can say to you we've gone up and down on the subject of possession. For a long time we didn't have anyone officially appointed as an exorcist. And we still don't do many exorcisms hereabouts, usually under extreme circumstances, when all traditional methods have been exhausted."

"Could you give me a number, per year?"

"I've heard a hundred or so a year within the American Catholic Church bandied about, but that's from writers such as yourself. I don't have a number like that based on my conversations with people. In our archdiocese, which is Manhattan, the Bronx, Staten Island, and some counties outside the city, a handful, less than a handful. Of course, if you go outside the Catholic Church, to the Protestant deliverance ministries of which there are hundreds, there are probably thousands of exorcisms per year. How many of those people we in the Catholic Church would categorize as possessed is another matter. I don't know where you are in your research. You do understand the distinctions in possession?"

This seemed like a test question. She felt he was entitled to assess his audience and she answered, "Demonic possession, full-scale possession, is usually defined as a person taken over completely by Satan or one of Satan's demons. The person no longer really functions as himself and is more of a vessel, an instrument of Satan. While a demonic oppression is more common, where the person is infected by the demon, but not taken over completely and the victim still functions as a person."

"I would give you an A on that," he said, confirming for her that he was administering a little quiz.

"Of course, there's another distinction," she said, "the fundamental one: Whether or not it ever really happens."

"That's why we're conservative here. In the deliverance ministries, when you read about some of the exorcisms they perform, I'd have to say the problems can be explained more easily by psychological factors than by invoking the demonic. I read your article, by the way. Very good."

"Thank you."

"What you said about self-help with Satan as a hook is relevant. I think sometimes beyond this archdiocese, beyond Catholicism, so-called demons are exorcised in what is closer to self-actualization, human potential movement kinds of things, with Satan as a hook, as you put it, than it is to religious belief. Depressed? It's demonic. Do an exorcism. And for many people it works. I'd hazard they never were demonically possessed or demonically obsessed as I understand the terms. Of course, if someone thinks they're possessed that doesn't mean they're trying to pull off a hoax."

He was so natural in his manner, direct, Ronnie made a fundamental error, misreading him as though she, as a nonbeliever, was in the room with another nonbeliever, ignoring his collar and the context of the conversation, that they were in a church office and he was an official of the church. And it was then he surprised her.

"But there are the times when a person *is* possessed."

She was so caught off guard she said, "I beg your pardon?"

"The rare, true possession. The Devil is an awesome thing. I know how he works. With the full force of his evil."

"You believe there are possessions that *are* Satan's work?"

"Definitely. And as you write your book, I would be so bold to suggest you never become so embracing of rational explanations that you fail to recognize that for those unfortunate to be chosen by the Devil, he is a fallen angel, of higher intelligence and higher will than mortal man. To be afflicted by the Devil is a dreadful affliction. It takes a great purity of faith by an exorcist to rid a person of his terrible power."

Ronnie asked about his direct experiences with exorcisms and he was vague, suggesting that any time it became known, "in a knee-jerk response, the people claiming to be possessed come out of the woodwork."

Lingering for her on the way home was the pure belief he expressed. She felt it was unprofessional on her part to have assumed his beliefs were hers. He was someone who could say to her sincerely, openly, "The Devil is an awesome thing. I know how he works."

She was in a hall of mirrors in an amusement park fun house. Her parents were there with her in the fractured reflections and then the image changed, she was an adult, and they were gone, no one else was there, and she was frightened. The expression she saw on her face in the reflection was fear, and she turned to leave, but she was lost, blocked by mirrors, and then coming into focus, in multiple images on all sides of her—front, left, right, everywhere she turned—was Satan, the dark angel with human features and lascivious lips, smiling, patronizing. The mirrors broke, shattered glass, and as she ran, new unbroken mirrors formed a tunnel, she ran through the tunnel, the Satan multiple images continued along the tunnel, moving with her as quickly as she ran, and she saw dim light at the end. She burst out into a street, it was night, the light was from a lamppost, and leaning against the lamppost, smiling, with an expression that said to her, Run, but you won't get away, was Satan, the last image when she awoke.

Her dream had movie qualities, an element of cinematography to it, and camera angles, as she later explained to Kaufman, Orson Welles's *The Lady from Shanghai,* and the therapist offered that people sometimes do copy movie techniques in dreams, that movies are dreamlike in the first place, in the way they reorder reality, and dreams can reflect movies we have seen.

"There's a new level here that interests me," Kaufman said. "Not Satan, he's a familiar player in your dreams and not the broken glass, also familiar. Your father and mother together. Is it possible, Veronica, that with all the other guilt you take on yourself, that you also take on survivor guilt, they're gone and you remain?"

"I never thought of it."

"Wouldn't seem likely, would it, the way you've described your relationship, that you'd put your father in the same frame as your mother? He was always distant, from eleven when your mother died, to the day you went off to college?"

"Pretty much."

"Did you eat separately at dinner?"

"We ate together. He'd call from work to pick up food if we needed it and usually he cooked something, short-order things, or I did when I was an older teenager."

"And you ate together and it was then in the evening that he would withdraw?"

"Pretty much."

"So your father sat down with you for dinner every night?"

"I suppose he did."

"And weekends you said sometimes he would take you to the movies."

"When I was younger."

"And it stopped when?"

"Sixteen or so, when I started seriously hanging out with friends."

"Did he ever take you ice skating or roller skating or museums or—"

"Baseball games. He took me to some baseball games, and the other things, too."

"Maybe he wasn't such an absent father. Maybe he was a man who couldn't cope with the role he was cast into, and he managed as well as he could, given his limitations. And so, he has a part of your heart, too, Ronnie, and you miss him, too, and you feel guilty that you're here, and he's not, and for the sadness you feel you created in his life that became such a burden for him. You know your mother loved you, you feel it. May not be such a bad thing for you to know, and my guess is it's true, that your father loved you, too. And he didn't blame you for your mother's death. His grief was profound and ultimately it overwhelmed him, but you were his little girl and he was trying."

Ronnie sat for a few moments, reflective.

"Possibly," she said, softly.

"I'll take 'possibly,' " Kaufman said.

Richard returned to New York, Nancy was with Bob, and to fulfill a fantasy of hers, they made love in Ronnie's bed, in the apartment, Ronnie wanting the feeling that he was there with her in the place where she lived, slept, so she could feel the added intimacy. She thought about her performance. She believed by the very nature of their sex together she was getting better at it and that she fulfilled him. She couldn't imagine how she might compare with some of his other women—she assumed there had to be others as he made his rounds, German actresses,

Swedish nurses, her fantasies about his sex life—but she was mainly comparing herself to herself and decided that he was with her, he returned to her, he must have thought she was worth it, and if it came to pass that he did limit his travel it might begin looking like a genuine New York affair, after all.

Richard told her they were invited to dinner at Antoine Burris's apartment and Ronnie was very interested to go, an opportunity to observe some aspect of Richard's private life. They went on a Saturday night, Ronnie wearing a new black dress, Richard picking her up in a taxicab, in his ever-constant blazer, jeans, and a white silk shirt this time, dress-up for Saturday night.

Burris lived on West Twelfth Street in a converted factory building, the apartment overlooking the Hudson River, the main living room/dining room area filled with books, outdoing even Richard's display.

"Tremendous," Ronnie said.

"I'm a collector," Burris responded. "I'm also compulsive, a deadly combination."

He introduced her to a woman he described as "my lady friend," Olga Sirvaya, six feet two, long black hair, pale white skin, hazel eyes, out of the pages of *Vogue,* wearing a skintight white dress.

"That dress," Ronnie whispered to Richard. "It's so tight, I'd say it was designed for her to ride the Tour de France."

"Olga is a model."

"No kidding. If I stand next to her I don't think we look like we're in the same species."

Olga barely spoke. She ate sparingly, a dinner of beef curry, prepared in the kitchen and then served by two elderly ladies in white server's outfits. The dinner conversation at first was dominated by Richard's recent trip and the feasibility of the Swedish behavioral scientist's findings, that there is a "joiner gene" that impels certain people to habituate toward groups, and in its extreme, to join cults. Her publisher then asked about the progress of the book and Ronnie gave a positive account of the work thus far. Knowing it would be of interest, she reported on her interview with Father McElene and the crystal surety of his beliefs.

They talked about faith among the clergy, to what extent, in their bones, modern-day clergymen still believed in the eternal struggle between God and Satan. The discussion shifted to Richard doing the book on satanic ritual abuse. The subject, which included satanic cult members possibly abducting children, with some accounts supposedly extracted from recovered memory, was fascinating to Ronnie, although it did not seem to register with Olga, who sat silently, bored and thin.

Ronnie considered the evening a great time. Michael was erudite, more so than anyone who preceded him, and he could have handled himself in the room, but it would have been as an observer. These men were right on good and evil, human behavior, satanic influences—the entire intellectual aspect of being with Richard that led her to sign on originally.

They went back to his place this time. He would be away about a week, research for the book. He needed to see a satanic cult in operation in Germantown, Maryland. The leader was ill and retiring, he had been in business for thirty years, and this was Richard's last chance to observe the Family of the Fallen Angel and talk to its main person.

"Looks like I very well may be around come the fall. You'll get bored with me."

"Bored is Olga. I'd have a way to go."

Ronnie rewrote the last paragraph she was working on, put her feet up on her desk, thinking about the material, whether to include her personal reaction to Father McElene's remarks, which was a larger concern; how much of herself to insert into the book or to keep it all detached third person. She originally assumed a traditional third-person style was the way the book should be written and was now not so certain, a major structural decision. She wouldn't solve it immediately and thought she might play with a portion of the text to see how it read.

Nancy came home from the office.

"So?"

"An excellent evening."

"Bet your Richard was nicer to his friends than he was to yours."

"He was. Except with Antoine Burris' date, it wouldn't have mattered. She was barely listening. Olga, the model from outer space. The guys were high octane, though, like talk show guests on some quirky religious channel."

Nancy was distracted. In the wastepaper basket next to Ronnie's desk were pages Ronnie had printed out and then doodled on. Nancy removed a page from the basket, her eyes enlarging. On the top of the page was a drawing of Satan, vengeful, threatening, and along the sides of the page were his minions, demons ecstatic-looking in their evil, the drawings exquisitely rendered, malevolently powerful.

"This is unbelievable." She held the page up for Ronnie. "I didn't know you could draw like this."

"I can't," she said, a headache suddenly rushing in.

"Did you copy it from a book?"

"I wouldn't've been able to, nothing like that," as she looked at it, bewildered, pressing her forehead for the pain. "I don't remember doing it at all."

12

She was afraid to sleep, fearful the creatures of the page would inhabit her dreams. She and Nancy had settled on an explanation. Similar to the manner in which Ronnie had previously dreamed images from her research, she had somehow created these drawings from what she had seen in the research material or from her own dreams. Ronnie's problem with the explanation was that never in her life had she exhibited the slightest ability at draftsmanship.

After lying awake for several hours she fell into a sleep of fatigue. In the morning she was relieved, not for the sleep, but because she could not recall her dreams. She was not due to see the therapist for another three days. She didn't know how she could go that long and left a message on Kaufman's machine asking if she could come in as soon as possible, that day. Nancy stood by while Ronnie placed the call, unsure if she should even go to work. Ronnie insisted she didn't need Nancy standing over her and watching her and Nancy, under protest, went to the office. Ronnie sat at her desk, staring at the drawings. She still couldn't make the connection, when she had done it, how.

She walked over to Broadway to buy a newspaper and the man in the box was in his place. He had disappeared for a while in one of his periodic absences, rather like Richard, she thought. Their last exchanges had been upsetting so she was going to give him a wide berth and walk past him. He noticed her, this man who didn't respond to anyone, and spoke in a husky voice, "Keep away from me."

He was in the rear of a television set box and tried to place more distance between them and there wasn't any room, his back was squeezed against the cardboard.

"What do I mean to you?" she said.

He didn't respond, within his private madness.

She moved on, feeling as though she could camp outside Kaufman's office if she didn't see her right away. She approached the building and became aware of a car cruising alongside her. The car stopped and Detectives Santini and Gomez emerged.

"Ms. Delaney, I see you're wearing a Yankee hat," Gomez said. She had popped it on when she was leaving the house.

"What?"

His voice was distant, outside her range of concentration.

"I said you're wearing a Yankee hat."

It still took a beat for her to concentrate, he was talking to her, talking to her about a hat.

"What of it?"

"You work out, Ms. Delaney?" Gomez said.

"Not really. I jog some. Look, I've got a lot on my mind."

Santini was not fully engaged in his partner's suspicions and let Gomez continue on his own.

"Sometimes a person's physical frame doesn't tell you how strong they are."

"Yes? And? You're a detective. Can't you detect I'm not in the mood for questions right now?"

"Randall Cummings was murdered, Ms. Delaney," Gomez said. "You were one of the last people to see him alive. If we're trying to find the murderer and you think we have to check your mood first, you're sadly mistaken. Familiar with Mariano Rivera, Ron Guidry?"

"Yes."

"Both of them, wicked fastballs, nothing you'd take from their physical frames. A person's size can be misleading. And someone who was harassed, in anger, might find the strength to perform a physical act on the person they thought was harassing them, an act you wouldn't predict, given their physical frame." She was overwrought, from everything, tapping her fingers on her side impatiently. "You're nervous, Ms. Delaney. It isn't easy living with something you're holding inside you."

She carried her cell phone with her and Kaufman hadn't called. She also left the number for the apartment. She needed to get upstairs to see if there was a message on her machine. She had to get in to see her right away.

"What?"

"I said it isn't easy living with something you're holding inside you. Is there something you should be telling us, Ms. Delaney?"

"We're in different solar systems," and she walked away from them.

"That was effective," Santini said as they observed her go into the building.

"Girl is a powder keg."

"Maybe she figured Cummings was harassing her, and now *we* are."

"Was worth a shot. Still is."

Ronnie placed another call to Kaufman saying it was imperative to see her. She couldn't work, she watched television, cable news, and finally a few minutes before 10:00 A.M. the phone rang.

"Hello."

"Veronica, it's Dr. Kaufman. What seems to be the trouble?"

"I can't tell you on the phone. Can I come in and see you? It's extremely urgent."

"I'll cancel a lunch. Come to my office at one."

Ronnie tried an experiment, sitting at her computer, surfing the Net, checking herself periodically. Did she go into a cloud, do another set of drawings unconsciously? She did not. The slow morning passed and she placed the sheet of paper with the drawings in an envelope and headed for Kaufman's office.

Ronnie immediately showed Kaufman the drawings, telling her she didn't remember doing them and was artistically incapable of anything like it.

"First, let's deal with the subject matter. It's consistent with your dreams and your book. Satan and demons. With which you're totally preoccupied within your work and within your personal psychology. Satanic images will eventually vanish from your reference, conscious and subconscious, when you come to terms with your guilt—over your mother, and may I now venture to say, your father. *And*—this is getting very significant in your life—*and* when you're finished with this book. Right now you're immersed in these images."

"Dr. Kaufman, I can't draw, I never could."

To prove the point she reached for a book on Kaufman's bookshelf, photography by Walker Evans, took a pen and a piece of white paper from the desk, and tried to copy an image from the book. The attempt was hapless, the work of a distinctly untalented person.

"All right," Kaufman said.

"Terrible. I'm terrible. How did it get there? It isn't some dark miracle. An outside force didn't come and draw on my paper."

"As a child, were you encouraged to draw?"

"No, not any more than other kids. I didn't have any talent in school either."

"But this is talented work, exceptionally so. It's possible you have ability that was repressed." Kaufman looked closely at the drawings. "Might be similar to automatic writing. Familiar with the term?"

"Something with séances."

"People used to believe you could write thoughts that came from someone else's mind, like a person who died. And they would attempt to contact that person. Very popular in the eighteen hundreds. Today we know there's a subconscious and the people themselves were doing the writing. Like when the pointer moves on a Ouija board, it feels to the people doing it that it's external. Subconsciously someone at the table is moving it."

"Even if you're saying I did this subconsciously, I still can't draw."

"Inwardly, evidently you can. A talent lost within you. Would we find that you actually drew well when you were little? And when your mother died, you stopped."

"I don't remember that."

"And your father's not here to ask. It could be that. Something else concerns me, though, how overloaded you are with this imagery. It's leaking out of you, Veronica."

Kaufman revisited what she considered the crucial source of Ronnie's preoccupation with Satan as a symbol, Ronnie's belief that she was the bad girl whose bad behavior caused her father to be distracted, the accident to occur, and her mother to die.

"You keep stressing various elements had to take place and I wasn't at the center of it. But what you don't have an answer for is if I didn't cause my father to turn around, the accident wouldn't have happened."

"I do have an answer. I still don't place you at the center of the events. Who told him to turn around, Veronica? People talk to children in the backseat of cars all the time without taking their eyes off the wheel. That was his responsibility, not yours. But we'll keep discussing it. We have to."

"I guess time is up."

"It's painful, I know." She looked closely at Ronnie. "Something else I must say. I don't like this book for you, Veronica. A person bedeviled, to choose an appropriate word, bedeviled by images of Satan, doing a book on satanic possession—by my estimation you're the worst possible person to write a book like this. Do you have a contract?"

"Yes. I made a commitment. I have an advance."

"I think you should consider terminating the book. You could give back the advance. If there's a legal issue, I'm an MD, I could give you a letter that will vouch for the injurious nature of your doing this book."

"That is pretty strong."

"I mean it to be. The Cummings article, all right, it seemed like a good idea for an article and it was, and you didn't get drawn in. But possession, bombarding yourself with satanic ideology and images, it's not good for you, a person with a deep affinity for Satan as evil, with feelings of yourself as an evil, bad little girl. Veronica, it would be criminal of me to sit here aware of your personal history and to know you're working on this particular book and not advise you to give it up."

"It's my work."

"This book isn't your work. *Writing* is. It's a project, one project, and for you, the wrong project, as I see it."

"I wonder if you're within professional bounds to come down so strongly—"

"I'd go so far as to say you shouldn't even postpone it. I think all it would accomplish is postpone these reactions. This is not the material for you, Veronica."

"A writer doesn't build a career abandoning projects."

"You could do articles again. You do them very well. You could do other books. This book, in my judgment, is overloading you with images of Satan, the worst possible images for you. Please consider what I've said to you."

Ronnie and Nancy sat in Ronnie's bedroom, Ronnie sitting up in the bed, Nancy on the floor, the two friends with various talks in the past between them about men and dating and single life and work, now with a crisis that went beyond anything in their experience. Kaufman's explanation for the drawings was close enough to their first instinct about it—Ronnie illustrated her research—and they found that plausible. Ronnie did not find plausible her technical ability to create the renderings. The dots seemed to connect on the Satan images in Ronnie's dreams—Ronnie thinking of herself as bad, hence, evil, hence, images of Satan. What she was supposed to do with the therapist's insight was elusive and she didn't feel immediately better for the therapist suggesting cause and effect. On whether or not to discontinue the book as Kaufman recommended, Ronnie and Nancy could deal with practical considerations. Ronnie had already spent some of the advance money for the work she had done. Nancy dismissed the money as a problem. If Ronnie wanted to get out of the project, she and Bob would lend her the money to drop it. Nancy called Bob for confirmation and he agreed. The money was off the table, leaving the core issue—was the book having a harmful effect on Ronnie and would dropping the book have an adverse effect on her career as a writer? Nancy sided with Kaufman, she didn't like the idea of the bad dreams, and the drawings were bewildering and frightening. She was troubled that her friend was capable of such dark imagery. If the book was pushing her in that direction, she didn't see Ronnie continuing it. What that meant professionally, abandoning your first book assignment, she couldn't tell, and suggested they talk to Jenna Hawkins.

"That's a baby thing to do, to tell an agent, 'My therapist says this book is bad for me, I'm being emotionally disturbed by it and I should drop it.'"

"I haven't been at it long enough. I don't want to be offering wrong advice."

"It's unprofessional. Asking her. Dropping the book. It's all unprofessional."

"Talk to Bob. Not his field, but he's a smart guy, he can give a practical opinion."

"Let's get him over here."

Bob came bearing a pizza and a bottle of red wine for dinner. He listened to Ronnie's presentation of the arguments pro and con, then asked to see the drawing in question. She brought it out and his forehead furrowed when he examined it.

"You drew this and you don't remember and you never had any skills for drawing anything like this?"

"Looks that way."

He reached across the table and gently touched Ronnie's hair.

"Such images churning around inside you. You've got to listen to the therapist, Ronnie. She's got your best interests at heart. And then . . ."

"And then what?" Ronnie asked.

"There's the other problem."

"What other problem?"

"Richard, he got you the book contract, didn't he?"

"Basically. Jenna made the deal."

"I don't like him, I don't trust him, I don't think he's the guy for you. And if you're working on a book that may be messing you up, makes sense to me he's the one who got you into it."

"What's in it for him—for me to be messed up?"

"Who knows? I'm just saying it's no big surprise that something bad for you comes from this guy. Maybe he likes his women messed up or insecure or vulnerable so he can come off the masterful stud."

"The assumptions here—" Ronnie said.

"Look at the way he treats you. He's dangling you like you're a puppet on a string. He's in town, he's out of town, he's in Europe, he's back, then he's gone, you don't know much about him. I Googled the guy and I went on his Web site, too."

"Really?" Ronnie said.

"I did it after the bowling. Does she know about it?"

"I never said anything."

"You should know about it. He wasn't great at the bowling if you recall, just average. When you were in the ladies' room, when no one was watching, he threw a perfect strike, like he could bowl a perfect game if he wanted to."

"So he was being accommodating with us," Ronnie said. "He didn't want to throw off the curve. It was social."

"It was strange. And I'm not sure but he *wanted* me to see it. An in-my-face kind of thing. Any way you look at it, it wasn't honest. So I tried to find out a little more about him. There are gaps in his bio. And his Web site, he comes off as an absolute true believer in Satan."

"Reasoned," Ronnie offered.

"Reasoned, yes, but a true believer. Okay, I'm Jewish, so most of the Christian God versus the Christian Satan doesn't speak to me, but he's in there, mainline. Can you really be serious about someone who truly believes the devil is not in the details, Ronnie, but in our lives? How much do you know about him?"

"Not a lot."

"Well, you know what you know, how he treats you."

"He says he's settling in, starting a book of his own, and he'll be around more."

"God help you. Drop the book, Ronnie, and then drop him. No charge for the advice."

Ronnie wasn't prepared to act on the advice; his assumptions were too extreme, the leaps too great, that it was in some way within Richard's interest to have her thrown off balance. Richard did get the book assignment for her and she didn't see how it was a negative thing; a natural outgrowth of the Cummings article, a step up for her writing career, an excellent contract, a fascinating subject. If the material was so fascinating that it was somehow getting into her psyche, that may have been a reason to soldier on; readers would find it fascinating, too. And there was also the raw work. She thought the outline was solid and that the pages she had written were well done. Bob was looking out for her, but she couldn't dismiss the possibility of some serious male-to-male competitiveness operating there.

Ronnie came to Jenna Hawkins's office and Nancy sat in on the meeting.

"Nancy tells me you're having nightmares over this book?"

"Nightmares would cover it," and deciding to go directly at the heart of the issue, "and the therapist I'm seeing, Martha Kaufman—"

"Yes, she's well known."

"She's advised me to drop the book, that there's an unfortunate conflict between my emotional DNA and the subject matter of the book."

"What would that be?"

"Along the lines that Satan is a heavy symbol for me, since I was a child, since my mother died when I was young, and doing a book on Satan brings out a lot of loaded responses, such as Satan showing up in my dreams, really bad dreams. And other things, too. She just thinks this project is not what I should be doing."

"I'm not in the psychology business, I'm in the book business. Martha Kaufman wrote a wonderful book, but that doesn't put her in the book business. So let's try to look at this in terms of the book business. Do you want to get out of this contract?"

"Everything I'm about says I should do it, finish, do the job. I signed the contract. I have a responsibility, and it's a terrific contract for a potentially terrific book. On the other side, a therapist with a good reputation is taking the position that I absolutely shouldn't be doing this book."

"If you drop the book is it that you'll never work again in this town—is that your concern?"

"I'd like to know that."

"You can get out of the book. Authors do it all the time. You *will* have to give back the advance. And in this case, you've just begun, it's not like it's even in their catalog. Probably Burris won't be keen on doing another project with you, but this won't disqualify you from working with other houses. How was the book going up to now?"

"Good."

"Would you like to talk to Burris about it, get an extension?"

"The therapist is saying I should just let go of it."

"As I said, I'm not in the psychology business. In terms of the book business, it's a good opportunity, but you don't have to do the book if you don't want to."

"I appreciate the advice."

"I would suggest if you decide not to proceed to get right back on the horse, start writing other things immediately, articles, perhaps try for a different book; don't create a writer's block for yourself."

"I won't."

She e-mailed Richard:

Been having really, really bad dreams. Seeing a therapist, Martha Kaufman. Strongly advises me to drop the book, says it's "bedeviling" me, bad images of Satan flooding in on me. Would like to proceed. I think it's going well and I love the idea of the book. But this is not good.

She suspected, with his general remoteness, he was not the kind of man likely to respond to any of the news bulletins contained in her e-mail, that she was in distress, sleeping badly, in therapy, and the big news, she was considering dropping the book. Her sense of him was that he abhorred complications and liked things one-foot-out-the-door clean. And yet if she couldn't tell him for fear he would disappear permanently, what *was* she doing in the relationship? Sometimes you need to reach out, you're in difficulty, and if the other person can't reach out to you, then you shouldn't be in the relationship; it isn't anything substantial, it's just sex, which is okay, except there are times when you need more.

Just when she had talked herself into having set in motion an end to the affair, she checked her e-mail to find:

So sorry you're not great. You are great and should always be great. Will be on the 7 P.M. shuttle. See you by 9. Will come to your place. Work here can hold for a day. We'll talk this out.

She was taken by surprise. He was dropping everything to see her. Ronnie asked Nancy if she would stay at Bob's that evening, and Ronnie bought ingredients for a salad for dinner and waited out the day. Unable to work and not knowing if she still was doing this project, she caught up on magazines, assessing the writers, then rereading her piece on Cummings. Good work, she concluded. But he didn't have to die.

Richard appeared in his blazer and jeans, carrying an overnight bag. He entered and without saying a word, placed his arms around her and embraced her, holding the back of her head with his hand, drawing her head to his shoulder, an enveloping, warm embrace that said, Don't worry, I'm here.

She was completely open with him. She showed him the drawings, told him about the dreams, the recurring images of Satan; reported Kaufman's view of the relevance of Satan imagery to her feelings of guilt over the death of her mother; spoke of her father; and then of blacking out, winning the race, and losing the day with Cummings, her voice breaking from time to time. His eyes narrowed several times in concentration as she presented herself in her vulnerability. He took her face in his hands and kissed her.

"So much to go through. Too much," he said.

And in a parallel gesture, she took his hands in hers and kissed them.

"I'm higher maintenance than you ever would have imagined."

"So am I, I suppose. You're a complex person with a complex life. And it does make you interesting," he teased.

She gave him an account of the meeting with Jenna Hawkins, and expressed how she was still conflicted. On one side was her sense of the right thing to do, finish the book, fulfill your obligation, and beyond that, write a terrific book on a good subject. On the other side was a respected therapist strongly opposed to her continuing the book because the project was dramatically ill-suited for her.

"I guess you're wondering where I come down on this, since I was in the chain of events."

"Yes, I'd say I'm interested to know."

"Could I possibly—and you can tell me no, and I'd respect that— could I read what you have so far?"

"What I have shouldn't be relevant. If it's good, it shouldn't be a reason to go on and if it's not good, it shouldn't be a reason to quit."

"I understand. It has to be a decision on the merits. Still, I'm very curious to see what you did."

She gathered the pages she had printed out, a preface and then a chapter on the satanic possession epidemics in sixteenth- and seventeenth-century Europe.

"You're going to take these with you?"

"No, Ronnie, I'm going to read them now, if it's all right."

"Oh."

He thumbed through. "Forty-two pages. Won't take that long."

She withdrew to the bedroom and watched a reality television program about singles and she thought it didn't have much to do with the reality of her single life. After a while he knocked on the bedroom door and she opened it for him. She sat back on the bed against the head-board and he sat on the bed near her.

"First of all, it's great. The tone, the voice, slightly dubious but in-trigued by the material. Perfect. Exactly what it should be, what I would expect from you."

"I was wondering at one point about making it first person."

"You'd lose that distance. It's the right voice, otherwise Veronica Delaney is too much in the narrative."

"That's where I ended up."

"Right. So the pages are great. Now, what you do? From my stand-point, if you decide not to go ahead with it, it will absolutely not mat-ter to me. I have no vested interest. None. I brought you and Antoine together, if it worked out, fine, if it doesn't, fine."

"Really?"

"Really. He's a big boy. He's in business. This wouldn't be the first book that didn't happen for him. And don't factor me into it. This is about you, what's best for you. And if at this time, with this tension in your life, and your therapy—the thing about therapy, sometimes it brings out dormant feelings that are better left alone, but that's another discussion—if the book's not right for you, don't do the book."

"Thank you."

"Having said that, my personal view is you've got a marvelous proj-ect going and it would be something of a loss if you didn't go on with it. I don't see this as the wrong book for you. I see you as the right per-son for, admittedly, not an easy book. But walk away, Antoine and I will still be pals, and so will we."

"Okay!"

"Enough about your book, how about *my* book?" he said lightly.

"How goes it?"

"This cult seems to have gotten softer over the years, where they're more about their community than their ideology. Not much so far that indicates any ritual abuse in their current history. I'm not sure yet of the past."

"Are you going to do it?"

"I am. Mainly write it in New York. We should look into some subscription series, music, theater, do the town."

He was especially tender with her in bed, gently caressing her as though he understood she needed, in her emotional stress, to be held, and that is why he was there, it was what she needed, until another need came to the fore.

He left early in the morning for the shuttle back to Washington, en route to Maryland. Essentially, he had given her permission to terminate the project and yet he was exceedingly complimentary of the work she had done thus far. She made her decision. With the help of therapy, and willpower, the kind of willpower she had shown in being on her own, in choosing to be a freelancer in the first place, she was going ahead with the book. She would stare down the demons.

She sent Richard an e-mail:

> Going ahead with the book. Seem to be possessed by the need to finish. Thanks for the support in whatever I would have done.

Later in the day she received an answer from him:

> Sounds good. I certainly would have supported your ending it. But now the world is going to have a terrific book from you. Back in about a week. Can't wait to see you.

He was away again, predictably, but she felt he had made a strongly supportive gesture by coming to New York. Eventually, he would be working there and they might indeed look into some traditional subscription series together, she speculated—theater, the Philharmonic. Autumn in New York.

She called Jenna Hawkins to say she was proceeding, the agent businesslike on the matter. Hawkins was not in the psychology business and didn't explore the emotional ramifications with Ronnie, principally concerned with stop, go. And it was a go.

The decision was not accepted as smoothly by Nancy, who was back from a weekend visiting her family in Connecticut.

"I'm sticking with the book."

"Why?"

"Because it could be something substantial, maybe even a breakthrough for me."

"You've broken through. Editors know who you are. You were getting work."

"I mean in book publishing."

"Ronnie, this book is giving you nightmares."

"Not the book per se, the nightmares are from a deeper place, apparently."

"You have a major therapist telling you to drop it because the book makes everything worse."

"I'm not a quitter. And it's clear to me, nothing I'm going through started with this book."

"Except it's where you are now. Blacking out. And those drawings. It's Spook-o-rama around here. This is what happens when Richard shows up. You're going ahead with a book you shouldn't be writing."

"He was very even about it, nonjudgmental. Basically said if I wanted to drop it, it was fine with him, no vested interest."

"That's all he said?"

"By and large. If the book worked out, fine. If it didn't, fine. I did show him some pages."

"And he loved them, I'll bet."

"He did."

"But that didn't matter to him. If it worked out, fine. If it didn't, fine."

"Exactly."

"Only he let you *know* he loved them. I'm beginning to see it the way Bob does. This was very manipulative because you end up doing the book a really smart therapist says you should get out of your life. And by the way, it accrues to his buddy's benefit."

"I can't believe that's his motivation."

"Maybe it isn't. Maybe it's worse. Maybe it's what Bob said, that he wants his women messed up."

"I don't believe that."

"So he rushed into town to aid a damsel in distress. Let me guess. Did he rush out again?"

"He's doing some research."

"In town, out of town, here, gone. He *is* dangling you like a puppet on a string. And now you're going ahead with a book that's bad for you. Really neat that he dropped in. This guy is the boyfriend from hell."

Martha Kaufman sat at the dining room table with her husband of thirty-five years, Elliot Kaufman, an orthopedist in his early sixties. Ronnie had informed Martha during her most recent session about continuing with the book, the therapist offering a last argument against doing it, which Ronnie rejected. Martha gave her husband background on Ronnie and the reasons she recommended Ronnie withdraw from the project.

"It's like watching the proverbial train wreck about to happen," Kaufman told him.

"I don't know what you can do. If she wants to go ahead—"

"She's sassy. One of those sassy young women today and that's wonderful. Imagine going into a satanic cult and doing an article about it. And she's being sassy by wanting to continue with this."

"She has some protection. She's seeing *you*."

"If she keeps seeing me. She probably thinks I crossed a line. For all her sass, she's very vulnerable, no family, a couple of nice friends, which is good, and someone she's having an affair with, and that may not be so good. *He* wrote a book on Satan and is probably doing one on satanic ritual abuse, as if she didn't have enough Satan references in her life. Apparently, he's very good-looking, worldly, but it seems he read her first pages, liked them, and the next I hear from her, she's going forward. Doesn't make me a particular fan of his."

"Possibly she'll be able to manage and it will work out."

"It will eat her up."

"Martha, that's very theatrical."

"Her dreams, the drawings, they're too intense. It's already eating her up."

13

"As you wander on through life, brother, whatever be your goal. Keep your eye upon the donut and not upon the hole."

A *Daily News* writer invoked the old legend from the wall of the long-departed Mayflower Coffee Shop on Park Avenue to enliven the reportage on a story already percolating in the tabloids. Felipe Ruiz, part owner of Fresh Donuts on Amsterdam Avenue and 114th Street, attempted to murder his partner, Angel Santos, by driving by and shooting him, hoping to make it look like a drive-by of drug dealers. He dropped a packet of cocaine in the doorway, waited in his car for his partner to appear for work, and drove past and fired at him. The bullets missed, shattering the window. The less-than-cool would-be killer, in appraising his handiwork, hit a bus stop pole, was knocked senseless, and found with the gun at his side.

THE DONUT MAN WHO COULDN'T SHOOT STRAIGHT was the story in the *Daily News*, while DONUT WAR! was featured in the *New York Post*.

For the detectives of the Twenty-sixth Precinct it was not the "coffee dunk" case the *Daily News* referred to—Felipe Ruiz would not confess, insisting the drive-by shooters drove past *him* and tossed the gun through the window of his car. He claimed the tossed gun caused him to crash. His fingerprints on the gun were the result, he said, of his picking it up out of curiosity.

Investigative work by the precinct detectives revealed a long-standing feud between the partners. The two had engaged in a punching match outside the store. Bystanders broke it up before the police were summoned. That episode was called in to the *West Side News,* a community weekly, and an item ran in the paper, according to information given to one of the detectives by the newsstand dealer next door to the shop.

Co-owners, Angel Santos and Felipe Ruiz, battled it out in front of their Fresh Donuts shop on Amsterdam Avenue and 114th Street yesterday. Punches were thrown. No arrests were made. What was the dispute, too much glaze?

The item was located by a detective going through back copies. He intended to confront Ruiz with the widely known antipathy between the men when Rourke leaned in to say that Ruiz's lawyer was talking about a deal. Gomez picked up the newspaper and was browsing through it when a photo caught his attention. The caption: "Winners of the Zip-Ade 5 K Run in Central Park, Bob Fox on the men's side and Veronica Delaney for the women."

"Look at this, will you?"

"So?" Santini said.

"You don't win a race by being a weak little thing."

"Please."

"Humor me."

Ronnie was at her computer working and answered the intercom to hear the unwanted voice of Detective Gomez.

"We need a few minutes of your time, ma'am."

"I'm working."

"Well, we're working, too."

They all stood in the small foyer to the apartment.

"We wanted to show you this," Gomez said, and offered the page of the newspaper. "How many women would you say were in the race?"

"I have no idea."

"Fifty-one, the company told us. Fifty-one women and you came in first."

"Good for me."

"How many races have you won?" Santini asked.

"One."

"This was the first time you ever won a race?"

"Yes."

"And how have you done in other races?" Gomez said.

"I haven't run other races."

Her palms began to sweat and she felt a trickling of sweat in her armpits. They were dead-on one of her unconscious moments and the strain showed in her face as she bit her lip.

"You all right, ma'am? Talking about this make you uncomfortable?" Gomez said with an edge.

"Detectives coming to my apartment in the middle of my workday makes me uncomfortable."

"No doubt. So I'm going to go back to my Ron Guidry–Mariano Rivera deal, that you can't tell someone's physical capabilities just by looking at them. Looking at your frame I wouldn't guess you could run faster than fifty-one women."

"Would you say that about Joan Benoit? Won the marathon in Los Angeles, a person same size as me."

"I'd say she was a strong woman, despite her physical frame. And you must be too, despite your physical frame, a strong woman."

"I am strong. I freelance. Takes some strength," she said with an edge of her own.

"I don't mean that kind of strong; running fast over a distance strong, lung capacity strong, athletic strong."

"Detective, I didn't kill Randall Cummings. I may have killed him in print, and that, retrospectively, may not have been the greatest thing I ever did in my life, but I didn't kill him. Now I've seen enough crime shows to know, if you want to book me for his murder, then book me. And I'll get a lawyer and we'll go from there. But this is becoming police harassment."

"You can't live a life with a secret, Ms. Delaney," he said, as the detectives turned to go. "Eventually it comes out."

"No doubt."

She closed the door after them and pressed her forehead against it, seeing herself again bewildered at the finish line with no memory of having run the race.

She forced herself to get back to work, writing material on some of the important exorcists through the years. She printed hard copies of her last pages, made herself a cup of tea, and then returned to her desk to read the pages she had just printed. On the top sheet in the upper right-hand corner was a drawing, elegantly rendered: Satan, the humanlike face, grinning mischievously, an expression she read as saying, Look where I showed up, I peek out of corners, you can't get away from me. She felt nauseous and tried to throw up. It was dry heaving. She went back to look at the page, perhaps she imagined it, but the drawing was still there and she couldn't remember drawing it.

"Hello."

"Uncle Jim, it's Veronica."

"Veronica!"

"How are you feeling, Uncle Jim?"

"Not good. My knees, both of them ache me day and night. Doctor says I could use surgery and my back isn't good either. Ever see that movie, *Seabiscuit*? Pain is what you get being around horses."

"Uncle Jim, I want you to try to remember me when I was a little girl. Say, around ten. Can you remember me when I was around ten?"

"Pretty little girl. Little Veronica. Didn't see much of you or my brother. I was up here in Saratoga."

"There were Christmas dinners. Easters. Did you ever see me draw, Uncle Jim, pictures?"

"Draw? Nothing comes to mind."

"Nothing?"

"I'm trying to put my mind there. Little Veronica around ten . . ."

"Drawing."

"Nope, can't remember."

"Never saw me with paper and pens or crayons?"

"Nope."

"If you happen to remember, will you call me? Do you have my number?"

"I've got it, drawer in the kitchen. How's school?"

"I'm out of school, Uncle Jim. I graduated and I'm working in New York as a writer."

"Did I know that?"

"You did, Uncle Jim."

"Fancy that, a writer. *I* ought to write a book. I could tell some stories."

"You will call me if you remember something?"

"Sure will. Good luck at school."

She looked at the drawing. She accepted that a person unconsciously moves the Ouija board, it is not done by an outside force, so she must have done this unconsciously from some dark place within her. She wondered if the woman in the psychiatric facility who had the same dream of Satan had ever done a drawing like this. She was unnerved by the possibility that an institutionalized woman might have done so, but she needed to know.

Ronnie went to the Web site and sent a message to CR.

I'm the person who shared a Satan dream with you. Something I must ask you. Imperative you respond. Please.

She kept checking her e-mail the rest of the afternoon and then a message from CR came up on her computer screen.

CR: What is so imperative?

RONNIE: I've been making drawings of Satan and demons. I
           don't remember drawing them and then they're
           there on pieces of paper. Doodles but elegantly
           done, scary images. Did you ever do anything like
           that?

CR: Oh, sure.

Nonchalant, "oh, sure." Ronnie's hands began to shake as she
typed.

RONNIE: Drawings of Satan, like he appeared in the dream?

CR: Yes. I couldn't draw as far as I knew and out of
       nowhere I started to, like professional drawings.
       Very frightening.

RONNIE: And then did they stop?

CR: After a few years.

Ronnie couldn't imagine how you could live with something like
that for a few years.

RONNIE: What caused it to stop?

CR: Just did. Everything strange stopped.

RONNIE: What else was strange?

CR: All the things that happened. The telepathy. I knew
       things about people I couldn't possibly know.

The exchange with Bob replayed in her mind, her saying his father
traveled so much and rewarded his patient mother by leaving her, which
Bob insisted she couldn't have known.

RONNIE: What else, please?

CR: Going into a daze. I would go into a daze and do what
       I never could do before. Like the swimming. I only
       swam sprints in college. Suddenly I could swim the
       English Channel.

Ronnie drew a deep breath in anxiety—it was like winning a road race over fifty-one women.

> **RONNIE: You swam the English Channel? When?**
> **CR: 1982. Just before they brought me here. These are**
> **all the signs. It happens when he gets into you.**
> **RONNIE: Who gets into you?**
> **CR: Satan. When he possesses you.**
> **RONNIE: You're saying you were possessed by Satan?**
> **CR: Yes. And then they brought me here. Have to go.**

Work was out of the question for her. She wanted to get to the *New York Times* microfilm collection immediately. She went to the Forty-second Street Library and looked in the index for 1982. Under sports she found a listing for a Connecticut woman swimming the English Channel and on the microfilm located an item in the sports section:

> *Claire Reilly, 22, of Bridgeport, a Connecticut woman with no long-distance swimming experience, swam the English Channel yesterday. Reilly formerly competed for the University of Connecticut in 100-meter races. She covered the twenty-one miles of open sea from Dover to Calais in twelve hours and ten minutes. "I just got it in my head to swim the English Channel and I hired a boatsman to track me," she said afterward. "I was able to keep going even though it was the longest distance I ever swam. It was like I was in a trance the whole way."*

Ronnie was desperate to get to Kaufman for her session the next day, deeply unsettled by the knowledge that she had the same manifestations as a woman who had been in a psychiatric hospital for over twenty years.

She presented Kaufman with printouts of the conversation with the woman and a copy of the *New York Times* article from 1982, along with the latest drawing. As Kaufman examined the material, Ronnie said, "I had the same dream as this woman. Did the same drawings. Had the same kind of out-of-the-blue physical act. We both had a telepathic experience. And she ended up in Empire State!"

"So many things going on, Veronica. The drawing is fascinating. Satan looks almost sly. It's really quite clever."

"I don't see anything clever about it. And I can't remember drawing it."

"You drew it. Nobody else did and to me it's your comment on the very fact of Satan as an image intruding in your life."

"Well, since you like it so much," she said sharply, "you can have it. My gift to you."

"Thank you. You might, as we proceed, see if you can give vent to this repressed artistic side of yourself with different subject matter."

"I have no control over it."

"Then there's another goal for us."

"I know where you're going. If I give up the book then I won't have this Satan overload. Let me ask you this. If I do give up the book, will I be all right?"

"You'd have a better path to being 'all right.'"

"I give up the book and there's still work to do. I don't give up the book, there's more work to do."

"Yes."

"I'm frightened. To be having parallel experiences with an institutionalized woman—"

"It's been a series of frightening incidents for you, the dead cat, and going further than that, back to your childhood. And now, Veronica, you have to be a grown-up. As to the book, could you work your way through it? Possibly. Why in the world would you do that to yourself?"

"Suppose I don't work on it for a while. Pick it up at a later date."

"You really think the book will be better for you at a later date?"

Ronnie took the drawing from Kaufman's desk and studied it.

"This isn't me."

"I'm afraid it is."

Ronnie drew a deep breath, then said, emotionally, "I don't want to end up in a mental institution." Kaufman waited. After a full minute of silence Ronnie finally said, "I'm going to drop it."

"Good! Excellent! I'll give you a letter if you need it. Now let's look at these parallels with this woman you're so worried about."

"They're signs of satanic possession, you know?"

"Don't you want to say 'presumed possession' or 'alleged possession'?"

"They're still the standard signs. Textbook."

"You said telepathy. You never told me about telepathy."

"Apparently I knew things about my roommate's boyfriend he never speaks about. I thought he told me. He may not have. How would I have known?"

"Intuition, coincidence, a lucky guess. I wouldn't make too much of it. As to the dreams and the drawings—Satan is not a symbol you and this woman invented. He's time-tested over centuries, and if you dream him or draw him, and she does, too, I'd hazard it isn't the first time more than one person ever did."

"But if it's happening to you, it doesn't matter if it happened to other people at other times."

"This is true. What we need to do is demystify these things. Swimming the English Channel, the Central Park race—I'm going to say that on the surface it sounds special, two unusual feats you share. It could be, though, like the drawings, a repressed ability. It's not like you never ran. It's not like she wasn't a swimmer."

"Not on that level."

"It's only a question of degree. A person, stressed, who regresses when stressed, writing a book on possession, which includes textbook signs of possession, begins to see signs of it within herself. Not supernatural to me. You're integrating the book into your life. And if a woman in an institution who thinks she was possessed shares similar experiences, parallel experiences to yours—a mathematician could probably explain it to you within the laws of probability."

"Maybe."

"Here's a question on an entirely different level, are you going to feel guilty about dropping the book?"

"A little."

"Because of Richard?"

"Perhaps."

This was an opening to a subject Kaufman was eager to pursue, Richard.

"Why, if this book is so wrong for you, did he leave you with renewed purpose in doing it?"

"He wasn't selling me on it. He made that clear."

"You *did* decide to go on."

"My friends don't think much of him either."

"I don't know the man."

"If he wanted me to go on with the book, and by the way, he never said I should, it could've been for the original reason, he liked me for the subject. Or because he liked what I wrote so far. Or he doesn't have access to the same kind of insights about me that you have."

"Fine. I'm only wondering why, on his watch, he would have you persist in doing something so completely wrong for you."

Nancy and Bob were delighted with the news of Ronnie finally abandoning the project. They talked over a spaghetti dinner in the women's apartment. Ronnie estimated she used about three thousand dollars in advance money for living expenses since the start of the book. Bob was willing to shoulder the amount as an informal loan. Ronnie thought she could handle it within her savings. They agreed it was important for her to write something else as far from Satan and demons as she could get.

Ronnie had been finding herself passing time spinning the channels on daytime television and thought instead of continuing to do it aimlessly, she might write about it, and was able to land an assignment from her editor at *New York* magazine for an essay on daytime programming.

Jenna Hawkins was unflappable, stop, go, go, stop. She drafted a letter to Antoine Burris saying the writer was withdrawing under medical advice and returning the advance. Hawkins told Ronnie she should prepare herself for Burris claiming ownership of her outline, since he sent a check for her research, and Ronnie said she didn't care. The agent liked the idea of the *New York* article and suggested she might eventually package an anthology of Ronnie's pieces, Hawkins coming up with a title on the spot, *In a New York Minute: Essays by a Writer on the Scene.*

Ronnie had yet to inform Richard and thought she had better do so before the agent's letter reached Burris. She called his cell phone number and, as usual, he didn't answer, so she left a message saying she would send him an e-mail.

> Have decided not to continue with the book. Was making me
> crazy. All being handled on the up-and-up by the agent. You
> said you had no vested interest. Hope so. Sorry.

Her friends and the therapist harbored a circumstantial case against Richard, anchored by the fact that he didn't stop her from continuing with the book. She granted him the presumption of innocence. She was curious about how he would react, though. Whatever his reaction, she was not going ahead with it.

Two days and not a word, electronic or telephonic, from Our Man in Satanic Ritual Abuse, she noted. She went out for a hamburger with Nancy and Bob and told them about the e-mail dialogue with Claire Reilly and the *New York Times* item.

" 'It was like I was in a trance the whole way,' the woman said. Sound familiar, road race fans?"

"She thinks she was possessed by Satan?" Bob said. "What does thinking you're possessed by Satan have to do with swimming the English Channel?"

"Yes, I'm sure it's not one of his events. But in possession, unusual physical strength is one of the so-called signs."

"But you don't believe in possession," Nancy said.

"I don't. Here's what's fascinating, though. On some level believing you're possessed becomes the same thing as being possessed, and I guess that's the case with this person."

"Ronnie, believing you're possessed is not the same thing as being possessed," Bob said. "One is possessed and the other isn't. And there isn't any such thing."

"God, am I glad you're out of this book," Nancy said.

"You two were right about it. Although, for a while there, I felt very ganged up on."

"We *are* your gang," Nancy said.

As she watched television and took notes she wrote something light-hearted for the new piece and it occurred to her that she would have been eighteen months on the book without ever going near lighthearted. "Although you have to admire," she wrote, "the athleticism of beach volleyball teams who show up on ESPN, if this is now an Olympic sport, shouldn't there also be an adjacent one for building sand castles?"

Richard called, startling her in the middle of the day.

"It's me, Ronnie."

"Hello!"

"Just emerged from some really interesting interviews. Years ago, this cult might very well have kidnapped some children. Doesn't appear to be any sexual abuse, at least nobody claims any. They did, it appears, force the children to participate in some animal sacrifices."

"Jesus, Richard, why ennoble these people by writing about them?"

"It's part of the story. So I've been around the clock unearthing this stuff. I just got back to checking messages. On the book, Ronnie, what's best for you is what's best for you. I feel that way completely. If it isn't the project for you, for whatever the reasons, walk away. Antoine will live, I assure you. It was a thought originally. That's all it was."

"You're totally cool with it?"

"Totally."

"Good. I'm moving on, doing something for *New York* on daytime TV. It's fun to do."

"Great."

"The book might have been important. But not fun. And not for me, ultimately."

"I'm with you. And I'll *be* with you. Coming back a week from Thursday. I saw they're having a night of swing dancing at the plaza in Lincoln Center with a live band. Ever do that kind of dancing?"

"A little. In college."

"I'll be back that day. Let's go."

"Somehow I don't think of you for that. Are you good at it?"

She was thinking of Bob and the bowling, wondering if Richard would say no, and then turn out to be a terrific dancer and thus curiously deceitful. This was a day for his surprising her.

"I am very, very good," he said with directness. "Follow my lead and we'll be stars."

"Richard, thank you for this call."

"Just direct your feet to the sunny side of the street," and serious Richard left her chuckling, also a surprise.

Jenna Hawkins called Ronnie to say Antoine Burris sent a letter back, confirming the author was withdrawing from the project, that the advance of the moneys received thus far, fifteen thousand dollars, would be returned by the author, and he would agree to a release from the contract. Ronnie estimated she had spent the three thousand she mentioned to Bob and Nancy in time given over to the project, she wouldn't be getting any of that back, and would have to take it as a loss. However, Hawkins was talking about making it all back on the *New York Minute* anthology of her articles. As Hawkins anticipated, Burris claimed ownership of the outline, a point Hawkins was prepared to negotiate. Burris asked if he could talk to Ronnie and Hawkins encouraged her to do so. A few days earlier Ronnie had been one of his authors and it was a courtesy she considered appropriate to the situation.

"It's Antoine. Richard talked to me. And I heard from your agent. But let me hear it from you. This material turned out not to be the right fit?"

"It was psychologically more demanding than I anticipated."

"It is an intense subject. Intellectually, did you find it interesting?"

"I did. If that were the only concern—"

"Fascinating, possession. Richard said your first pages were wonderful. More's the pity. Ronnie, I'm not going to reassign this as yet. On the grounds that interest in the subject seems to be ongoing, I'm going to set everything aside for three months. If after three months, you've possibly had a change of heart, we'll draw up the papers again and the project is yours."

"That's very nice of you, Antoine, but frankly—"

"Don't commit yourself. You don't have to do anything or say anything. This is all on my end. Legally, we'll close this out for you. Informally, it remains your project if you happen to feel more inclined to do it."

"You're being very nice about it."

"Self-interest. You may yet come around and then we'll all have a wonderful book. All the best, Ronnie."

"Thank you, Antoine."

She couldn't determine if he behaved responsibly because of Richard or was trying to find a way to hold on to a project he thought promising. Whatever the reason she was pleased to have received the call, which was better than a lawsuit.

Richard sent Ronnie an e-mail saying he would be dressed in period for their dance event, an unusually playful choice for this straight-arrow man. To match his style she went to a vintage dress shop and bought a 1940s blue and white polka-dot dress with an imitation gardenia for her hair. He arrived in a taxicab wearing a full-fitting blue pinstriped suit with wide lapels, wide slacks with big cuffs, a white shirt, and a period painted tie.

She laughed when she saw him, and was beaming over her own outfit.

"You're going to die in that," she said in the ride to Lincoln Center.

"I'll take the jacket off," and he opened it to reveal that underneath the suit jacket he was wearing broad suspenders.

A portion of the plaza was cordoned off for the people attending the event. The Lincoln Center Big Band was set up with a bandstand and sound system. At the sides were a couple of bars for drinks, and for those paying a surcharge on the night, Richard one of them, seating was available at tables ringing the dance area.

The band played "Take the A Train" and the evening was off to a fast start for the two hundred or so people participating. Ronnie's swing dance experience was limited to a couple of college parties, but she had a sense of the lindy. Richard, though, was extremely deft and guided her through the moves. She blended with him and on a couple of the faster numbers a few of the senior citizens on the dance floor stopped dancing to watch them. On the slow dance portion, to "Star Dust," Ronnie said, "Now I know why this kind of thing was popular," as he drew her to him, their bodies pressing together.

They sat and sipped their Tom Collins drinks, a theme drink of the evening. Richard excused himself to go to the men's room. Ronnie watched the dancers and then turned to look at the people seated. At a nearby table, holding a wineglass aloft, tipping it toward her as if to toast her, smiling a taunting smile, was Satan.

Horrified, she turned away and struggled for breath, then staggered from the table. The Satan of her dreams, of the drawings, had broken out of the confines of sleep and her unconscious and appeared in her conscious, waking life.

14

As the band played "Polka Dots and Moonbeams," wildly irrelevant to her state of mind, she held on to a stanchion for the sound system to keep herself upright. She was trembling and soaking with perspiration. Richard found her there, outside the outer ring of tables.

"Take me home. I'm sick."

"What's wrong?"

"Take me home."

They rushed toward the taxicab area, Richard supporting her stooped body with his arm.

"We should go to a hospital."

"Take me home, take me home."

After traveling a few blocks she asked the cabdriver to stop, went outside the taxicab, and vomited the sweet alcoholic drink and bile.

"You must have food poisoning."

"It was the drink. Let me just get home."

———

Nancy was in the living room reading a newspaper when they entered the apartment.

"Ronnie?"

"I got sick. The heat, the drink—" and she rushed to the bedroom and lay on her back.

"Maybe you should sit up," Richard said, standing over her, Nancy next to him.

"I just want to rest. I need to rest."

"Get you a cold towel?" Nancy asked.

"Good."

Nancy brought in a moist washcloth and placed it on Ronnie's forehead.

"I'm going to sleep now."

"You sure you're okay?" Richard asked.

"She's obviously not okay," Nancy said sharply.

"I'll be fine, let me just close my eyes. Sorry I ruined the night."

"You don't have to apologize to him," Nancy said.

"I'll call you in the morning."

He took a last look and headed out of the apartment, Nancy not acknowledging him.

Nancy stroked Ronnie's hand and Ronnie slipped into sleep, like a child exhausted by a most terrible day.

In the dream she was on a ballroom floor, the dance area enclosed by mirrors. She wore a white gown. Satan came forward, ludicrously wearing a tuxedo. He extended his hand to her to dance and she shook her head, no, and ran away from him in anxiety, the movements outsized, theatrical, as if it were a dance performance. She looked in the mirrors, which reflected her anxiety back to her as Satan hovered in the background, smiling, and in the repeated motif, the mirrors suddenly shattered. She awoke, soaking in her polka-dot dress.

———

She sat on the floor of the kitchen with the lights out, sipping a bottle of water. She saw Satan *in* her life, *in* her very life? "What?" she said aloud.

She changed into pajamas and went back to sleep. Nancy looked in on her in the morning, saw her sleeping, and waited for her to awake. Nancy left for work only after assurances that Ronnie was feeling better.

Moving slowly, Ronnie showered and emerged to answer a ringing phone.

"How are you today?" Richard asked.

"Better than last night. Not terrific."

"What was wrong?"

She was not inclined to admit, Oh, I merely saw Satan at an adjoining table, just sitting there among the dance patrons.

"Probably what I drank."

"Are you going to be all right?"

"I hope so."

"This is a bad time to be slipping out again, but the cult leader, the guy who hasn't been well, he took a turn for the worse. I need to go there, see if I can get in a last interview—"

"Whatever."

His career was the least of her concerns.

"Probably back within a week. And that should do the traveling for a while. You sure you're going to be okay?"

"I'll manage."

"Feel good, Ronnie. We'll be in touch."

"Sure."

She watched television for her article. Nancy called a couple of times. She and Bob had theater tickets that night, would Ronnie need anything from her, she could drop by after work.

"I'm just going to have a light bite for dinner."

"Richard, is he going to look in on you?"

"He went out of town again."

"Of course he did."

She slept peacefully that night, not expecting to, and in the morning willed herself to work. She was scheduled to see Kaufman at 2:00 P.M. She anticipated what Kaufman would say, that the scene at the plaza was a variation on the drawings with the same root causes.

She took a crosstown bus at Ninety-sixth Street to the East Side and transferred to the downtown bus at Second Avenue. She casually looked out the window. A black sedan drew next to the bus and in the second seat a window rolled down, and looking up at her from the open window, smiling, was Satan. She covered her face with her hands and sat that way until the driver announced Thirty-fourth Street, where she got off.

Ronnie described the manifestations to Kaufman slowly, haltingly.

"It was like Satan was trailing along as I went to my therapist, a superior look to say, It won't do you any good, honey."

"These fantasies, they're similar to the drawings, aren't they? Except you're giving the symbol of Satan full dimension."

"It's worse, because it's in my walking-around life."

"Veronica, we know you're fit, physically. And you don't show the symptoms of schizophrenia. You're functioning. You're working."

"More or less. But that's great news, Dr. Kaufman. I'm not schizophrenic."

"Why are you doing this to yourself?" she said bluntly.

"What kind of question is that?"

"A direct question. There is no Satan, Veronica. No Satan who rides around in the back of a car, or sits at a table at a dance in Lincoln Center. You're imagining him, dreaming him, drawing him, seeing him. And I'm asking why you're putting yourself through this."

"I don't want to go through this."

"I wish I were sure of that. You're punishing yourself." She observed Ronnie, who was looking at her hands in discomfort. "Who gets punished in our culture?"

"I feel like a schoolchild answering. Someone who's been bad."

"Someone who's been bad. It's the same origins, the bad girl conjuring up the embodiment of evil—Satan."

"I knew you'd say that."

"Knowing I'd say it doesn't mean it doesn't have validity. Once you think of yourself as bad, it keeps building on itself."

Kaufman urged Ronnie to go back once again, painful as it was—and Ronnie was very uncomfortable—and talk about her mother's death, which Kaufman characterized as "your original sin." She then prodded her to talk about her father's death, and the sex with Richard, whether she thought taking pleasure in it made her bad, and the article about Cummings, how she was prepared to believe writing it somehow led to his death and made her bad, until Ronnie was weary, eager to get out of there.

Kaufman wanted to increase their sessions from once to three times a week, "on the clinic's nickel," she said, and strongly advised it, to which Ronnie said, "So it's not just similar to the drawings. This is obviously crazier, these 'sightings.'"

"I didn't say that. I merely feel you could use additional therapy."

"I appreciate it, Doctor. I'll ponder it, with all else."

She dared not look out the window in the buses that took her home. In the apartment, she turned on the television set to watch people parading problems that didn't seem to be in the same world as hers. Nancy came home from work and found Ronnie lying in bed on her back staring at the ceiling. The nightly news was on. Ronnie wasn't paying any attention to it.

"This doesn't look good."

"Satan's been showing up, Nancy. *In* my life. Not in my dreams, not in drawings. I saw him today, he was in the backseat of a car, and I saw him when I went dancing with Richard, which is why I got sick. It made me sick to my stomach. A horrible face. Human, but not really.

A dark angel with a human face and he smiles at me, a sort of condescending smile."

"Ronnie!"

"Dr. Kaufman says I'm not schizophrenic. Just having your run-of-the-mill, explainable hallucinations."

"What's explainable?"

"I'm someone reliving her mother's death and a whole arsenal of other guilt. Thinking of myself as bad and conjuring up the ultimate symbol of badness."

"What can I do for you?"

"Seems to be between me, and me. Right now, I'm going to try to get some writing done. I'll just have a yogurt or something for dinner. And pretend normal."

"She's supposed to be very good. Is she?"

"She's smart. She's offering me three sessions a week. But it feels like I'm on a train heading toward a station and the station is where it's safe and I'll be fine, but the train is moving very slowly and the station is moving, too, even faster than the train, and I'm not catching up."

When she met with her husband, Kaufman was not nearly as guarded as with her patient.

"I told her imagining you're seeing Satan when you're conscious is similar to drawing Satan unconsciously. And it is, in a general sense, a variation on her theme."

"But it's more extreme."

"It is more extreme. I didn't want to alarm her. I need to keep her focused on understanding her own guilt. She's placed a huge burden on herself and she's accelerated her self-recrimination. A lovely girl and she's unraveling."

"So how wise is it not to alarm her?" he asked.

"It's a balancing act. She has to concentrate in the sessions, not be unhinged by what I say. Frankly, I'm a beat away from trying to keep her inside."

Ronnie was reading between the lines of Kaufman's responses. She knew that seeing Satan at a nearby table or through a bus window was a more powerful aberration than illustrating him without being aware of the act, or merely dreaming him. A therapist's restraint could not conceal from her that a nightmare by day was more serious than a nightmare by night.

The following morning she sent an e-mail to CR:

> I need to ask you, did you ever see Satan when you were awake? Not in a dream. In a waking state?

A few hours later she received a response. She stared at it, not wanting to believe what she was reading on her screen.

> I did see him when I was awake. Several times. The first time I remember as if it was today. I saw him across a dance floor.

On the words "across a dance floor," Ronnie began to feel ill again. She sent CR an instant message.

> **RONNIE:** These things are happening to me. I'm desperate. Could you please consider having a visitor?
> **CR:** My name is Claire Reilly. I'm at Empire State Psychiatric Facility in Cold Spring, N.Y.
> **RONNIE:** May I come today? Are there visiting hours?
> **CR:** Visiting hours are open. Come when you wish. I never have visitors.

Ronnie took the train, an hour and a quarter ride from Grand Central Station, unable to concentrate on the magazines she brought. She resisted looking out the window. She took a taxicab for the remaining ten-minute ride to the facility.

The main building resembled a penal institution: a three-story un-adorned red brick structure half a city block in size. The grounds were more felicitous: a tree-lined campus with a rolling grass lawn. Ronnie passed through a security guard and electronic scanner and announced herself at the front desk. The guard there called on his phone and she was told to wait in the visitors' lounge off the main lobby, a room with fluorescent lighting, cafeteria-style tables and chairs, a few unmatching sofas and chairs, and yellow walls decorated with fading art posters. The place had a point-of-no-return atmosphere. The time was approaching 3:00 P.M. No one else was in the lounge.

After a few minutes a woman in her forties entered in the company of a nurse in a white uniform. Claire Reilly was five feet six, the trace of attractive features in a puffy face; wearing a print dress twenty years out of date, her auburn hair in a ponytail with a pink ribbon. She carried a little matching pink handbag, as though she meant to be at her best for a visitor. Ronnie wondered if she was looking into her future, if this was who she could end up being, in a place like this.

"Ms. Reilly, I'm Ronnie Delaney."

"Will you be all right, Claire?" the nurse asked.

"Fine. We're going to sit under a tree. Is that all right with you?" she said to Ronnie. "This room is so institutional."

As they headed for the front door, Claire walked slowly, her gait un-certain, and that, along with the puffy face, indicated to Ronnie the woman was living with the effects of heavy medication.

Claire guided them to a shaded bench. A few patients wandered around the grounds listlessly, with nurses nearby watching out for them. Ronnie felt as if she had stepped into a Diane Arbus photograph.

"So, my dear, I can see the anxiety in your face."

"Terrible things have been happening to me, Ms. Reilly."

"I gather. It's an exclusive circle."

"An exclusive circle?"

"We ladies. I assume we should be flattered. If you read about it, you'll see some people think we invite Satan in by our behavior. I'm not sure of that."

"I've been having parallel experiences to yours. I won a race in Central Park. I never ran like that before. Like you swam the English Channel."

"The English Channel. It not only feels like another life—here's the irony, it felt like another life at the time."

"And the telepathy and the drawings and the terrible dreams, and now I see him, Satan appears when I'm awake. In a car. Across a dance floor."

"Sounds very familiar. You're possessed, my dear. He's found his way into you."

The chilling remark was said casually and Ronnie shuddered.

"You say that very confidently."

"Well, I don't have to *examine* you. I see it in your eyes. Same eyes as I had." She suddenly became secretive, unbalanced, and whispered confidentially, "You have to watch out for the medication. They start you out to keep you calm, but after a while it becomes how you live. You don't belong to yourself anymore."

"Dear God, what am I doing here?" Ronnie said aloud to herself, softly, rhetorically, but Claire answered.

"Looking for an answer. What's happening to you, how can you stop it? I was a teacher. I wanted to live a responsible life. And this is what happened to me. If you read about these things, if you're possessed, completely, you're not functioning, Satan takes you over entirely. What I was, what you are, is a form of possession they call 'obsessed,' where you still function, but he gets into you."

"Yes, I know the distinction," Ronnie said.

"A complete possession is the easy one. Because you're taken over, you're not really conscious of what's happening to you. But obsession, that's the true act of cruelty, when you're aware of your torture and not able to do anything about it. It's satanic in its cruelty."

"I've been seeing a psychotherapist who feels everything can be explained."

"Then why are you here? Too much of a coincidence, the two of us? Be interesting how many others there've been like us. Maybe some of them killed themselves. I should consider myself fortunate."

"Could I ask, please—how is it that *you're* here?"

"It happened very quickly. I was going along, with the various signs of obsession that you know very well by now building in me. I was confused, not knowing what was happening to me; functioning, not normally, but not where you'd have to send me to a place like this. And then it accelerated. Satan himself appeared when I was awake. I didn't know where or when he was going to show up next. All this while, Satan, in his human form, was inhabiting my real world. First one Satan, then the other, and I couldn't keep everything together. Eventually, I just couldn't function."

"Satan in his *human* form?"

"When he assumes the aspect of a human being."

"What do you mean?"

"Part of his guile, his evil. First he uses your body, which he can only do if he appears to be real. And then he works on your mind. That's what he's really after, I believe, to destroy your mind, which is infinitely more cruel. He must think of you as virtuous." She was still for a moment, reflective. "The evil angel appears to me from time to time, just to make sure I stay here." Changing moods, she said, "The sex is fantastic, isn't it, with our Raymond?"

"Raymond?"

"Aren't you seeing someone; talk, dark, handsome, fantastic sex?"

Ronnie couldn't bring herself to answer at first.

"Yes," she said quietly.

"I knew that. Goes with everything else. Raymond Scott. Also known as Satan."

"I don't follow . . ."

Claire opened her pocketbook.

"We were in a club and a photographer wanted to take a photograph of the two of us. Raymond didn't want that. How can you be sleeping with someone and not have a picture of the two of you? So I had a friend take one secretly when we were on the street."

She removed the photograph and showed it to Ronnie. It was a younger version of Claire. She was with a man who looked exactly like Richard. Ronnie stared at it, astonished.

"He looks just like the man I'm seeing. But his name is Richard Smith," she said, her heart racing.

"Smith, Scott, Satan."

"You're saying this man was Satan in human form?"

"Absolutely."

"Why do you say that?"

"I know now. I didn't know then. His behavior: itinerant, unreliable, drawing me in, letting me out, using sex to hold me in place, playing cat and mouse; and the books he gave me to read, rare books with drawings of Satan, powerful images that embedded themselves in my mind, found their way into my dreams, until I was drawing them, seeing them, and he was doing this to me, working on me, finding the weakness in my mental state and breaking me down."

"What did he do for a living, Raymond Scott?"

"He was a Satan scholar. He lectured on Satan." Claire suddenly noticed something behind Ronnie. "No!" she gasped. "No!"

Ronnie turned. Nothing was out of the ordinary.

"He's back. Satan is back."

"Where?"

"Right there. He's grinning at me."

"I don't see anything."

She started to run awkwardly, heavily, toward the main building.

"Claire!" Ronnie ran after her.

While running, Claire looked back apprehensively to the place where she said Satan appeared to her. She stopped. "He's gone now." The woman looked forlorn; the bad thing had happened again. "Talking like this, it isn't good for me."

"I didn't mean to upset you."

Out of compassion Ronnie kissed her gently on the cheek.

With compassion of her own, Claire said, "Be the mouse that gets away."

On the trip back to the city Ronnie's mind was so flooded with bits and pieces of the conversation with Claire Reilly, she thought, ruefully, she didn't even have room for her own sighting of Satan. She wrote down everything she could remember of the meeting and when Nancy entered the apartment Ronnie overwhelmed her with a report.

"Whoa. You're saying Richard was with this woman twenty years ago?"

"It looked exactly like him, and he was a lecturer on Satan, and the things she described, how he manipulated her, planted images of Satan with her, how he came, went. It's describing Richard."

"And he's *Satan in human form*? Ronnie? Could we just settle on he's a really bad guy?"

"This woman, she knew it all, the whole relationship with Richard. Maybe Satan *does* exist. The old argument, if innate good exists, innate evil can exist. And if innate evil can exist, it can . . . materialize, as an evil angel, as an evil person. I am so messed up. I am so messed up," and she began to cry, a deep, heaving cry. Nancy put her arms around her.

"Easy, girlfriend, easy. It'll be better. You got yourself out of the book. Next, you'll be out of this guy. And little by little you'll be yourself. You have to be yourself, Ronnie, you have to," and then Nancy, too, began to weep, and they held each other.

"Crazy people look in my eyes and they see something. I've been having absolute signs of possession, Nancy."

"It's the book. It's got you totally screwed up, like you're living out your research."

"I went on Google. Nothing for a Raymond Scott. Is it possible he *is* the same person, Richard *is* Raymond Scott? But he hasn't aged. There's got to be like some Dorian Gray portrait turning old somewhere. This is so weird. I'm in something so weird."

"*He's* weird. And if this is his pattern, and he changes his name, and manipulates women, he's a goddamn sociopath. Even if he isn't Raymond Scott, he's still a terrible, terrible guy. You have dated the worst guy ever."

"I'm beginning to think he isn't for me," she said, deadpan.

She dialed his cell phone and left a message. "Richard, it's Ronnie. Most important you call me." She went to her computer and e-mailed him the same message.

―――――

"What we need are spareribs," Nancy announced.

"Yes! That'll definitely fix everything."

They ordered the food, and when it arrived, Ronnie unearthed an album and for inspiration played Paul Simon's "50 Ways to Leave Your Lover." As they were finishing dinner, Richard called. Ronnie sat on the bed, Nancy seated herself on the floor of the bedroom to listen to Ronnie's end.

"Yes?"

"What is it, Ronnie?"

"Does the name Claire Reilly mean anything to you?"

"Claire Reilly. Swam the English Channel in 1982."

His directness was audacious, Ronnie granted him. Are you onto me? he seemed to be saying. Well, you can be onto me. So there.

"You knew her?"

"Briefly. We both lived in Bridgeport at the same time."

"Did you have an affair with her?"

"Nothing like it. I didn't know her very well, an in-the-library, small talk acquaintanceship."

"Charming. And you lived in Bridgeport, Connecticut. How come I don't see you as a Bridgeport-Connecticut kind of guy?"

"A sad story," he said, brushing past her remark. "She became mentally ill, apparently."

"Apparently. But you didn't know her very well."

"No."

"Does the name Raymond Scott mean anything to you?"

"Raymond Scott. He was on the Satan circuit for a while. Don't know what happened to him."

"So here's the question everyone loves. If the book, given my psychology, was the absolute wrong book for me, once I said I wanted to drop the project, why did you encourage me to go on with it?"

"You're presuming I know your psychology. And I didn't encourage you, Ronnie."

"But that was the effect. Seductively, you encouraged me. In a subtle, seductive kind of way. Reading what I wrote, praising what you read."

"I still think you were right for the book and perhaps one day you will be again."

"Working me a little, still?"

"I don't know what you mean. Ronnie, the tone here troubles me. I think we've had something special together and when I get back I'd like us to see more of each other, become—more intimate."

"Slip out the back, Jack."

"Excuse me?"

"Make a new plan, Stan."

"Ronnie?"

"We're not going to become more intimate, Richard. We're not going to become anything. You're too manipulative for me. You're too—everything for me. I'm going to say good-bye now. Like *good-bye* good-bye."

"Ronnie—"

"I'm not the girl for you, on whatever level you want to take that. Good-bye."

Ronnie hung up and she and Nancy slapped double high fives.

She nestled into bed for sleep, relieved, a weight lifted, singing to herself, "Just drop off the key, Lee, and get yourself free."

A priest at an altar, an impressive man, tall and elegant, an El Greco figure, the church interior ornate. The priest speaks in Spanish. Ronnie is in a pew in a summery white cotton blouse with a yellow skirt, sandals, a red flower in her hair, dressed like many of the other women who are present. The men are in European working men's Sunday suits and ties. As the priest intones, suddenly Richard appears at the side of the church. He wears tight black pants and a black silk shirt open at the neck. He carries a guitar case and opens it. The worshippers gasp. He has a gun. She is dreaming Richard as Antonio Banderas in a Robert Rodriguez movie. Richard/Antonio speaks argumentatively in Spanish to the priest.

"En la guerra entre Dios y el Diablo, el ganador será el Diablo. Porque en la tierra, Dios encontró a los débiles y los humildes, pero el Diablo encontró a los fuertes y bravos, por lo que las fuerzas del Diablo en la tierra serán más poderosas y más peligrosas . . ."

She begins to speak the words he speaks, along with him, in agreement, *". . . y ellos pueden encontrar formas de destruír a los débiles y los humildes."*

"Ronnie, for God's sake, Ronnie, wake up!" Nancy was standing over her, shaking her hard, and she was roused out of sleep.

"What?"

"You were shouting in Spanish."

"I was dreaming, a church—"

"You woke me. What kind of dream was it? You don't speak Spanish."

"I don't. I don't. Oh, Jesus Christ." She held her face in her hands, sitting upright now. "It's another sign."

"What sign?"

"Of possession. Speaking in a language unknown to the person."

Nancy attempted to make sense of it. "Look, we live in New York. It's getting to be a bilingual city. You must've picked up more Spanish than you think you know. Or you heard something and memorized it without realizing and it came out in sleep."

"Right," Ronnie said, largely to release her. "Go back to bed."

"When is your next session?"

"Couple of days."

"You've got to get in earlier," and Nancy withdrew to her room.

Ronnie lay awake waiting for the morning sun. However she arrived at this point, by being suggestible in stress, by exposure to the research, or by something beyond logic and rationality, something was in her, she could feel it, and it was taking her over.

15

Traditionally, many New York psychotherapists planned their vacations for the month of August, a practice Claire Kaufman followed for her private patients, whom she felt welcomed the respite. She and her husband favored a warm weather vacation in the dead of winter, however, and took their time then. In August she maintained her hours at the clinic, where her patients' mental health issues did not seem to abate with the heat of summer. She received the call from Nancy at her apartment. The outgoing message on her office phone gave Kaufman's home number for cases of emergency and Nancy called her there.

Nancy identified herself as Ronnie Delaney's roommate and told Kaufman that Ronnie had fallen back to sleep after an extremely troubled night in which she shouted out loud in Spanish while sleeping, a language Ronnie did not even know. Nancy was intervening to say her friend, in her opinion, had taken a turn for the worse, and that Ronnie had raised the possibility of satanic possession. Kaufman, concerned, told Nancy she was coming to the apartment, Nancy should make certain if Ronnie awoke that she waited for her. Kaufman set out for the roommates' place on 111th Street and West End Avenue, an uncommon occurrence, a New York psychotherapist making a house call in August.

Nancy and Kaufman talked softly in the living room while Ronnie continued to sleep.

"Everything she says is a sign of possession, I can see an explanation for," Nancy said. "The race—she's a closet runner. The telepathy—that was pretty weak, she knew something about my boyfriend's parents, except he might've told her. The language—she said some words in Spanish. Okay. She may have memorized something she heard and it emerged in sleep. It's the other things that worry me. The nervous breakdown things. Seeing Satan. Thinking Richard Smith could be the human embodiment of Satan."

"What's that?"

"She went to see this Claire Reilly at Empire State."

"Did she?"

"Not a mentally well person. Thinks Satan takes a human form and that she was possessed by him, as a Raymond Scott, who might also be Richard."

"Really?"

"This Raymond Scott's behavior was the same as Richard's. Same planting satanic images in her thoughts. Same manipulations. She showed Ronnie a picture that was taken of her with this Raymond Scott and it looked to Ronnie like it *was* Richard. Anyway, she broke up with him yesterday, and you'd think she'd be on the way back, but last night—"

Ronnie entered the room, apprehensive.

"Dr. Kaufman, what are you doing here?"

"Nancy called me. She was worried about your episode last night."

"You came to my apartment? I must be in pretty bad shape." She sat in a chair and kneaded her forehead to relieve the tension. "Nancy told you about the Spanish?"

"She did."

"Last item for my résumé on possession."

"Veronica, possession does not exist," Kaufman said. "It has absolutely no basis in fact or science."

"There are more things in heaven and earth, Horatio, than are dreamt of in your philosophy."

"You know the subject of possession as well as anyone by now. People need to believe in it, and so they do, but that doesn't mean they *are* possessed."

"But for those people who believe, and who begin to manifest the symptoms, believing is the same as *being* possessed. They end up in the same place."

"Are you telling me you believe you're possessed, Veronica?"

"Technically, it's *obsessed,* or we wouldn't be having this conversation. In a full-scale possession, I'd be bouncing off the walls. I believe I have the symptoms of satanic *obsession.*"

"Which you've been recycling from the book," Nancy said.

"If you begin to believe it," Kaufman said, "you'll only reinforce the belief. The more you believe you saw Satan, the more likely it is you will 'see' him, in quotes. And it should come as no surprise that I would say to you, someone who believes they are obsessed by Satan must believe they *deserve* to be obsessed by Satan."

"Your basic theme."

"No, yours. Veronica, I have access to an excellent residential therapeutic facility. It's in a townhouse on East Ninety-third Street. Run by a colleague of mine, Philip Wheatley. Private, very effective. You'd have your own room, there's a lovely library. We'd work something out on the costs, so you needn't concern yourself about that."

"You want to put me away like Claire Reilly?"

"This is not putting you away. It's therapeutic. I'd come by for our regular sessions, you'd have additional therapy with Dr. Wheatley, who is brilliant, and you'd be in group therapy with other people who've experienced childhood trauma."

"Is that my category?"

"You're defying category. But childhood trauma is at the core of things. And the combination of individual and group therapy over a period of time—"

"Would I be medicated? Is that part of the therapy, finding the right antidepressant?"

"Not without your consent."

"And do I give up my rights? Once I'm in, can I just leave, or don't I own myself anymore?"

"You wouldn't be there against your will."

"And if my situation deteriorates, if the therapy isn't working, do you have the right to keep me there?"

"You wouldn't sign yourself over. You'd have the right to leave. But anyone, Nancy, me, if they're a threat to themselves or others can be remanded to a psychiatric facility. It's the law. But you're asking the wrong questions. It isn't what happens if your situation deteriorates, it's what do we do to get you better."

"They're the right questions. I know the case studies; people live like I am now, normal at times, crazy at other times. And they're in and out of facilities. And they drug them up. And their minds are never the same. All I have is my mind," she said, her voice trailing off.

"I wouldn't let any harm come to you," Nancy said. "But you can't live like this, ranting in the night, thinking you see the Devil. What kind of life is this?"

"I appreciate your coming, Dr. Kaufman, and Nancy, you *are* my true blue friend, but I'm not going to do it. I'm not going down that road and risk ending up like that woman. What I'm going to do is go right to where the symptoms are, to the kind of symptoms they are, and deal with them on that level. I'm going to have an exorcism."

"Veronica, it's completely artificial!" Kaufman said.

"A lapsed Catholic girl, maybe they've got the right mumbo jumbo for me."

"You have unresolved problems an exorcism isn't going to touch."

"People behaving like I am *have* been helped by exorcisms."

"Some people. In a placebo sense. But for some people, it's destabilizing. You can get worse."

"It's what I'm going to do. I have a contact in the church. Now

I'm going to go inside, take a shower, get dressed, and fix up my life."

Kaufman left, but Nancy wasn't prepared to let Ronnie out of her sight. Ronnie insisted she didn't want her as a bodyguard, that was no way for either of them to live either. She was rational, she had made her way to Cold Spring and back, she could get in a taxicab and go to the archdiocese office and then get back to the apartment. She called Father McElene, however, the priest was out of the office. She reminded the secretary she had been in to see him before and the furtiveness in Ronnie's voice led the secretary to suggest she come to the office and wait, he would be in at 11:00 A.M. She took a taxicab downtown, looking straight ahead, not wanting to make eye contact with anything.

Father McElene was back in the office when she arrived, and she went over her notes while waiting, having written down the various manifestations and approximate dates. The secretary said he was ready for her, he greeted her warmly, and she sat with her material in front of her, thinking this man was in the Roman Catholic hierarchy, he could make this happen, she had to be persuasive.

Soberly, carefully, she presented the record of the accumulating manifestations, with a light dusting of the Raymond Scott as Richard Smith as Satan scenario, not wanting to appear to be merely a mixed-up New York girl caught in a bad relationship. She described in general terms the therapy she was in with Kaufman and Kaufman's thoughts about the cause of her behavior, largely to convince him that she had tried therapy, and wasn't getting better. She admitted that writing a book about possession might lead an observer to assume the subject matter combined with her suggestibility could bring her to this state. Whatever caused them, the manifestations *were* happening. And she had stopped working on the book. She repeated the position she took with Kaufman, she needed to go directly to where the symptoms were, and to the kind of symptoms, and was imploring him to arrange for an exorcism.

He did not respond immediately; he had made notes of his own and he looked them over before addressing her. He had surprised Ronnie in their first meeting by embracing the idea of possession; he seemed like such a sophisticated man, and yet he told her then that he believed in Satan, and in Satan, on occasion, possessing people. Possibly it had been a pose, created for a writer, and here, in this room, they were now into a test, this time Ronnie testing him—where did he really come down on the issue, and was he prepared to allow an exorcism if the person believed it would be the solution?

"There is always someone," he said quietly. He paused a moment, leaving her to wonder if he meant there is always someone who *believes* they are possessed, or if he himself was indeed a true believer, and meant there is always someone who *is* possessed. "You're such a valuable person," he said. "Exactly whom he would want to take down with his evil," indicating he did believe it was possible.

"Then will you help me? Please say you will, Father."

"I'll do my best. But it isn't that easy and it isn't that fast. The church has procedures. First, we have to do an evaluation. A priest needs to observe the manifestations, if possible. I realize in your case, in an obsession, it may not be predictable, for someone to be right there when you're in difficulty. Even short of that, we have to do a proper interview, make a report, and I'm not the one to do it, an exorcist has to do it."

"Fine."

"We really haven't done many lately, as I indicated when we talked. In our church a priest performing an exorcism has to have purity of faith and experience in exorcism. We've been training people. This is a terrible way to put it, given your immediate need, but we have a backlog of cases."

"What do people do?"

"Some aren't really afflicted. The symptoms vanish on their own when the person is denied the attention they might have been seeking out of narcissism. Some are helped by other means, psychiatric treatment, drug therapies. Some are lost to us. And some live interrupted lives."

"Interrupted lives. I've read that. The manifestations come and go, over years, over a life. It frightens me."

"Ms. Delaney, let me work on it. See if I can pull some strings, move this along."

"How long would you say?"

"Several weeks, and that would be a miracle."

"And several weeks is how many weeks?"

"Let me see. I'll look into it."

"I'd also like to talk to my childhood priest."

"You should."

"Maybe he could do it right away."

"If he's qualified. And he'd still need permission. Let me get started. You're going to get through this fine," he said. "You have the power of God on your side."

"I haven't been around that sentiment in a long time," she said. "Thank you, Father."

She placed a call on her cell phone to Father Connolly in the Bronx.

"Saint Christopher Church," a woman answered.

"Hello. My name is Veronica Delaney and I'm looking for Father Connolly. Is he in?"

"This time of day he plays chess with the youngsters in the park. Should be back in about an hour."

"If he comes in, would you tell him Veronica Delaney is on her way to see him? And could he wait for me, please? He knows me."

"Yes, I will."

"Appreciate it."

She couldn't find a taxicab and headed toward the subway. She reached Lexington Avenue and was about to enter the station. She saw him in the mix of pedestrians on the other side of the street, a winged presence in with the crowd. She stopped walking, closed her eyes, her heart pounding; waited, hoping this would pass; and looked again and saw an ordinary street scene. He was gone. He had not been smiling this time. He seemed to Ronnie to have been studying her, or possibly just checking in.

She emerged from the station at Fordham Road and Jerome Avenue in the Bronx and walked toward Saint James Park, located near the church. This was her childhood park. She had not been in this place for years and when she entered she remembered being a little girl here, being pushed on the swings by her mother, and yes, her father, dancing around a maypole with other children to mark the start of spring, walking hand in hand with her mother; the memories an intermingling of the joyful and the achingly sad.

The chess tables were in an area behind a recreation center building and Father Connolly sat with an African American boy of about eleven, the two engrossed in their game. Father Connolly had grown older in the service of his faith since she had last seen him. He was a small, white-haired man, seventy-eight, five feet four, unimposing but for the face, and she nodded her head affirmatively seeing that face again, a wrinkled face with soft brown eyes, a countenance of endless empathy. He looked up as she approached the table.

"Father, it's Veronica Delaney."

"Veronica, my dear. Tony, we'll finish tomorrow, all right?" The boy nodded and Father Connolly came to her.

"It's so good to see you, Father."

"What brings you here?"

"I'm not good. I'm not good," and she began to sob. He held her until she subsided and then guided her to a patio table and chairs near the chess area and helped her sit. She told him her story—Richard, the signs of possession, the Satan manifestations—and he appeared to draw the pain unto himself.

"An exorcism? You must understand, it doesn't always work, Veronica."

"And sometimes it does. Father McElene said purity of faith was a main requirement for the exorcist. He's talking about you."

"I'm not the person for this."

"You are to me. If you could call, they could give you permission—"

"Veronica, do you really believe in your heart of hearts that the Devil is in you?"

"I don't know anymore. But even if it's all psychological, which is what the therapist says, I've read that an exorcism can still help on that level, if the person believes it will help. I believe it will and that you can help me."

"During the Second World War when I was a chaplain I did several exorcisms. The results were mixed. There were demons of war, as much as anything. Years later, a young woman in my parish claimed she was possessed. I wanted her hospitalized. I believe Satan *is* present in our world. I did not believe it for this woman. My superiors pressured me to perform an exorcism. It wasn't successful. Soon after, she died in a drowning. I don't know if it was an accident. I never performed an exorcism again."

"But I want to live. That's why I'm here."

"I can't do it for you, Veronica. I can't take the chance if it's the wrong remedy."

"It's my chance, not yours."

"No, I would be very much involved."

"Would you call Father McElene? At least tell him we spoke."

"I'll call him."

"And would you please think about it? He said 'several weeks.' Can I hold myself together 'several weeks'?"

"Stay here with us for a while in our convent. We'll exorcise your demons with prayer and guidance and counseling."

"You see how little good counseling did for me, Father. As for prayer, when my mother was dying, I prayed. It didn't help." She wrote her phone numbers down for him on a piece of paper. "You'll think about it? You'll call me?"

"I can't let you just go like this."

"I'm fine when I'm fine." She patted him on his hand. "This is what I need. And you can do this. You're a kind man. I trust you."

She found a taxicab on Fordham Road and went back to the apartment. Bob came over for a dinner Nancy prepared and he was as upset as

Nancy at the notion of Ronnie soliciting an exorcism. He blamed
Richard for everything; "a terrible guy who turned you upside down."
Nancy was concerned with details, was Ronnie going to continue seeing Kaufman while her exorcism was in the works. Ronnie hadn't
given it any thought, but as she considered it she decided until she went
through the exorcism, therapy might be counterproductive—two different belief systems. They managed to arrive at something of a com-
promise, she would consider returning to therapy, but only after the
exorcism was performed.

As Bob was leaving he said to Ronnie, "I wish we could do more."

"You've *done* more."

Like a sleepwalker Ronnie arose from her bed. She put on her jogging
outfit, sneakers, placed a few dollars in her pocket as she usually did before leaving for a run, and left the apartment to go jogging. She went
past the sleeping doorman and jogged along the street toward Riverside
Park. She was running, eyes open, oblivious, unconscious, at three thirty
in the morning.

She was unaware of a figure in a car parked across the street. As she
left the building the person made a call on a cell phone.

She entered the park and stopped to sit on the ground with her
back against a retaining wall. She remained there awhile, drifted into
sleep, then her eyes opened, she stood, and began to run through the
deserted park, her face devoid of emotion. A few yards in front of her
something was moving in the darkness. Her trancelike state lifted and
she became aware of the movement. A man was in her path facing her
menacingly. By the light of a lamppost she saw the man's face. It was
Randall Cummings. He had a lifeless expression, the walking dead. She
tried to run past him, around him, but she had come upon him too
quickly and he tripped her with his leg, sending her sprawling to the
ground. As she turned to get up, he lunged at her with a knife. She spun
out of the way and with a rapid swipe of her arm knocked the knife out
of his hand. She was on her feet and now he came toward her, his hands
outstretched to choke her. She ducked under his grasp, got to him first,

her hands at his throat, and began choking him, pushing him backward, choking the air out of him as he gasped, pushing him as she choked hard, and then he tripped on a tree stump and as he fell back she saw it wasn't Cummings at all, it was the man in the cardboard box. He was the reality, not Cummings. He fell away from her, tumbling down a hill that sloped from the walkway, screaming at her from the bottom, "You crazy bitch, you goddamn crazy bitch!"

In a panic she ran fast in the direction she had come, back toward the apartment, but in her path, swarming in front of her, were several howling, hissing black cats. She turned in the other direction to run and a few of them scampered across her path, howling as she ran faster, as fast as she could along the walkway to get away from the creatures until, finally, she was beyond them, the sound of the cats descending, and she was by herself running in the night. She ran at full speed in her panic until she was out of breath, and sprawled onto a bench on her stomach, gasping, bewildered, horrified—she nearly killed someone, nearly strangled him to death. The next thought was more than she could bear—did she kill Randall Cummings?

On a promontory in the park above the walkway was a figure who had been observing the near-strangling and Ronnie's terrified run, watching with a look of amused satisfaction as if it were his entertainment for the dead of night. It was Richard.

16

She arose in the morning, her body aching, and made her way out of the park. She had to get to Father Connolly. She couldn't wait on the bureaucracy. She knew that she was dangerous and losing her hold on reality. If he refused to perform an exorcism, at least he promised her haven in a convent. The sisters and their symbols of faith might help until the church worked through their procedures and found someone for her.

She had a few dollars in her pocket, she bought a newspaper to get change and dialed information at a pay booth. The church was listed, Father Connolly was not. She called the church, receiving an outgoing message; no one was in the office to take her call. She didn't have enough money for a taxicab to the Bronx and went to the nearest subway station. She was going to sit outside the church to wait for someone to arrive. Proximity to the church seemed to her a better idea than being in the city at large.

––––––

Shortly after 8:00 A.M. she arrived at the simple gray brick Roman Catholic church. She rang the bell for the office, located in a small annex adjacent to the main building. No one answered. She sat on the church steps, in despair over the events of the night.

She was unaware that out of her line of sight, watching her down the street, was Richard, who had followed her.

Rourke asked Santini and Gomez to come into his office, where Maria Sanchez, a uniformed officer in her twenties, was seated.

"Maria—" Rourke said, prompting her.

"We got a call a few minutes ago," she told them. "Guy said a crazy woman tried to strangle him last night, middle of the night in Riverside Park. He was sleeping in 'his apartment,' he said, referring to the park, so it must have been some homeless guy. Said he was letting us know to spare 'future victims.' The woman was young, he said, in jogging clothes. He thought maybe he scared her in the dark, but he said that was no excuse. She choked him like she wanted to kill him. He tripped and fell down a hill and she lost her grip and ran away. That's all he wanted to say. Didn't want anything to do with the police. Just wanted us to know so no one else gets hurt. He was moving away. Didn't want to be in any neighborhood where crazy women tried to kill you."

"Can't blame him for that," Rourke said, "but here's the kicker. Tell them where he said it happened."

"Riverside Park around 113th Street."

"Is that a fact?" Gomez said.

"Yes. And the Delaney girl lives?" Rourke asked.

"On 111th. Right near the park," Gomez answered.

"Same MO as Cummings. Right near her apartment. Let's bring her in."

Nancy didn't see Ronnie in her room when she awoke and assumed she went jogging early. She checked and when Ronnie's jogging shoes weren't in the closet, confirmed for herself this was the case. She left for a dental appointment prior to going to work and was not in the building when Santini and Gomez arrived looking for Ronnie. The doorman, who came on at seven, said that he had seen the roommate leave. He hadn't seen Ronnie that morning. They buzzed up and when there was no answer Santini asked for the superintendent of the building. A muscular man in his forties appeared wearing work clothes. When he heard they were from homicide and needed to talk to Veronica Delaney, he got very excited. His cousin was a cop, he told them, and he opened the door with a key Ronnie and Nancy had left in case of emergency; not the emergency they had in mind.

When the detectives saw Ronnie was not there they went back down. A search of the apartment was not their priority, they had to find the suspect quickly. They spoke with Carter and Greenberg, who had arrived, and who were going to position themselves outside the building and intercept her if she appeared.

Gomez asked the superintendent and the doorman where in the vicinity Ronnie might be at this time of the morning, did they know if she had a favorite breakfast place? They didn't know of any. A gym where she worked out? She jogged in the park, the doorman said. She jogged. They knew that. The detectives had Nancy's work address from their earlier interrogation and needed her for Ronnie's whereabouts.

First, they drove through the park, hoping to spot Ronnie, and when they did not they headed downtown for Nancy. They arrived at the Hawkins Literary Agency a few minutes after nine. Nobody was at the office yet. They were going to wait for the business day to begin and for Ronnie's roommate to appear.

During this time, a picture of Ronnie taken from a magazine head shot was printed with her vital statistics under the line, "Wanted for questioning in the murder of Randall Cummings" and sent out as a police bulletin to all precincts. Rourke was furious when someone leaked it and this appeared on the cable channel New York News, a tip-off to the suspect and an invitation to flee. Ronnie, however, was not going anywhere. She was sitting on the steps of Saint Christopher Church in the

Bronx, out of range of this activity, desperate, waiting for someone, any-one, from the church.

A few minutes after nine a robust African American woman in her for-ties approached the door leading to the church office. Ronnie quickly came over to her.

"At last."

"Did you want to see Father Flynn? He's out of town."

"Father Connolly."

"Father Connolly? He's semiretired, you know. If he's coming in today, won't be until much later."

"I have to see him right away. It's an emergency."

"Your name is?"

"Veronica Delaney."

"Oh, right." The woman unlocked the door. "We can call him up. He lives nearby."

The church worker led Ronnie into a small, cluttered office, dialed a number, and handed the phone to Ronnie.

"Father Connolly—"

"It's Veronica, Father. I'm at the church. I have to see you right now!"

"My goodness. I'll be there in five minutes."

She sat on a worn upholstered bench in a dimly lit waiting area outside the office. Father Connolly hurried in and she greeted him with an ex-plosion of her torment.

"I almost killed a man last night, Father! I went running in the park in the middle of the night and I didn't know I was doing it, like other times I blacked out, and then I saw what I was doing. I was choking somebody. The man could've died, I could've killed him, and if I could do that, then maybe I killed Randall Cummings. I was there, I was at his place the day he died, and he died from being choked to death, so it could have been me. Evil is in me, Father. I'm going out of my mind. We have to have an exorcism. We have to do it right now. You have to do it!"

He took her by the hands and said, "Veronica, I'll try to help. But what you're looking for can't be something *done* to you. It has to be something from *within* you." He put his arm around her gently. "Let's go into the chapel. It would be a good thing."

The chapel was a small, simple space in the annex portion of the building; basic artifacts for worship and a few pews. Father Connolly led Ronnie to sit in the first pew.

"What can get you through is faith. Faith in God. Faith in your essential goodness."

"I lost my faith a long time ago."

"You had it once, when you were a little girl. You have to find it again."

The office worker entered, flustered.

"I'm sorry, Father. This man insisted—"

Richard brashly entered the room with a look of amusement at the entertainment value of the proceedings.

"Hello, Ronnie."

"Father, this is the man!"

"What are you doing here?" Father Connolly said. "You've been stalking her?"

"I wouldn't call it that. I'm a friend of Ronnie's. And she was very—abrupt with me. I wanted to say to her, you can't get rid of me so easily once you let me in, so to speak."

"Father, make him go away."

As Richard stood there, imperious, amused, Father Connolly studied him, trying to take his measure.

"What kind of behavior is this?"

Richard looked at him patronizingly.

"Who are you to ask?"

"Get out of here," Ronnie said. "Father!" she appealed.

Father Connolly studied Richard in his arrogance.

"If he is the demon in your life, I'm afraid you're the one who has to will him away."

Suddenly, Randall Cummings's assistant Cosmo Pitalis materialized, dressed in black, white-faced. He was livid.

"You killed Cummings."

"No," Ronnie said, terrified.

"You were angry with him and you snapped. You grabbed him by the neck, the last thing he expected, and it caught him off guard. He began to gag, and he couldn't catch his breath, and you choked him to death."

"I didn't!"

Pitalis was gone, Ronnie saw just the two of them, Father Connolly and Richard. She was breathing rapidly, panicked.

"Say good-bye to yourself, Ronnie."

"What is your purpose here?" Father Connolly said. "Leave this chapel!"

"And then? I'll only follow her somewhere else. This is the confrontation, old man. Are you up to it?"

The man in the box suddenly materialized in front of Ronnie.

"You tried to kill me, you crazy bitch. If I didn't trip, I'd be dead. Crazy killer bitch!"

He was gone, but she saw the scene in the park unfold again, her choking him, him falling backward.

She was shaking, overwrought.

"It's over," Richard said.

"He's playing with you. You have to pray to God to give you the strength to deal with this."

"Your mind is never going to be the same."

"I don't know who you are, but you might as well *be* Satan," Father Connolly said. "You're the purest embodiment of evil I have seen in a long, long time."

"Is that a fact?" Then he turned to Ronnie. "Sad, isn't it, when you have a good mind and it goes?"

"Don't listen to him. Pray, Veronica. The words will lead you back to your faith and give you strength. Our Father, who art in heaven . . ."

The black cats suddenly appeared, hissing, scrambling through the chapel, in and out of the pews, under her feet. She screamed in terror. She was cold, shivering. She was holding herself in fear, feeling her strength dwindling. The cats vanished.

"Give in, Ronnie, let go," Richard said. "It's not a bad life, having people take care of you."

"Don't let him get to you. Say those beautiful words, Veronica. Our Father, who art in heaven . . ." He kneeled and looked into her eyes. "Your faith is deep within you. It never left. Find it and it will lead you out of this."

Struggling, barely audibly, she said, "Our Father, who art in heaven . . ."

"Hallowed be thy name . . ."

"Hallowed be thy name . . ."

"Go on."

"Give in, Ronnie, give in."

Where Richard was standing, she now saw the dark angel, winged, menacing.

"No!"

"The words will lead you."

"I can't."

"Yes, you can. Thy kingdom come . . ." She was shivering, disoriented, her eyes darting, looking for what terrible thing would happen next.

The dark angel was gone, Richard was back.

Father Connolly took her hands in his, willing her. "I remember that special little girl you were. Come now. Pray with your old priest."

She was in the car again. Her father turned, took his eyes off the wheel. A crashing sound, then shattered glass.

The stained glass window of the chapel disintegrated. The glass shards struck her face. She touched her hands to her face and then saw her hands were covered with blood and she screamed. She couldn't take it any longer. She felt weak, fading.

"Game's over, Ronnie. We can bring an ambulance for you and you'll be fine. You and Claire Reilly will be fine."

The blood was gone. The stained glass window was intact. Richard came toward her and patted her on the arm condescendingly.

"Ready, Ronnie?"

Father Connolly shoved him away.

"Don't you touch her! Veronica, look at me. For your mother, who loved you so much. Give us this day . . . You can do it. Do it for her. Give us this day . . ."

"Give us this day . . ." in a weakened voice, "our daily bread."

"And forgive us . . ."

"And forgive us," haltingly, weakly, "our trespasses as we forgive those . . ."

"Yes, go on."

". . . who trespass against us."

"It won't work, Ronnie. Satan is real. Too strong for this."

"And lead us . . ."

"And lead us not into temptation. But deliver us from evil," she managed to say, her voice barely audible.

"Say good-bye to the world as you knew it. Your mind is going to belong to Satan for as long as you live."

She felt herself slipping away. If she let go of the reality of this place, and of herself, it would finally be peaceful.

"That's right. Give in to it."

Father Connolly took his cross and placed it in Ronnie's hands. He closed her hands over it and shook her hands hard to get her to focus on him.

"God's light is your beacon. Follow that light. It will lead you to everything good and true about you. Concentrate with every ounce of your soul and follow God's light. Follow the light, Veronica. The light of your God when you were a little girl." Weary, she shook her head no. "You can do it. You have to try." She looked at him, at his soulful face, and closed her eyes.

She began to see a faint light. It began to grow stronger, white, incandescent. Images played in and out of it. She saw Nancy and Bob, the three of them were laughing together. She saw children's faces, the children from the recreation center, and she was with them. She saw herself as a child. She was about six. She carried a flower, a dandelion from the park, and she gave it to her mother, who was overjoyed at the sight of her. She tried to absorb it, that her mother was so resplendently happy with her, that the joy in her mother's face was so radiant. For her to have made her mother so happy had to mean something. She opened her eyes and Father Connolly was with her, holding her hands over the cross.

"Pray to God in your own words. Pray with your heart."

"It's pointless. Satan owns you now."

"Find the God of your childhood. Pray, Veronica, pray."

Gripping the cross, she cried out, "Lord, please save me. I pray to you to save me. I didn't kill my mother. Mommy, Mommy, I'm so sorry. But it wasn't my fault! It wasn't my fault! I didn't kill you. I didn't kill anybody. I'm not bad. I'm not bad!" She wept profoundly, her body rocking.

Slowly, as if a fever had broken, everything began to come clear, where she was, the chapel, Father Connolly, Richard.

She turned to Richard in his imperiousness. "You evil bastard. Get the hell out of my life!"

"Look at this," Richard said.

"It was you from the beginning. You sent the black cat. All that was you. Well, now you can get the hell out of here!"

"Really, now? If that's the way you want it."

"That's the way I want it."

He turned to leave, but with a last thought. "I'll still be around."

"Not with me you won't."

Arrogantly, calmly, he walked out of the chapel and she watched him go.

Father Connolly took Ronnie's hands in his.

"He can't hurt you anymore. You're too strong for him, you and God."

She was emotionally and physically drained and he brought her into his office and guided her to lie down on his couch.

"You're the special person I always knew you'd grow up to be."

He placed a blanket over her and she fell asleep.

———

Santini and Gomez never reached Nancy as to Ronnie's whereabouts. In Staten Island, Beattie Ryan, the retired mail carrier whose religious beliefs originally led her to join the protest against Randall Cummings, underwent a challenge to her faith. She was watching television and Ronnie's face appeared on the screen—wanted in connection with Randall Cummings's murder. She called her priest for guidance and he suggested the Christian thing to do was contact the police immediately, and he was obliged to do so, if she did not. She located a number that had been given to her by Santini and called, the call routed to Rourke. She told him she had allowed the detectives to be misled as to the circumstances on the day of Randall Cummings's murder. John Wilson was not with her the entire time. He left their position across the street and went into the church a few minutes after the girl came out, the girl who was wanted. Wilson was inside for a while and after he rejoined her he told her that he took care of it, that they wouldn't have the evildoer to worry about anymore, and instructed her to say they were together the entire time. He told her he had done "God's work."

John Wilson was taken into custody for the murder of Randall Cummings.

Ronnie awoke and came into the office where Father Connolly was sitting with the secretary and a young man; a church volunteer whom Father Connolly called to drive her home. She asked to use the phone and dialed Nancy at work.

"It's me."

"Ronnie! You were in the news! They were looking for you! But they just said they arrested someone named John Wilson!"

"John Wilson."

"Where are you, are you all right?"

"I'm good. Everything is good. I'm in my childhood church. Can't beat the old favorites."

———

As Father Connolly led her to the car, she said, "I can never thank you enough. This is beyond thanks."

"The best thanks you can give me is to take a little advice. Now that you found it again, keep your faith. I venture it could be as important as your computer."

Father Connolly continued along the street to a local coffee shop. He hadn't eaten breakfast in the rush of the morning. Standing on a street corner was Richard, talking on his cell phone. He ended his call as the priest approached. The two locked eyes.

"You're pretty good, old man," Richard said.

"It *is* you, isn't it?" Father Connolly asked.

He didn't answer. He smiled and walked on.